GLIMMER TRAIN
STORIES

EDITORS
Susan Burmeister-Brown   Linda B. Swanson-Davies

CONSULTING EDITOR
Roz Wais

COPY EDITOR
Scott Stuart Allie

TYPESETTING & LAYOUT
Paul Morris

COVER ART
The Corn God *by Jane Zwinger*

ESTABLISHED IN 1990

PUBLISHED QUARTERLY
in spring, summer, fall, and winter by Glimmer Train Press, Inc.
P.O. Box 80430, Portland, Oregon 97280-1430
Telephone: 503/221-0836   Facsimile: 503/221-0837
www.glimmertrain.org

PRINTED IN U.S.A.
Indexed in *Humanities International Complete*
Member of the Council of Literary Magazines and Presses

Glimmer Train (ISSN #1055-7520), registered in U.S. Patent and Trademark Office, is published quarterly, $36 per year in the U.S., by Glimmer Train Press, Inc., 4763 SW Maplewood Rd., P.O. Box 80430, Portland, OR 97280-1430. Periodicals postage paid at Portland, OR, and additional mailing offices. POSTMASTER: Send address changes to Glimmer Train Press, P.O. Box 3000, Denville, NJ 07834-9929.

STATEMENT OF OWNERSHIP, MANAGEMENT, AND CIRCULATION. Required by 39 USC 3685, file date: 10/3/11. Publication name: Glimmer Train, publication #10557520. Published quarterly (4x/yr). Publisher and owner: Glimmer Train Press, Inc. Complete mailing address of known office of publication and headquarters is P.O. Box 80430, Portland, OR 97280-1430. One-year subscription price: $38. Editors and co-presidents: Susan Burmeister-Brown and Linda Burmeister Swanson-Davies, P.O. Box 80430, Portland, OR 97280-1430. Known bondholders: none. Extent and nature of circulation: a) average number of copies each issue during preceding 12 months, b) actual number of copies of single issue published nearest to filing date. Net press run: a) seven thousand, two hundred eighty-two; b) seven thousand. Paid or requested mailed outside-county mail subscriptions: a) three thousand, nine hundred forty-four; b) three thousand, nine hundred seventy-nine. Paid or requested mailed inside-county mail subscriptions: a) none; b) none; Sales through distributors: a) one thousand, one hundred ninety-three; b) one thousand sixty-seven. Other Classes: a) fifty; b) fifty. Total paid/requested circulation: a) five thousand, one hundred eighty-seven; b) five thousand, ninety-six. Free distribution outside-county by mail: a) one hundred; b) one hundred. Free distribution inside-county by mail: a) none; b) none. Free distribution, other classes: a) none; b) none. Free distribution outside of mail: a) four hundred fifty; b) four hundred fifty. Total free distribution: a) five hundred fifty; b) five hundred fifty. Total distribution: a) five thousand, seven hundred thirty-seven; b) five thousand, six hundred forty-six. Copies not distributed: a) one thousand seven hundred nine; b) one thousand three hundred fifty-four. Total sum of distributed and not distributed copies: a) seven thousand, four hundred forty-six; b) seven thousand. Percent Paid and or requested Circulation: a) ninety; b) ninety. I certify that the statements made by me above are correct and complete—Linda Swanson-Davies, Editor.

ISSN # 1055-7520, CPDA BIPAD # 79021
DISTRIBUTION: Bookstores can purchase *Glimmer Train Stories* through these distributors:
DEMCO, Inc., 4810 Forest Run Road, Madison, WI 53707 ph: 800/356-1200
Peribo PTY Ltd., 58 Beaumont Rd., Mt. Kuring-Gai, NSW 2080, AUSTRALIA
Small Changes, P.O. Box 70740, Seattle, WA 98127 ph: 206/382-1980
Source Interlink, 27500 Riverview Center Blvd., Suite 400, Bonita Sprints, FL 36134
Ubiquity, 607 Degraw St., Brooklyn, NY 11217
SUBSCRIPTION SVCS: EBSCO, Divine, Subscription Services of America, Harrassowitz, Swets, WT Cox, Blackwell's UK.

Subscription rates: Order online at www.glimmertrain.org
or by mail—one year, $38 within the U.S. (Visa/MC/check).
Airmail to Canada, $48; outside North America, $62.
Payable by Visa/MC or check for U.S. dollars drawn on a U.S. bank.

Glimmer Train Press also offers **Writers Ask**—nuts, bolts, and informed perspectives—a quarterly newsletter for the committed writer. One year, four issues, $22 within the U.S. ($24 Canada, $28 elsewhere), Visa, MC, or check to Glimmer Train Press, Inc., or order online at www.glimmertrain.org.

At 7:15 p.m. on October 15, 1945, our father came home on the train to Long Island after four and a half years in the army, the final two years of that on the European front, as one of the Ritchie Boys.

In those years, he'd changed from a newlywed who'd married our mom just six weeks after meeting her, and who thought maybe he'd raise dogs for a living (though he'd only had one for a week when he was ten), to a man who was amazed to have survived, didn't know his young daughter, and prayed he and his wife would still recognize each other.

Eighteen years earlier, he'd left Hamburg for New York under the sponsorship of his mother's flighty sister; eleven years later, from his 8x8 office in a building that would be torn down and replaced by the Twin Towers, he sold every chair for the new United Nations building, paid off our mortgage, and bought a small sheep farm in Pennsylvania, where he and Mom celebrated by having one more baby. Five years after that and nearly broke, we moved to Oregon—a new life ahead.

Twenty one years ago, we were seeking stories for our very first issue.

We are always transitioning. Sometimes the transitions feel gigantic at the time, and sometimes they seem subtle, but continue to ripple, and every single one of them helps to make us who we are.

Like a river, we are never the same water.

It is good sharing these years with you.

Susan & Linda

Submitting Work to Glimmer Train

Your short-story manuscripts are welcome all year. To make submissions at our site, go to www.glimmertrain.org and click on the yellow *Submissions* tab. Complete writing guidelines are at the site. Prefer snail mail? Click on the *help* link for instructions.

SUBMISSION CALENDAR

January .... **Standard** submission (up to 12,000 words). No reading fee. Payment for accepted stories: $700.

Very Short Fiction Award. Any length under 3,000 words welcome. Prizes: 1st place – $1,200 and publication, 2nd/3rd places – $500/$300 and possible publication.

February .... **Short Story Award for New Writers**. Any length under 12,000 words welcome. Open only to writers whose fiction has not been published in any print publication with a circulation over 5,000. Prizes: 1st place – $1,200 and publication, 2nd/3rd places – $500/$300 and possible publication.

March .... **Fiction Open**. Any length from 2,000 to 20,000 words welcome. Prizes: 1st place – $2,000 and publication, 2nd/3rd places – $1,000/$600 and possible publication.

April .... **Family Matters**. Any length under 12,000 words welcome. Prizes: 1st place – $1,200 and publication, 2nd/3rd places – $500/$300 and possible publication. Also **Standard.**

May .... **Short Story Award for New Writers**

June .... **Fiction Open**

July .... **Very Short Fiction Award** and **Standard**

August .... **Short Story Award for New Writers**

September ...... **Fiction Open**

October .... **Family Matters** and **Standard**

November ...... **Short Story Award for New Writers**

December .... **Fiction Open**

One of the most respected short-story journals in print, *Glimmer Train Stories* is represented in recent editions of the Pushcart Prize, O. Henry, *New Stories from the South*, *New Stories from the Midwest*, and *Best American Short Stories* anthologies.

In a year's time, we pay writers over $45,000, nearly a third of that going to new writers. Your subscriptions directly support those writers and help keep literary short fiction alive and vibrant. *Thank you.*

CONTENTS

I swear the snow seemed deeper then.

Paul Rawlins's fiction has appeared in *Glimmer Train, Epoch, Image, Tampa Review, Prism*, and America West's in-flight magazine, among others, and has been anthologized in *Dispensation, Where Love Is Found*, and *Listening to the Voices*.

THE CORN GOD

Paul Rawlins

Two weeks after the army sent my father to Afghanistan, my mother drove me to my grandparents' farm, explaining that she had to find a new job now that our daddy was gone and promising she would come back for me soon. She gave me a huge *abrazo*, reached down to pinch my bum, which was a habit of hers, and then left me, telling my grandmother, no, she couldn't stay for dinner, my grandmother saying, nonsense, it was a long way she had come.

"I have to go," she said, in her samba accent. These were my father's parents, and I think we both felt like strangers there without him. Or maybe she thought my grandfather's eyes lingered on her a little too long, like men's eyes always did. Or maybe, as things turned out, she just had a plane to catch.

I had worked up a heart full of venom for the farm on the drive up, knowing I would be left there alone. We had visited every July when I was little. For a week I would drink thick, whole milk, always poured from the same yellow pitcher, eat homemade scones and mounds of my grandmother's pickles, tag behind my grandfather on his chores, and chase cats around the barn—and cry when we finally had to go home. That was then. We hadn't been back now for a couple of summers, since my father had changed jobs and had little vacation time. My mother didn't really like the farm and would never have gone there with just the two of us; I cared less about it myself as I grew into bikes and rollerblades, sleepovers, and morning crafts classes under the pavilion at the park with two other girls who had just moved in on the next block. And my grandmother, we knew, was in the early stages of dementia.

But while I stood in the driveway, staring at the skinny white house, taller than it was wide and standing in a swamp from the water turned out of a ditch that ran along the road; the milk barn with the muddy corral and row of plastic calf sheds behind it; the fields of tall corn and drying windrows of green and blond alfalfa waiting for the sun and the bailer, my hate cowered and left me only desperation.

My grandfather came down from the porch while my mother drove off, toot-tooting the horn and waving at me out the window, over the top of the car. My grandmother had wandered across the lawn and was staring up into the crabapple tree with her hands held behind her back, the irrigation water covering the tops of her shoes.

"We put you in the upstairs room," Grandpa said, which was where my mother and dad had always stayed, while I slept downstairs on the foldout couch. "These all your things?"

I nodded, and he reached down for my suitcase and the overstuffed backpack leaning against my leg, while I stood hugging my pillow in my arms. My grandfather looked at it.

"We got pillows," he said. "She knows that." Then he took my bags and headed up the cement steps into the house. I looked back at my grandmother, who was whistling now, and waving her fingers at something up among the leaves.

"Mom," I whispered. The word came out a mist, a trace of vapor that floated up toward the electric wires, where it broke into its tiny pieces and scattered on the air.

Nobody bothered me in the bedroom.

Nobody came upstairs at all.

Though somebody, I was never sure who, had been before I got there: the bed was newly made, corner-tucked, with a prim stripe of sheet folded down over the top of the blanket, making a tight pocket

I would worm into that night and, with my pillow squeezed between my arms and curled-up legs, sob myself to sleep.

It was a loft room, and the outside wall came up maybe three feet high where it met the pitch of the roof, with a window at each triangle end—one to the west, one to the east. A sagging twin bed, a chest of drawers, a little table with a lamp, a little chair that had once been painted a minty green with a picture of a large-eyed puppy with a bow around its neck on the backrest: these were on the east end of the room. Along the walls were boxes, two old Samsonite suitcases, a trunk. The suitcases, I would discover later, were empty, except for an old wheat-back penny and a safety pin I found when I turned out the sock ruffle in one of them. The trunk held clothes from when my grandfather had been in the army, old and permanently creased. I would take them out—the shirts, the pants, the tie, the little pup-tent cap—and lay them around me carefully on the floor, unpacking the trunk until I reached the bottom, then running my hands along the edges and into the corners for anything I'd missed, every time thinking there ought to be something more—a letter, a photograph, a bullet, a ribboned medal.

"Were you in the war, Grandpa?" I asked him on my third night while we each sat in our own chair in the living room. I was so lonely—worse, I was very bored.

"No," he said.

"He was a sailor," my grandmother piped in.

"That was Dennis," he told her, an uncle. "Dennis was in the navy."

"He sent me that little hula girl there, on the shelf. From Borneo," she said, pointing until I looked.

"He never left North Island," my grandfather said as he got up and walked through the kitchen on his way outside. "That came from Disneyland."

Grandma had called my father more than once to tell him that his sister had died, which had happened years ago, or to accuse him of taking away her old blue Buick. My grandfather would come in several times a day to check the stove and the taps, and he had installed a door at the top of the stairwell to the basement that he kept locked. He stocked the cupboard with extra bread and cans of potted meat, easy dinner fixings, because Grandma cooked sometimes with handfuls of salt or soda, or she might set a pot of vegetables on for soup and neglect to add the water or light the burners on the stove. He locked up the cleaning chemicals and his gun, and they stayed away from church most Sundays because my grandmother might refuse the Sacrament bread, complaining out loud that it was only crumbs, or, I heard once, stand up and start taking off her blouse.

Sometimes she knew me; sometimes she thought I was one of her sisters. Sometimes I was just a stranger she asked my grandfather to make go away.

It was Nancy, the neighbor who lived on the opposite side of the mile-square block, who arranged school for me. Her kids were younger than I was—the oldest was only nine—so she had none of her own at the junior high, but whether my grandfather had asked her, or she, with a mother's knack, simply sized up the situation and took things in hand, I was registered and added to the bus route at the end of August. Back home I had already been in middle school for a year; here, as a seventh grader, I would be back on the bottom rung again, and the new girl besides.

It didn't matter. I couldn't wait to go.

I don't remember if I noticed the girl with a fat ponytail of auburn hair when she got on the bus two stops after I did that first morning. (Grandma had left me flustered by calling me Nora, her sister, when I came downstairs, and warning me not to wear her blue dress.) But I had two classes with her that day, pre-algebra and P.E., and on her way off the bus that afternoon, she gave me a little finger wave and said, "Don't forget your hygiene form." She pulled a face that made me smile, then said to save her a seat tomorrow morning. In that instant—when Steph Saunders said hello—life was better.

Liesel rode the bus, too; we had English together, and pre-algebra with Steph. Missy had home ec, drama, and a dance class two nights a week with Liesel, and she knew Steph from half a dozen different places their paths had crossed growing up in the same rural valley. Within two weeks, I was part of a new quartet.

We made our first trip to my house after school, mostly because no one had seen inside it before. Not that it was anything spectacular, but it was someplace new at least. And they envied my room. Steph and Liesel both had to share with sisters, and nobody else had her own room on the second floor with a pitched ceiling and a window at each end.

Missy peered out the east one and said, "You ought to put a window box right here. They have them at Smithfield Implement. We could paint it blue, with sunflowers on it." Missy had a thing for sunflowers that fall.

"It's too late now," Liesel said, coming over beside her and leaning down to see.

"We'll get some artificial ones then," Missy said, measuring the width of the sill with her hands. "That way Deeds can change them whenever she wants something new." That was the first time anybody had called me Deeds. I liked it, and I waited to see if Liesel or Steph would take it up. I'd had nicknames back home, but nobody wants to be called Deedle Bug in junior high.

I was always Deeds after that, which I counted as more good fortune, and my house became our hub. Steph and Missy both had big families, and there were always kids around—and chores at Missy's. Liesel's sister practiced her clarinet every day after school, or her little brother was there with a bunch of friends, tossing ropes around the handlebars of their bicycles, playing rodeo, or floating junk boats down the drainage ditch. In my attic room and Grandpa's fields, nobody paid us much attention, and that was perfect for a private, four-girls' world.

Except for a freeze in September that blackened the squash leaves and ended the tomatoes, the fall was warm, and most days, after we went inside and found a snack, we wandered down the road that bordered the cornfield. About half a mile from the barn it made a T, to follow the fence line of the neighbor's pasture, and the land began to slope at the top of a hill that tumbled down to the sloughs along the river bottoms. Down the slope just far enough to be hidden from the house, we'd tromp nests into the long, sallow grass underneath the spread of the Russian olives, where we could lie out of the wind with our faces toward the westing sun and talk about secret or forbidden subjects: boys and the specifics of sex as best we knew them, diet pills and meth, the girls at school or church. I mostly listened. I was young for my grade, with no signs yet of monthly periods or breasts. I didn't worry about boys at school I didn't even know; I worried about my dad and wondered about Mom. I didn't have sisters or brothers or even chores to complain about, though I had assigned myself some—I swept the kitchen floor and the back steps each day, made my bed, cleared the table after breakfast and dinner. But no one demanded even that of me, and no one seemed to notice.

I would drift along at the edge of their daydreams until they insisted that I tell them something. Then I would make up lies about my life back home, full of boys and rich friends and danger. The best lies, the most extravagant, I told about my mother.

I was the mongrel offspring of both my parents: I had my mother's dark hair and a bit of dusk in my skin, but my father's genes had left me stumpy legged and blue eyed. My mother said my look was exotic; all I knew was that I didn't—and I would never—look like her. She was from Brazil, which I was convinced was a sort of factory that turned out the most beautiful women in the world. No matter how she wore her hair, it teased so you wanted to touch it, and her silk blouses shifted along her body like a pearly second skin.

"She's a model," I said. They had seen her picture, and none of them doubted me. "Or she was, before she met my dad."

"How did they meet?" Liesel said.

I took a little more risk here.

"Do you want to know the real story?" I said. The real story was my mother had come to be a nanny for a family whose son had been a missionary in Brazil and met my father on a blind date, where he'd tried to show off with his high-school Spanish. But they were all listening now. Liesel had looked up from where she was braiding Missy's hair. Steph leaned back on her elbows, and Missy sat cross-legged with her arms wrapped around her knees.

"My dad was down in South America, with the army. He was doing what they call black ops, secret stuff. They were hunting down this big drug guy." I was improvising as I went, but the pieces just seemed to appear and slide into place as I kept talking.

"I don't even know what country it was," I said. "He can't ever say. And nobody knew they were there; even the government would have denied it if they had been caught. But they were looking for this guy in the jungle. They found his camp, and there was a firefight. He wasn't there—he'd found out they were coming—but he left a bunch of other guys behind to guard the cocaine." It was all sounding good.

"Anyway, you know how they're always kidnapping people down there and holding them for ransom? That's what had happened to my mom. After the army guys had taken over the camp, they were setting fire to the place, and they found these hostages in one of the huts. And one of them was my mom."

"Really?" Missy said.

I nodded.

"She was only fifteen. But my dad told her before he left that he'd come back and marry her when she was eighteen. And that's what he did."

I told them that's where Mom was now—she had gone back to be in a soap opera. The drug lord who had kidnapped her was dead, so it was safe. She would be down there until they finished filming the season, and then she'd come get me. Dad was over on secret missions in Iraq and Afghanistan, but when he got back from the war, we might all move to Brazil.

"Do you speak Spanish?" Missy said.

"They don't speak Spanish there," I said. "They speak Portuguese."

"Do you speak Portuguese, then?"

"*Um pouco*," I said.

"What's that mean?"

"It means I speak a little."

"Does she call you?" Missy asked.

She didn't—she hadn't called at all.

"Not very often," I said. I started to choke up. "She's busy."

"When is she coming back?"

"I don't know for sure."

We all sat quiet until Steph stood and brushed the slivers of grass off her jeans.

"We'll ask the corn god," she said.

The west end of the field had once been a sand hill, where my grandfather said corn used to grow as tall as a man on a saddle horse. On the west side of the road that bordered the field stood a dozen volunteer stalks in a staggered row that had escaped the combine, the only things left standing in the field. The middle two stood tallest, topped with tufted crowns that looked like dipping heads of wheat, their leaves tattered into pennants of parchment, thin fingers that lifted up to point the direction of the wind. The stalks, desiccated canes with the outer skin stripped away, fit together like sections of pipe. A few ears still stood erect and sheathed in their husks against the stalk, but most of the remaining ears hung down, dry, rough-edged cobs with flaky, empty sockets and a few golden kernels at the tip, knobby and smooth, like the last stray teeth in an old man's mouth. Most of the yellow had faded out of the leaves and stalks, like a sun bled of heat, but they were not quite white. They were the color of grass in the fall, pale, yellow-tinted bone, with stains of dark rust along the stalks. One of the stalks was bent, fractured at a ninety-degree angle and barred across another, like a pointing or a broken arm, and they rattled with the wind—even when we couldn't hear the breeze that moved them. Liesel said the row reminded her of chess pieces, and we decided the queen was in the middle, and the king a little higher at her left, both taller than any of us. Next came the bishops, Liesel told us, but there were extras, so we gave the queen two attendants besides, and the king had one. Then the knights. And on the ends, again, the one on the left a bit higher and coming up about to the tops of our heads, were the rooks.

It was Steph who turned the line of stalks into an altar—or a deity.

"It's the corn god," she'd said, after we had finished naming the chess pieces.

"That's not nice," Missy told her.

"It's *god* with a little *g*," Steph said. "Like they have in Africa."

"Since when were you in Africa?"

Steph sighed.

"I just mean that primitive people, like in Africa, worship the earth and the sun and trees and things like that."

"Why would you want to worship feed corn?" Liesel said. "You can't even eat it."

"The corn's just a symbol," Steph said. Then she'd knelt in front of the row of stalks, spread out her arms in a huge Y, and bowed her head.

"O great corn god," she said. Missy sniggered.

"Ignore her," Steph said. "Show mercy to the nonbelievers—or smite them, as you will."

"Don't say that," Missy told her.

"Stop laughing," Steph hissed over her shoulder.

"I wasn't."

"You were."

"Well I've stopped. Don't say that anymore."

Steph turned back toward the row of stalks.

"Great corn god," she said, "giver of the harvest, hear me, your daughter."

"With your ears," Liesel mouthed to me. I put both hands to my face and stumbled into the field, trying to make my laughter sound like a cough. Steph must have looked back again because I could hear Liesel saying, "Keep going."

"Hear me," Steph said. I broke out laughing just as Liesel chanted, out loud this time:

"With your ears."

Everybody was laughing now. Steph stayed on her knees, looking at us over her shoulder and trying to keep a straight face. Finally, she got up and found two old cobs.

"Hear me, with your ears," she said, shaking them over her head. "Now can I finish?" Liesel nodded, grinning. She had one hand on her hip, a leg thrust out to the side, a dancer's pose, her body long and taut. Missy stood with her arms wrapped tight across her front, biting at her thumbnail.

This time, Steph leaned forward and touched the ears to the ground in front of her.

"Great corn god, giver of gifts, hear your daughter," she said. "And let Tyler Pond ask me to winter formal." She paused like she was thinking of what else to say, and then added, "Amen."

She got up, brushed off her knees, and handed the cobs to Liesel. Steph might get asked to the winter formal at the high school if Tyler Pond, who was a sophomore, dared ask a seventh grader. Steph was pretty; she had her dark, red-brown hair and clear skin, and boobs already the size of softballs. Steph didn't look thirteen.

"Your parents wouldn't let you go," Liesel said, drumming the air in front of her with the pair of cobs. "And the high school wouldn't let a seventh grader go to winter formal anyway."

"I didn't say I would go," Steph said. "I just want him to ask me. So go on." Steph nodded toward the row of stalks. Liesel knelt down and asked for a good grade on her next math test. Missy declined, shaking her head while she bit her thumb, and saying she couldn't think of anything. I had shrugged, taken the cobs, and asked the corn god to keep my dad safe.

Tyler had not asked Steph to winter formal—not yet—but he did call her one night. Liesel had gotten a B. I got a call from Dad telling me not to worry; he had left messages everywhere for Mom, and they'd have everything worked out soon. So when Steph handed me the ears after I told them my story, I took them, knelt, and asked when my mom was coming home.

Liesel had another test coming up. Steph wanted a new pair of jeans that cost a hundred and thirty dollars. Missy said she was still thinking. Our petitions didn't take very long. And it wasn't as funny this time.

"You should probably leave something when you ask for something," Steph said.

"Leave what?"

"A sacrifice. Like when they throw virgins into volcanoes. People in the old days would kill a sheep or burn something on an altar," Steph explained.

"We can't start a fire out here," I said.

"You bring gifts. That makes the god happy, and then you get what you want. Otherwise, the god gets angry and wipes everybody out with a drought or a plague."

"What sort of gifts?" Liesel said.

Steph shrugged. "Food. Something you like. You always have to give up something to get something." She thought for a moment. "And if you don't, the corn won't grow."

"I don't care if the corn grows," Missy said, though I thought my grandfather might.

"If the corn doesn't grow, nothing grows."

"That's stupid."

"No it's not. Corn is the sign of life. It comes from the sun and the earth and water. And then the animals eat it, and it gives them life. And then we drink the milk and eat the animals, and it gives us life."

"Sounds like biology class," Liesel said.

"All right, if the corn doesn't grow, it means you won't grow either," Steph said.

Liesel plucked out the front of her blouse.

"So what have you been bringing?" she said.

Steph actually blushed. Next time, we agreed, we'd all bring an offering.

I got a card that week from Mom. It had foreign stamps on it and no return address. But she said she loved me and she'd see me soon.

I put the card in my jacket pocket and walked out in the field until I stood looking at the row of stalks. Their fingers lifted to point at me in the wind that was blowing in my face and toying with my hair, which had grown long and shaggy. Nancy had offered to trim my bangs, but most days I just pulled it back into a ponytail and let it be. It was loose now, shifting and falling with the gusts, and I squinted against the bits of dust the breeze kicked up.

The corn god seemed to be looking back at me, waiting for me to speak. The crowns on the tall stalks nodded. The attendants rustled in conference, the broken arm on the queen's bishop clacking like a door banging open and shut on a hinge. I lifted a hand in greeting, then let it fall.

I didn't come any closer, just stood watching, until I saw something shiny at the foot of the queen. I brushed my hair back, then walked forward and knelt down to look. It was a muffin. It had been wrapped in foil, but the silver had been carefully folded back and curled like petals. There was a candle, too, with a little silver necklace wrapped around it. The wick was black, but there was only a tiny dimple in the wax beneath it, so it hadn't burned for very long. The muffin was banana walnut, Missy's favorite. You had to give up something you wanted, Steph had said. I picked up the candle and turned it in my fingers. Then I saw the rock that had been laid there. Under it was a piece of paper, and on the paper was Missy's wish—her prayer. I unfolded the note and read it, but Nancy had already told me how Missy's mom had found a lump in her breast and had to go into Logan for tests.

I folded the paper and tucked it back under the rock, then stood and held up my mother's card to show the stalks.

Soon. She hadn't said when, exactly. But she had said soon.

Missy was first up every week after that, with a muffin and a candle. Liesel would raise her eyebrows and lick her lips behind Missy's back where I could see her, though Missy would never say what she wanted out loud.

"You can tell," Liesel said finally. "It's not like a wish."

"He knows," Missy said, getting up from the ground.

Liesel hauled out her math book.

"Not even," Steph said.

"You can't leave that out here," Missy said, wiping her nose with one of the wads of Kleenex she kept stuffed in her coat pockets.

"I figured that way he could read up a little bit," Liesel tipped her head toward the corn god, "and maybe I'd get an A next time." I laughed. Missy insisted she couldn't leave the book. Liesel said it would only be for overnight, but she shoved the book back into her bag and pulled out a tube of lip gloss. Steph shook her head.

"No good," she said. "Unless you want someone to kiss you." Liesel thought a minute, shrugged, and stuck the tube into the ground.

Steph had brought a little stuffed bear.

"What's that got to do with jeans? Or is his name Tyler?" Liesel said. Steph pointed to the tiny blue shorts it was wearing.

I don't know why, but I had taken the little hula dancer from my grandma's shelf. I could come back later and get it. What I always asked for now was the only thing I had wanted since I had gotten the card: I wanted "soon" to be "now." I prayed for my mother to come and take me home.

When I stepped up for my turn, Steph said, from behind me, "Where's your mom, really?"

I didn't turn around. Something had been funny for almost a week now. It felt like Steph had taken a step away from me. She was there, just like she had been since the second day of school, but it was like she was watching instead of being with me. First Steph, and then Liesel and Missy.

"South America," I said.

"That's a whole continent," Liesel pointed out, while she rubbed the tops of her folded arms with her hands.

"Your mother's not a model," Steph said.

I took a long breath.

"She was."

"She's not an actress. And your dad's only a supply sergeant."

"He is now," I said feebly.

"That's all he's ever been," Steph said. "My uncle's in his unit."

I stood holding the little hula girl in front of me, thumbing her skirt.

"Why did you lie to us?" Liesel said.

"I didn't," I tried.

"Stop lying." Missy had been quiet for a couple of weeks, and she had started to cry over everything. Now she sounded angry.

I turned to face them, casting around for something to say. I put a hand in my pocket, found my mother's card, and squeezed it in my fist.

"Why'd she leave you?" Steph said.

"She went to get a job."

"But why'd she have to leave you here?"

I didn't know why. I had never known why.

"I'm sorry," I said.

"Why should we believe you now?" Missy said.

"True," Steph agreed.

I stood with the three of them in an arc in front of me, waiting, until Steph said, "We'll fix it. Come here." She squatted to tug a piece of orange bailing twine from the dirt and told me to hold out my hands. I set the hula dancer down, and she wrapped the twine around my wrists, tying it in a triple knot on top.

"A little dolly's not going to do it. You'll have to be the corn god's bride." She waved an arm in front of the stalks. "We'll need to make a bed, here," she said. Missy and Liesel went to work gathering together bunches of grass and laying them out on the ground Steph had swept with her foot. I was crying.

"I'm sorry," I said.

"Don't tell me," Steph said. She tipped her head toward the line of stalks. "You need to tell him."

While Missy finished straightening out the grass nest, Steph said they needed to do my feet, and Liesel tied the laces of my shoes together.

"Lie down here," Steph said.

"I didn't lie to the corn god," I said, kneeling down, then dropping onto my rump on the frozen grass.

"How do we know?" Missy said. She looked over to Steph and Liesel. "What should she have to do? Maybe she should stay here all night."

"Someone would have to stay here with her to make sure," Liesel said.

"We wouldn't have to do that, would we, Deeds?" Steph said. "Not on your wedding night." Liesel giggled.

I shook my head no. No, they wouldn't have to. No, they couldn't leave me here all night. Just no.

They stood around me in a half-circle, chewing at their lips, scrunching up their foreheads to think. The sun was almost gone, and from my back, I could see the night sky's first cold star.

"I know," Steph said. She searched for a good-sized ear and snapped it off a stalk. She came back and stood at my feet, peeling back the husk and exposing the cob. Liesel had a quizzical smile on her face. Missy stood in front of the king, the hood from her coat pulled up, biting at her thumb.

"What's that for?" Liesel said.

"For the sacrifice."

Liesel made a chopping motion with her arm, her fist closed as if she were plunging a knife. Then she started to chant.

"Un yah un yah un yah un yah."

"Lying is a serious offense," Steph said, looking down at me. "There's a price that has to be paid."

I stared up at her. Liesel started chanting again.

"Un yah un yah un yah un yah."

"Are you ready?" Steph turned to Missy and Liesel. "You're going to have to help."

Steph raised the peeled cob above her head, while Liesel started around to my other side, but I had already worked my lashed-together shoes off at the heels, and I rolled to my knees and up on my feet, biting at the orange twine that tasted of waxy plastic and dirt as I stumbled away.

"She went to go get a job," I said, spitting grit from my mouth. "She's coming back."

"Not now," Steph said, shaking her head and waggling the corncob at me.

I worked the card out of my pocket with my tied hands and shook it at them, backing into the field, feeling the corn stubble jab into my feet.

"She already told me," I said. "She said soon."

"That was before. Now the corn god's going to be angry."

"You probably sent that card to yourself," Missy said.

"You asked about your mom, too," I reminded her. Her face clouded.

"But she didn't offend the corn god," Steph said. "The corn god will listen to her."

I shook the card.

"She already said."

"I'd hate to be your grandpa next spring. The corn's going to be about this high," Steph tipped to one side and held a hand to her knee. "If it even sprouts."

"Well...I saw you and Tyler," I yelled at Steph. I was panting now. "I was over at Nancy's. You were out back...you were behind the trampoline."

Steph stood with her mouth hung open.

"Liar," she said.

"You were, he was—"

"Everything you say is a lie!" Steph threw the cob at me. "No wonder the corn god hates you."

"I don't care," I cried, tripping over the stump-littered ground while I backed away. "I come out at night and pee on it."

Missy hurled a cob at me with murder in her face. Liesel stared at her, while Steph found another.

"Go on, then," Steph said, chucking the cob. "And don't be surprised what happens."

"I saw you," I tried again. More ears landed around me, and I scrambled across the field for the road. I could hear them arguing behind me after the cobs stopped, Steph shouting, "You think I care?" And then Liesel, yelling from the end of the field while I ran in my stocking feet along the flat rise in between the two ruts that made the road, the sharp breeze snapping at my face and ears:

"It was a game, Deeds."

From my upstairs window, I imagined I could just make out his crown, the shadow of the wheat-headed tassels at the tops of the tallest stalks. I couldn't remember a moon so bright: you could see the road through the field, the cows bedded down in the mouth of the hay shed in the corral, the dark pole of an old derrick like a long gallows, and far to the west, the dim white luminescence—a science word that week—resting on the corn god.

He would kill my father in the war and keep my mother, ruin my grandpa's farm. Or if the corn god wouldn't, the real God would, for bowing down in front of the stalks. Maybe it had happened already, with Missy's mom—and now with Grandma. Nancy had been at the house waiting for me when I got home, shoeless and bawling. After she had calmed me down, made me wash my face, and got me in my slippers, she told me that my grandfather had run Grandma into Logan to the doctor. She wouldn't tell me exactly what had happened; she said it would be all right, but I didn't think she sounded sure.

I didn't change out of my clothes when I went up to bed. I had shivered since I had gotten home that afternoon, and I didn't know if I would ever take my clothes off again. I stood shivering at my windowsill, cold from the inside out, my mind churning, until finally I felt my way down the dark stairs, running my hand along the wall, feeling over the edge of each step with my foot for the next one. I turned the knob to the hall closet slowly, pushing against the door with my other hand, because it shut tight and sprang when it opened. I reached down my coat, slid my arms into the sleeves, and left the door ajar as I headed for the kitchen cupboard, where Grandpa kept a flashlight and matches.

"DeeDee?"

I hadn't seen my grandfather sitting in the corner at the kitchen table. I shook when he spoke, terrified and struck dumb, until I knew the voice was his.

"It's the middle of the night," he said. He didn't turn on the lamp hanging above the table. I knew he was there, a shadow in the corner, but I couldn't make him out distinctly, and he didn't stand.

"What you got your coat on for?"

"I was cold. Where's Grandma?"

He didn't answer.

"Nancy was here," I said. "She made me supper. She was just going to go check on her boys. I told her I'd be all right, she didn't have to stay." I liked Nancy. I didn't want to get her in trouble.

"She was here when I got back. We thought you were asleep."

"Where's Grandma?" I said.

"They kept her at the hospital."

"What happened?"

"She was cooking dinner at the stove."

"Was it bad?" I said.

"No," he told me. I would learn the details later, how she had said to him, "Earl, look," and held out her nightie from the sides, watching the flames twirling around the hem, snaking their way up toward her waist.

He stood and walked to the sink. I went to the wall, found the switch, and turned on the light. He pulled away from the brightness of the bulb. A day's beard made his face gray, and he wore a suit jacket on top of his overalls. He had the face of a sad-looking dog; loose folds of skin hung down around his mouth, and the eyes were stunned. I didn't understand, then, how my grandfather was a disappointed man. He had never gotten ahead as he had hoped to; his small herd of Jerseys stayed small, his fields never expanded in the way he had dreamed, and he owed more and owned less now than he had when my father was my age. There had been the daughter, long dead from drugs, and a silly try at local politics that had left him looking like a fool. He had already borne a thousand failures, large and small. Now his crazy wife had set herself on fire.

And I knew why.

"He hurt her," I said. "Just like Missy's mom."

"Who? What's the matter with Missy's mom?"

I explained about the cancer, the lone stand of corn and the prayer hid under the rock, the gifts Missy brought every week now.

"Next year," I told him, "the crops won't grow. He won't let them." I was desperate by then, my body bent forward, every sinew, every pulse begging.

"And Mom won't come back. Dad will get hurt."

Something in him stirred, and he seemed to wake.

"Who said?"

"He did."

"Who?"

"The corn god," I told him. "Bad things will happen—they said don't be surprised."

My grandfather looked down at me, his hands resting on the counter behind him. I had time for half a dozen panting breaths before he spoke.

"Out there?" He pointed down the hall toward the back door.

I nodded.

"He's out there now?"

I nodded yes again.

"That why you got your coat on?"

Was that where I had really been going?

"Show me," he said. He handed me down a flashlight from the

kitchen cupboard, then lifted his own coat from a peg by the back door.

The night air bit at us as we stepped into it, trying to herd us back inside. The air, the crackle of the crisp grass as we walked, made the world seem brittle. At the barn, my grandfather took the flashlight and told me to wait. He went inside, and I listened to the low murmurs and shufflings of the cows around the corner, smelled their ammonia scent. They heard or sensed us there and began to stir and move our way. "Shh," I told them, but it was comforting to know they were close. My grandfather came out with a round, metal can, handed me the flashlight again, and walked toward the road. He seemed to know where we were going; I followed along in a rut in the frozen clay, still in my slippers. He spoke only once; always frugal, he told me to turn off the flashlight, as the moon was bright enough that we didn't need it.

Where the road made its T, I pointed to the north, and as we came up to the file of stalks, I turned the light on them, scanning up and down their length, then panning over the ground in front of them. There were my shoes, the laces still in knots. A little half-circle of cobs stood in the soil where the girls had apparently stuck them near the head of the grass bed after I had run. I hung back while my grandfather walked forward and stood a few steps in front of the row of corn.

"You girls been playing out here?" he said. I nodded.

"This what done it? Brought your bad luck?"

"Yes," I told him. I kept moving the light's beam up and down the rank of stalks. In the dark, they seemed to rustle and whisper amongst themselves, then froze, morphing into plain dried leaves and stems when I trained the light on them. My grandfather brushed at the arc of buried cobs with the toe of his boot, and looked at the nest of grass; then he took something from his pocket and turned back toward me.

He had a sickle in his hand. I didn't know what it was called then; I just saw the curve of the knife, the point at its end. It was only a crescent shadow in the dark, but I thought I could see its edge, honed down to silver on the whetstone in the barn.

I dropped the flashlight and ran.

"DeeDee," he yelled. I dove into the cave made by the drooping arms of the Russian olives. He could have followed me if he'd wanted—there was nothing to stop him, only the branches hung so low, I thought they might give me an advantage. I rolled in the grass, wet and cold with frost, panting, then scrambled on my hands and knees over toward the fence, away from the opening, back from where he might think I was, and peeked out from the branches.

He had picked up the flashlight and was scanning with it over where I had crawled under the tree.

"DeeDee," the same impatient yell, loveless, bitter.

He stood with the flashlight pointed at the tree, the sickle resting against his leg. I worked myself further down the hill until I felt the fence at my back.

"DeeDee," he called again after a while. His voice had softened, not from compassion, not some sweet lure to bring me into the open, but because he'd given up. Then he set the flashlight down on the can, walked over to the row of corn, and got down on a knee.

I couldn't really have believed that he would kill me, so maybe what prompted me to run was what he did next, when he grasped the first stalk, the king's rook, a foot above the ground, swung the sickle, and chopped it from the roots—the rook, the knight, then the bishop and his attendant, on his way to the king. The sickle was actually dull maybe, or the stalks were tough and fibrous, or my grandfather was tired, because some of them he beat at, slashing and chopping until they came away from the earth, and he laid them down behind him. He cut down the whole stand, kicking at the stumps when he stood, pushing the leaves and stems together in a pile with his booted feet. Then he poured gasoline from the can over the pile, stepped back, and tossed a match he had pulled from his pocket and lit by scraping it beneath his thumbnail. The flames were instant—a poof of sound, and they appeared, a magician's trick. He took a few steps back, then sat on the can to watch the orange pennants rise and then bend before a bit of breeze.

I crawled out from under the trees while he sat there, hunched low to the ground, elbows on his knees. I came up to the fire from behind him, watched it for a moment, then gathered up a handful of cobs and flung them into the flames one by one.

My grandfather looked my way and nodded.

I gathered every cob and leaf and stem I could find and hurled them in. I threw in pieces of orange bailing twine, tufts of grass I jerked out of the ground. I threw in everything I could pick up that would burn, working my way around to the front of the fire, where I found Missy's necklace. I squatted by it, flushed warm from the fire and my effort, and looked into the flames that had made quick work of the weeds and were already dying, curling into little dots of embers, as though in their hurry they had mistakenly consumed themselves. It was just a game. That's what Liesel had said: It was a game. But Liesel had only wagered on a math test.

"She's not coming back," I said out loud.

"I don't know," my grandfather replied.

We were thinking our separate thoughts, each of our own losses.

I scanned the ground for Grandma's little hula dancer, but it was gone—in the flames, or maybe one of the girls had taken it. I picked the necklace out of the dirt and laid it under a rock at the edge of the blackened circle of ashes. Then I turned to my grandfather, who handed me the sickle to carry and picked up his gas can.

He did not take my hand on the walk back to the house; this was not a movie or a play; we were not sudden friends or newly reconciled. But we were allies now, at least. Nature makes an indifferent god, and the winter in the valley would be long and bleak, because that's what winters were here. Grandma would come back after New Year's for a while. Liesel talked to me at school still sometimes, and in my prayers at night, kneeling on the old rag rug beside my bed, I dutifully remembered Missy's mom (who would have a double mastectomy and then start training to run marathons) when I asked for my own.

In the spring, I'd ride with my grandfather while he planted, sitting on the fender high above the giant, turning wheel of the tractor, waiting for a card or a call, each with far-flung promises to see me soon, each gap between the last one and the next a little longer, weaning me away. And in the scorching heat of summer—this one, or the next, or one of many that would follow—life would rise: during one, the war would end and the soldiers would come home; over another, I would tend an enormous crop of pumpkins; I would marry (like my mother, young) in another; and in the next would have a baby of my own. They would always end, as summer always does, with a tinge of sadness, and at the far edge of the field, looming tall as a man on horseback, the corn would always grow.

INTERVIEW WITH
LAURA VAN DEN BERG

by Jeremiah Chamberlin

Laura van den Berg grew up in Florida and received her MFA from Emerson College. Her stories have recently appeared or are forthcoming in such places as Ploughshares, Conjunctions, American Short Fiction, One Story, *the* Boston Review, Literary Review, Epoch, *and* StoryQuarterly. *Her work has also been anthologized in* The Best American Nonrequired Reading 2008, Best New American Voices 2010, *and* The Pushcart Prize XXIV: Best of the Small Presses. *Her first collection,* What the World Will Look Like When All the Water Leaves Us, *was published by Dzanc Books in the fall of 2009. The book was a Barnes & Noble Discover Great New Writers Holiday Pick, a finalist for* ForeWord *Magazine's Book of the Year*

Laura van den Berg

Photo credit: Miriam Berkley

Award, long-listed for the Story Prize, and short-listed for the Frank O'Connor Award. A former assistant editor at **Ploughshares,** *van den Berg is now a fiction editor at* **West Branch.** *She has taught writing at Emerson College, Gettysburg College, and Grub Street, as well as in the PEN/New England's Freedom to Write Program as the recipient of a Dzanc Prize. In addition to scholarships from the Bread Loaf and Sewanee Writers' Conferences, she is the recipient of the 2009 Julia Peterkin Award from Converse College, the 2009-2010 Emerging Writer Lectureship at Gettysburg College, and the 2010-2011 Tickner Fellowship at the Gilman School. She currently lives in Baltimore with writer Paul Yoon, where she is at work on both short fiction and a novel.*

Let's begin at the beginning. Were you someone for whom writing was always important, or did you come to it later in life?

I came to it later, which I think is a bit unusual. Most writers I know were at least really big readers when they were younger, if they weren't already writing. Yet I had no interest in literature at all. My literary education had ended with *To Kill a Mockingbird.* Then, when I got to college, I wanted to be a psychology major. But two things happened simultaneously in my first year of school: one, you have to take math for a psychology major, and I was failing statistics because I can't do math at all; and, two, I took a creative-writing workshop as an elective. That was where the switch flipped for me. I was twenty, and I think the biggest thing apart from starting to write my own work was the reading. We read Lorrie Moore, Amy Hempel, and all these fabulous short-story writers. I'd just had no idea that literature like that was even out there! So that was a total revelation. I was seeing a sense of reality in literature that really resonated with me.

How so?

I think because it was more contemporary. Reading *To Kill a Mock-ingbird* or *Sounder* or any of the other books that you read in freshman English—these weren't worlds that I could connect to. They felt like relics from a different time. So somehow I had gone through life not really knowing that contemporary literature existed, which I know now sounds crazy, but I felt like these authors were speaking my language. I love Lorrie Moore's viciously dark humor, for example. And the beautiful fragility that a lot of Amy Hempel's characters have. After that, I switched my major to English with a minor in creative writing, and started writing seriously.

Where was this?

This was in Florida. I grew up in Florida and I went to school at Rollins College, which is a little liberal-arts school in Orlando.

Let's talk about how Florida either did or didn't shape your sense of aesthetic, because none of the stories in your collection are set in the state. In fact, I was surprised to learn that you'd grown up there after I finished reading the book.

It's such a bizarre state, you know? There are so many different worlds. I grew up in Orlando, which is very suburban. So as I got older, I was really unhappy to be a resident of Florida. I longed for the Northeast, even though I'd never really been there. I imagined it as the epitome of arts and culture. So my dream was to get out of Florida. And because of that, because I didn't have a real interest in the place—or maybe I couldn't fully appreciate the place—I didn't want to write about Florida. So both literally and in terms of my writing, this was a place I was looking to move away from. Of course, in hindsight, I can see now that there's a kind of surrealism to the entire state. I mean, as a kid I liked to go to Gatorland, where you can pay to see people wrestle alligators and feed these huge creatures that would really like to do nothing more than eat you. [*Laughter.*]

A good place to take your kids, right?

Yeah! My dad would take me and my sister there. And many other parts of the state are just as strange. So I think without me knowing it, the strangeness of that place was actually very important to my writing. Because with a lot of the stories in my collection—even though they don't take place in Florida—there is a kind of strangeness to the landscape. That felt normal to me. And I think a lot of that had to do with growing up in this sort of odd culture.

So what did you do after you finished college?

I went straight to graduate school at Emerson, which is in Boston.

Emerson was a great place for me at that particular time. I made a lot of friends there, I had some great teachers there, and that's where I wrote most of my stories that are in my book.

Who did you work with?

Don Lee, Jessica Treadway, Pamela Painter, Margot Livesey. They were all wonderful. Margot's amazing strength as a teacher is the ability to look inside a story and understand what the author wants to do with it, and then help them work toward that. Margot helped me better understand what I was trying to do, but wasn't yet accomplishing.

How so?

Margot is Scottish, so her whole manner is very British in that she is the most polite person you could ever meet. She is very direct, but has her own way of saying things. So she'll say, "You know, I had questions about the ending," which you learn in Margot-speak means, "I don't think this is working very well." [*Laughter.*] Her approach is Socratic—she asks you questions and tries to get you to understand the world you're trying to put down better than you do.

Was there a particular story in the collection that she really helped you turn around?

She was immensely helpful with all of them, because I wrote nearly every story in graduate school, but "Up High in the Air," in particular. When I showed it to her, I knew it wasn't very good. And instead of the husband being obsessed with the lake monster, he was randomly obsessed with the yeti. The words Margot used to describe that element were "willfully strange." It was a strangeness that didn't really have roots in the character's lives. Rather, it felt more like the author *imposing* strangeness upon it. So she helped me rewrite that story through a different lens.

Nearly all of your stories do have a "strange" or mystical element to them— the Loch Ness monster, Bigfoot, et cetera. So did those concerns arise naturally within the stories, or did you set out to write a book with this subject matter?

It happened by accident. When I got three-fourths of the way through drafting the book, I did notice these recurring elements, which was when I started thinking of it in terms of a potential collection. But I don't really know where all the monster stuff came from. [*Laughter.*] Again, I guess from the strangeness of the landscape I grew up in. Though it's interesting to hear some people read the stories and describe them this way. I mean, I understand they're not all straight-up realism, they're moving in the direction of fabulism or magical realism, but these sorts of fascinations felt normal, you know? Frankly, it felt like realism to me at the time! I loved that stuff as a kid—I was totally interested in the Loch Ness monster and Bigfoot—but my *real* interest in these stories is why we become obsessed and fixated on things. And the ways in which we try to give our lives a story, to give our lives purpose and direction. The various ways that that can take shape are not always the most helpful sorts of ways. I inexplicably love monsters and myths, but I think that within that there's a kind of ineffability about the human experience and being in the world. Because I've always felt like there's so much about the world, so much mystery, that I would never understand. I was really interested in exploring that mystery in my own work, and the monsters became a way to do that.

Perhaps because your work walks that line between reality and magical realism at times, part of the mystery becomes trying to understand what's real and what isn't. For example, in "Goodbye My Loveds," there may or may not be a hole that leads to the other side of the world. Certainly the narrator's younger brother, who she's taking care of after the death of their parents, thinks it exists. But as readers, we're never quite sure.

As an author I don't really have an opinion on whether the hole is just a hole, or whether it's a tunnel that might not lead to the other side of the world but *could* lead to something magical. I mean, I believe that it could be either. I'm just really interested in people who live in the world of the imagination. For example, characters like McKay, who really believes that the Loch Ness monster is out there, and Denver, who really believes that this hole is going to lead him someplace. I think it's beautiful and terrifying at the same time, because it's easier to *not* believe in things in a way. To decide these possibilities don't exist, that there aren't things out there, that there's only daily reality. So I think there's a beauty to people who do live in the world with imagination, and who embrace the mystery of the world at large.

At the same time, this can be terrifying because people can be totally engulfed by that belief, and they can disappear into the mystery, disappear into the fog. That's a contradiction that I'm interested in as both a writer and as a person.

I have to say I find myself increasingly drawn to this type of fiction—writing that isn't quite so neat and tidy, that isn't built with the intricacy of a pocket watch. Certainly I can appreciate the craftsmanship, but I'm rarely moved by it on an emotional level. It's almost too perfect. Everything fits and makes sense. My students, on the other hand, want a clear "message" or "lesson" to take away from the story. They're not interested in ambiguity.

Yeah, my students are very much the same way. I think that has a lot to do with why, on a cultural level, there's such an interest in memoir. Because memoir seems to be very much about the "why," you know?

Cause and effect.

Right. Cause and effect—this happened to me, I went through this experience, and this is what it meant. Or, this is how I got to this point, and this is how I got out.

Well, we want to know that every child molester was abused so that we can explain this sort of pathology. It needs to have a definable and identifiable cause, or the world fails to make sense.

Right. And that goes back to what I was saying about monsters standing in for this sort of unknowing. Whether we acknowledge it or not, most people are facing this on some level in their day-to-day lives. Life so rarely gives us that "why." We try to understand inexplicable things, but usually the explanations we come up with tend to fall short. There are so many things that can't really be understood.

To me the difference between positive and negative ambiguity in fiction has to do with the central concerns of the story. The logic system of the story should determine what is and what isn't answered. It doesn't need to necessarily give the reader answers, but I think it should give them something to take away. So when you're working with a student and they say, "I didn't want to explain anything—you were supposed to be confused," my experience in reading those stories is not that I'm getting something but I can't quite make sense of it, but that as a reader the story is giving me nothing. It's communicating nothing to me.

Another common element in your fiction that has to do with the "unexplained" is the way in which relationships often simply come to an end. This then leaves your characters struggling to understand why that happened.

In a number of ways the characters in this book are all dealing with loss of some kind, and the end of relationships is one of those types of loss. I'm interested in people grappling with absence, and trying to figure out what to put in that absence, or how to make sense of the absence, when usually you can't make sense of it. So that's Part One of the answer.

Part Two of why I'm interested in characters whose relationships just fall apart…I mean, I've been in a really happy relationship with another writer for the last six years, and so I think having that platform of security in my personal life gave me space to explore relationships that I had had that perhaps weren't so happy. In my family there were a lot of complicated relationships, and quite a bit of divorce. So I never perceived marriage—even as a child—as something that was intended to be happy and harmonious. I mean, I've often perceived marriage as a source of strife. So that, again, was my own reality that I was bringing to the stories.

And I think that what draws people together and what keeps people together is mysterious. Oftentimes it doesn't really have a lot to do with love. People need each other to fulfill certain roles. Then, at a certain point, maybe that runs its course. So, yeah, I guess for a very long time I had always viewed relationships as things that end. And even though my personal opinion on that has shifted a little as I've gotten older, I think that that worldview is part of the landscape of the stories.

What I also liked about the collection that made it feel very unified to me is the emotional atmosphere that permeates the book. In many of the stories there's a kind of joyful sadness. The Greeks have a word for this: harmolypi. *Joy and sadness at the same time. Was that something you were conscious of as you were crafting the stories?*

I became more conscious of the emotional landscapes once I was in the final stages of revision. But it's true that some of the characters are in a kind of deep sadness, and that they don't exactly have an epiphany, but rather a transcendent moment in the sadness. I think it's probably pretty clear to the reader that Jimmy [in "Where We Must Be"] is not long for this world. But when they have that moment couched on the bank of the lake and he asks Jean to help him wade out…for me, at least, Jean is kind of having this beautiful moment. It's a horrible moment, but it's a beautiful moment at the same time. And, frankly, it's just very rare to have a moment that's completely agonizing or completely beautiful that isn't tinged with something else. So I guess I'm interested in that complexity of experience. But at the level of the *moment*, if that makes sense.

It does. It's more about "gesture" than "epiphany." So how do you find those moments? Are you someone who writes through the story looking for the end? Or are you somebody who writes toward an end that you've already seen?

I wouldn't say I've seen the ending, per se, but what I have often seen is an image of some kind in almost all of these stories. I didn't know what action would happen, but I was writing toward that particular image. Like a distant light that I was moving toward.

Was that the case in the story we were just talking about?

Yes. I had the image of them out on the water. I had no idea how they would get from A to B to C to D, but I *did* have that image. Similarly, in the title story, one of the first things I had was the image of the mother walking away and the daughter watching her.

How do your stories begin?

They start in all kinds of ways for me. With "Where I Must Be," for example, I was doing something really mundane, washing the dishes, and I just heard that first line: "Some people dream of being chased by Bigfoot." It's one of those moments as a writer where you're like, "Am I on to something or am I just going crazy?" [*Laughter.*] So that was a voice thing for me. And I just started following the voice.

Some pieces, like the title story, started with a word. I just randomly fell in love with the word *Madagascar.* I would walk around saying it to myself: *Madagascar, Madagascar.* [*Laughter.*] It sounds exotic, sort of like a Jacques Cousteau kind of thing, doesn't it? I knew nothing about Madagascar except a vague sense of where it was located in the world, and that there were lemurs there. But I just fell in love with that word and that grew into a story.

Since we're on the topic of Madagascar, I want to ask about the role of science in these stories. So many of the adults in this book are either explorers or biologists. Were your parents scientists?

No, not in the literal sense. But I think both of my parents are very curious people in different kinds of ways, and are interested in the world. So I guess on an intellectual level the idea of exploration was not unusual to me. But I always thought that was just the coolest thing ever—to be an explorer of some kind.

Several years ago I was interviewing Peter Ho Davies, who had a background in science before he became a writer, and he said that the disciplines aren't as separate as people often think. That, in fact, he often approaches writing stories like a scientist: asking questions, probing hypotheses, trying to uncover what's hidden.

Yeah. Absolutely. I know nothing about science and have no background in science at all, but I'm interested in this idea of seeking knowledge. And, specifically, seeking answers, and answers that aren't always accessible. It seems like a fundamental part of the human condition to quest for this knowledge—to try to understand what the solar system looks like, and how atoms and particles function, and how to cure things.

Were the scientific elements of these stories put in place to create a comparison between the mystical and the mythical? Or did they just naturally come together?

They naturally came together. I didn't ever say to myself, "I will now align the knowable and the unknowable!" If only I could have that kind of foresight when I'm actually sitting down at my desk, it'd be immensely helpful. [*Laughter.*] But, alas, not the case. I always think about that E.L. Doctorow quote: "Writing is like driving at night in the fog. You can only see as far as your headlights, but you can make the whole trip that way." That's very much my writing process—groping through the dark, trying to find things in that darkness.

In "Inverness," for example, Emily is questing via science, and McKay is questing via something that is much more unscientific; Emily is looking for the twin flower, which is rare, but exists, whereas

McKay is looking for something that arguably doesn't exist at all. But to me their searches are very similar. In terms of the emotional trajectory of the search, there's really no difference between the two. So rather than consciously putting the mythic and scientific side by side, I think I was more interested in the different ways we search for things, and how those searches help us uncover the self at the same time.

So if you're "groping through the dark" while you write, does revision play a large role in your process?

Absolutely. I tend to write drafts quickly, and they're usually messy drafts. When I'm done what I have is a skeletal thing, so revision for me is putting flesh on the bone. But the main thing for me in revision is just figuring out what it is that I've actually written—what kind of story is here, what kind of story *could* be here, uncovering what the real story is and who these characters are. There's a lot of imaginative excavation that happens in revision.

Do you mean in terms of voice, in terms of emotional payoff, or in terms of structure?

I think those things are all very intertwined. If you figure out what the story is, then you find the right structure, which means the emotional payoff is much more likely to appear.

Why is that?

Well, I think when you figure out the story, you start writing things that are true for that story, or at least start moving in a truer direction. I don't see structure as being a separate thing. The whole purpose of structure is to reveal, to put characters in a situation where whatever emotional truth the story is getting at can be revealed. So when I'm revising, I'm trying to figure out all these things—not just structure, but also what it is that I think I want to be revealed in the first place. They're connected. That's when the emotional payoff comes onto the page. When I'm drafting, I really don't know what I'm writing. It's a mess. [*Laughter.*]

Another thing that changes for me as a writer during the revision process is how I think about audience. During the drafting stage, it's just me and the characters. But once I start revising, I'm aware of a reader. How do you approach this?

That's so crucial. When I'm drafting it's very important for me to think of it as speaking into the void, and to not consider an audience or a reader. Then I revise up until the point where I know the story still has problems, but I don't know exactly how to fix them. That's when some really dear friends who are wonderful readers of your work become immensely helpful, because they can help you understand the gap between what you think you might have put on the page and what's *actually* on the page. Because you know the world and you know the characters, you might think certain elements are in play when they're actually still in your head.

In terms of a broader audience, short fiction is often accused of being too insular, of being less focused on "important" issues like politics and social justice and more concerned with the individual experience. In an article he wrote for Mother Jones, *Ted Genoways, the editor of the* Virginia Quarterly Review, *said, "Writers need to venture out from under the protective wing of academia to put themselves and their work on the line. Stop being so damn dainty and polite, treat writing like your life blood instead of your livelihood." Do you think that's a fair accusation?*

I do think that fiction should say something. I don't mean it has to be a political statement or anything like that, but something that matters. Not long ago, the *Guardian* had a feature called "Ten Rules for Writing Fiction," and they invited authors to submit their best writing advice. Anne Enright said, "Remember that all description is an opinion about the world. Find a place to stand." I think that that's very true. Aesthetically, we should find a place to stand and own it. In that way fiction can say something.

This also reminds me of the piece Stephen King wrote about the short story in the *New York Times Book Review* ["What Ails the Short Story"] several years ago. He said that when he reads a story he wants it to be like "a big, hot meteor screaming down from the Kansas sky." He said that fiction should be vivid and exciting and adventurous, which I don't disagree with. I mean, I want that experience as a reader too; it's not like I'm sitting here saying, "Oh, no, I would like my stories to be gray and pallid and unexciting." [*Laughter.*] But this seems like an easy argument to make about the state of fiction. Because I *do* think that every writer wants their work to be compelling, whether or not it fits this definition.

Insofar as "the protective wing of academia," I know writers who really thrive off their academic jobs, and others for whom it's been really bad for their writing. For some, an academic job is the greatest thing in the world—they do amazing work while they're also teaching. But when a writer has been on campus a really long time and has tenure, it can take away a sense of urgency or ambition to create work with broader relevance. I mean, it's not uncommon to find writers teaching who wrote great books when they were younger, but who haven't published a book in ten years. I don't think that's academia's fault, but it seems to be a fairly common story for writers in academia. I wonder if some people would have been better off doing something else.

And this is what I think, personally, has gotten a little bit dangerous about going through an MFA program: it's assumed that you want to seek out an academic job afterward. Again, I have no objection to writers working in academia. But I think the assumption is that this is the normal thing to do. Some people fall into academic jobs without really asking themselves the hard questions: "Is this a good fit for my writing? Would I be better off having a nine-to-five job?" Those are questions I'm still grappling with for myself.

Similarly, some people believe that an MFA program will automatically make them a writer. So when that doesn't magically happen afterward, it's very difficult for them to sustain their writing, particularly without the encouragement and support of their peers. Yet it takes an immense amount of work and patience and luck to break into publishing.

My experience in my MFA program was very positive. I don't think I could have written this book if I hadn't have been in a program at the time. But my boyfriend, Paul Yoon, does not have an MFA. He graduated from Wesleyan, and afterward he just went out into the world and worked. He published his first book [*Once the Shore*] in 2009. People often ask him, "What program did you graduate from?" And when he says, "I didn't get an MFA," they're flabbergasted. As if it were impossible to be a writer without an MFA. I think that that is what bothers me—not the existence of MFA programs, but the idea that you can't be a writer if you didn't go to one. That's just crazy. If the tide continues in that direction, I think that that's not necessarily a good trend.

Speaking of publishing, let's talk a bit about your experience with Dzanc Books. How did your collection end up with them?

After I won the Dzanc Prize in 2007, they asked to see the whole collection. I was working with an agent at the time, and we sent it to them, they made an offer, and we accepted. [*Laughter.*] It was all actually quite painless, which I feel is not the typical story. And they were really enthused about the book, which seemed good. We decided that Dzanc would be a great home for the collection, and it absolutely has been.

I think that a lot of writers—young writers, in particular—have their eyes on big houses and don't realize some of the benefits of working with an independent press like Dzanc.

Yeah, I had a long conversation about this last night with some fellow writers. Something that I've loved and valued about Dzanc is that they tend to publish only one book a month, or every other month. If you're their October release, it's very personalized. Their focus is completely on your book, which would certainly not be the case at a big house where they're juggling many more titles. I know that this is my first experience with a publisher, but something I've loved about Dzanc is their hands-on approach and enthusiasm. The whole process was very collaborative. From the cover design to the font, I really had a say in everything, so as an author, I felt like I had a real voice in the process. They were also great in terms of offering support for the book tour.

Which is vanishing.

Which is vanishing! Exactly. I know people who have published books recently with bigger houses, but who got absolutely nothing for tour support because so many publishers feel there isn't a strong enough correlation between touring and book sales. But Dzanc was great about helping me get out there.

The book has certainly gotten noticed, too. The collection was a Barnes & Noble Discovery Pick, selected for Andrew's Book Club, long-listed for the

Story Prize, and short-listed for the Frank O'Connor Award, among other accolades.

Yeah, maybe there was a time when if you published with an indie press you were only reaching a very specific audience, and it was harder to get broader attention for your book. But I think that's really shifting. And to use Paul as an example, too, when he published his book with Sarabande, if I may brag about him for a moment… [*Laughter.*]

Please.

…his collection was a *New York Times* Notable Book, as well as being selected by the *San Francisco Chronicle* and the *L.A. Times* as one of their best books of 2009. He was in no way hampered by being with an indie house, and I don't feel that I've been, either.

Speaking of touring, Julie Barer, who is an agent, recently visited Ann Arbor and told our MFA students that the days of writers locking themselves in a garret is over. That in order to develop an audience, authors need to put themselves out there more than they once did—that they've got to be involved in a literary conversation that's happening on the internet and on blogs, as well as attending conferences and festivals. Is that something that you enjoy doing? Would you say that you're involved in the broader literary conversation?

Yeah, it is. I mean, I wouldn't do it if I didn't enjoy it. I think Julie is right. But I also think that writers—and this might sound a little idealistic—I think writers should just be who they are. And do what feels true to themselves. Again, to use Paul as an example, we're opposites in many ways. He totally believes that the writer *should* be in a garret removed from the rest of the world. So he said, "I'm not touring. Nothing." That's just not who he is, and I really admire that he knew that about himself and really stuck to his guns. He understands that this might have consequences—it's not like he was being naive about it. But life is too short, you know? We should just be who we are.

But me, I love this stuff. I'm the classic extrovert personality—I love to travel, I love to go places and meet people and hang out with friends. Going on a book tour, then, was an opportunity to have a big adventure. Community is also very important to me. So to be able to enlarge and cultivate community, and to be part of the larger literary conversation, was incredibly valuable and important to me as a writer.

Jeremiah Chamberlin lives in Ann Arbor, where he is the Associate Director of the English Department Writing Program at the University of Michigan. His writing has appeared in such places as *Glimmer Train*, the *New York Times Book Review*, *Poets & Writers*, the *Michigan Quarterly Review*, *Flyway*, and *Fiction Writers Review*, as well as in online exclusives for *Granta* and the *Virginia Quarterly Review*. His short fiction has received a Pushcart Prize Special Mention and has been twice nominated for Best New American Voices. He is the Editor of the online literary journal *Fiction Writers Review* and a Contributing Editor for *Poets & Writers*.

1985. I spent the year naked, in sunglasses.

Lydia Fitzpatrick received her MFA from the University of Michigan in 2010, where she won a Hopwood Award for short fiction. She was the 2010–2011 Carl Djerassi Fiction Fellow at the Wisconsin Institute for Creative Writing. Her fiction, nonfiction, and interviews have appeared in *Mid-American Review*, *Opium*, *Fiction Writers Review*, and *Devil's Lake*, and she is a recipient of the 2010–2011 Sherwood Anderson Fiction Award. She lives in Wadmalaw, South Carolina. "In a Library, in Saltillo" is part of a novel-in-progress.

IN A LIBRARY, IN SALTILLO

Lydia Fitzpatrick

Sadie wiped her mouth and flushed the toilet. Her throat burned, and the morning light leaking through the blinds made her brain spin.

"You throwing up again?" Her mother's voice came from down the hall, from the couch.

"Nah!" Sadie yelled, as she felt her stomach lift and flip. She clamped her lips shut, pictured steady ground, and waited for it to pass. The mirror over the sink was flecked with bits of toothpaste. She'd blown out her hair, but now there was vomit in it, clumped in one of the dulled black streaks Kayla had put in that fall, when they were still friends. She washed it out, careful not to smudge the smoky cat-eyes she'd drawn, and pulled on a pair of jean shorts. They weren't nice, she knew, but they were the only thing that still fit her, and she figured they wouldn't for long. She wasn't sure how much weight she'd gained—she hadn't dared stand on the scale in the girls' locker room—but her skin had started to feel taut, like she was a water balloon filled too full.

In the den, her mom had her eyes closed. Sadie could tell she wasn't sleeping. When she slept, her wrinkles eased, became thin, white fault lines. The den—the whole trailer—smelled of cigarette ash and boiled eggs. It always had, Sadie guessed, but she'd just now started to notice, to feel her throat bottom out when she opened the fridge, when she emptied the dregs of her mom's wine coolers into the sink.

Glimmer Train Stories, Issue 81, Winter 2012
©2011 Lydia Fitzpatrick

The TV was muted. A newscaster's mouth moved. Her lipstick was perfect and her teeth shone. Behind her, a car burned, sending a wave of black smoke into the New Orleans sky. The only news they got was New Orleans news, news from two hours away.

Her mom stirred. "Let me feel your head. Come on. I want to see if you're hot," she said, eyes barely open. Her toes were curled around the arm of the couch. Her knees up, her crotch a shadowy region Sadie tried not to see.

"No, Ma. I'm fine. I'm late."

"You should stay home. You look like shit, honey."

Look in the mirror, Sadie wanted to say, but her mom wasn't malicious, just lonely. She'd call Sadie in sick every day of the week, if Sadie let her, and they'd eat cheese curls and watch *Real World* reruns, and every once in a while her mom would shriek at the TV, like she could change what was about to happen. Her mom would be happy drunk by ten and sad drunk by noon and talking nonstop about Sadie's dad the Non-Entity by two. The first time her mom had called him that—a Non-Entity—Sadie had been thirteen and mean enough to say the things she thought. "Non-Entity. Well, look who finally found a fucking dictionary," she'd said, and her mom's voice had been shaky for days.

"I gotta go," Sadie said. "Love you." She leaned over and kissed her mom on the forehead and grabbed her backpack off the kitchen table. The night before, she'd packed it with everything she'd need for J.T. and Javier.

"I love you too. Don't push yourself, honey." She paused and reached a hand toward Sadie, then let it fall back on the couch. "It won't kill you to miss a day. Tenth grade. It's not rocket science."

Sadie nodded and let the screen door slap behind her. Next door, Lottie Budreau's double-wide was sagging in the middle, like it had lost something vital inside, and the yellow paint job was pruning in the humidity. Lottie had put the garden gnomes out last week, as she did the first week of spring every year, and the whole army of them were peering toward the highway with chipped, hopeful eyes. It wasn't a neighborhood at all. Only the two trailers, hers and the Budreaus', set down like forgotten Monopoly pieces on the sunny side of the highway. Just past Bulah or just before it, depending on which way you were going.

Sadie started down 90, headed south, toward Bulah. She walked along the edge of the road, where the gravel cracked and sprouted dandelions. Dew soaked her sneakers. The silver spray paint she'd used on them bled onto her ankles. Trash was scattered in the weeds: waxed-paper cups and hubcaps and diapers and ragged, stuffing-less animals. Once, Sadie had found a black leather shoe, like a ballet slipper. She'd kept it for a while, hoping the other might turn up, but it hadn't, and her left foot outgrew just the one. Behind her, a semi groaned, wheels hissing against the dew-damp pavement. Sadie stopped and gripped the straps of her backpack. As the truck passed, her hair snapped at her face, snagged on the tiny onyx stud in her nose. Her ears popped, like she'd entered a different altitude. The trucks passed all day here, clattering the dishes, sloshing the toilet water. At night they made her dreams shake.

She could see J.T.'s pickup from a mile away. It was bright banana yellow, with tires as high as her shoulders and a flame that sprang up from the grill and licked at the windshield. He was parked in the Red's Rockets lot, between the two giant plywood rockets that Red had erected when the Fireworks Emporium moved in off Route 54. Red had gone out of business anyhow, and now the senior boys drank in there and set off fireworks. Sadie had been a couple of times, passing a warm bottle of Malibu, her ass sunk deep in a damp mattress, the glass crunching under her sneakers when she moved. Other nights, she and her mom dragged beach chairs onto their lawn and listened to the crack and sizzle of roman candles and black cats and bottle rockets, of all the goods Red had left behind. They watched fire split the sky.

J.T. must have seen her, too, because when she was still a ways away, he revved the engine, twisted the truck toward her, and left the parking lot in a plume of dust. He drove past her on 90 going the wrong way, then pulled a U and cut onto the shoulder in front of her.

"You're late," he said. "You couldn't have niced up?"

J.T. was in a collared shirt, working his fresh-shaved jaw so it popped in the socket. He was her cousin, but whenever she saw him, she was surprised that they shared blood. Everything about him was quick— his eyes, his brain—he even talked quicker than Sadie, but he didn't have anything better to say.

"My mom would've noticed."

"Uh-huh. 'Cause Jamie's so fucking observant. You got everything?"

Sadie nodded and opened the passenger door.

"Get in the back. Javier gets the front. That's customer service."

"It's Javi-er," she said, landing heavy on the *er*, even though she had no idea if that was how you pronounced it.

"Good. Practice saying it," J.T. said. "You gotta know that shit cold."

J.T. had gotten the looks of the family, with a face that should have been on glossy paper, in a frame, not right there where you could reach out and touch it. Her aunt Sharon always said, "Nobody's an angel who looks like one," and she meant J.T. Sadie slipped her backpack into the truck, then went around back and hoisted herself in. Once she was settled, with her spine curled against the cab, J.T. slid open the window, and handed her a McDonald's bag splotched with grease.

"Breakfast," he said.

Beneath two wadded wrappers, Sadie found a sausage-and-egg biscuit. No cheese. That was the way she liked it. And that was enough for her to forgive J.T. That and the fact that two weeks ago, when she'd told him about the baby, he'd spread open his hands and said, "Here are your options." Kayla, her former best friend, had looked affronted at the news, but J.T. had made it seem like three frenzied eighth periods with Danny Makin in the dark room had given Sadie choices, not taken them away.

"J.T.," she said, "you think Javier'll like me?"

"I don't give a shit," he said, pulling the truck into gear. "And neither should you."

"But what if I do."

"It's business, Sadie. Please don't fuck this up," he said.

She nodded, thinking of the one picture of Javier that J.T. had given her. He was sitting at a table in front of an empty plate, with a crumpled napkin on top of it. He had glasses, and cheeks that bowed inward, and a neck too long and thin (and this worried Sadie, that she might be fatter than him, that she'd surely be fatter than him in six months). He was older than she was. Twenty, J.T. had said, and he looked older than that. But it was his eyes that struck her. They stared into the bottom left corner of the picture, toward nothing Sadie could discern, and they were wide with wonder. She wanted that expression. She wanted to be the source of it.

"Javier José Mercado," she whispered, as they smoothed onto the highway. Once the truck was going fast, blurring Weeks Bay and the sugar cane fields and the dump, where gulls twisted in slow circles in the sky, like they were strung to a mobile, she said it louder, "Javier José Mercado." She let the wind whip the words from her mouth.

"Nice to meet you."

She smiled, mouth open. The insides of her cheeks vibrated with the road.

"Nice to meet you," she said.

Javier's place was north of town, almost to Delacroix, where most of the black kids at school lived, but J.T. said he had money, that that was how he'd gotten a tourist visa in the first place. They had to loop up past the hot-sauce plant to get there. Brenda's Shake Shack flashed by, all shiny red and chrome. Sadie worked the dinner shift there, four nights a week, the same shift her mom had quit a year before. Her mom had just stopped showing up—not a word to Sadie—and as soon as Sadie realized it, she went in and begged for the job. Brenda's was the only place in town that tourists ever went, besides the sauce plant. On weekends there'd be a line of them—parents on cell phones with a string of sticky-faced kids—waiting for vinyl booths and overpriced hot dogs, their eyes streaming from the plant tour, from the vats of vinegar and chili peppers that made the air burn in Bulah.

It was Javier's uncle's house, and it wasn't nice. A split-level. Small, just a room or two bigger than her trailer, but the windows looked clean, like they'd been scrubbed on both sides, and there was a woven mat with flowers outside the door, and in the yard sheets billowed on a line like in a laundry commercial. A Camaro sat in the driveway, six inches off the ground, if that, with gold paint as glossy as nail polish and a rosary dangling from the rearview. Sadie wondered if it was Javier's, if he was a guy like J.T., who'd ride around in a car that cost more than his house, more than his mom got in disability in a year. But it couldn't be his, she reminded herself, because he'd only flown in from Mexico a week ago.

"Sit tight," J.T. said, and he slapped the side of the truck and jogged up the front walk. The door opened as J.T. got to it, and Sadie couldn't see anything or anyone inside before it shut again.

She unzipped the front pouch of her backpack, and pulled out a compact and a lipstick—Brick House—that she'd stolen from her mom. The lipstick was mashed and dotted with crumbs. It had sat in the bottom of her mom's purse too long, through seasons, and as she put it on, a pain gripped her stomach. It made her close her eyes and suck in air, and then it was gone, leaving her insides wrung out. These pains had been coming—two or three a day—for a week, and Sadie had thought at first that it was the baby kicking. But she'd looked online, and the baby was the size of a prune. Its feet like tiny leaves, she imagined, not big enough to kick and make her feel it.

The front door opened again, and Sadie heard a little girl shriek, and then a wave of laughter, and someone yelled, "*Suerte!*" J.T. stepped out onto the walk, and behind him was Javier. He was even slighter in person than he'd seemed in the photo. Willowy, Sadie thought, but he moved like a Jacob's ladder, like his joints didn't have enough cushion.

Sadie raised a hand. "Hi," she said, but they weren't close enough to hear her. J.T. was talking over his shoulder. Javier was shaking his head. Sadie couldn't tell if he'd seen her yet. The sun caught his glasses, made them gleam silver. She should have gotten out of the truck, she thought, as they crossed the street toward her.

"Hey," she said again, and her voice came out thick.

J.T. shot her a look.

"Hi," Javier said, with barely an accent. His eyes hit hers for a second, then he squinted, like she was too bright to look at, and dropped his chin toward the pavement. J.T. got in the truck, but Javier stayed by the passenger door. He seemed suspended, Sadie thought, like the air was heavy enough to hold him in place. Then his cheeks bunched. The pearly point of a canine jutted over his lower lip. He smiled up at her. "Thank you," he said. "For doing this."

He reached in his pocket and pulled out a tiny plastic bag, the kind drugs came in, the kind she'd found, a few times, in J.T.'s glovebox. A ring glinted in the corner of the bag. As he handed it to her, she could feel the heat rising up her throat, onto her cheeks. Her face felt like the front of J.T.'s truck, those flames, on fire. She thought she might cry, or throw up, but then J.T. honked the horn, and Sadie wrapped her fist around the bag, wanting, instinctively, to hide it from him.

"Nice to meet you," Sadie said, and it came out sounding half normal. Javier wasn't smiling anymore, but he wasn't *not* smiling, and he hadn't flinched at J.T.'s honk. He just kept looking up at her.

"We better get going," she said, and he nodded.

The ring was a simple gold band with a tiny turquoise stone in the shape of an egg. She was too scared to slip it on her finger in the truck bed. She imagined hitting a pothole, a red light, the ring spinning out of her hand, shimmering in the air, disappearing. She folded the bag and slipped it into the front pocket of her shorts.

The courthouse sat way back off the town square, separated from the street by a tree-lined walk that tapered into a flight of stairs and a squat, brick building. Sadie had been inside once, when her mom had gotten hauled in, drunk, for defacing an ex-boyfriend's car. She had made J.T. drive her, with the intention of pleading her mom's case, but when she'd seen her mom, sleeping, her body unfurled and at ease on a concrete slab in her cell, she'd turned around and told the deputy not to wake her.

But today, she was getting married. Not married, J.T. kept saying, but close. If they made it through today, Javier would get a fiancé visa, and she'd get a thousand dollars. If they made it through the next few months, if they got the marriage license—she'd get five thousand, minus whatever J.T. was taking for his troubles. A thousand was enough for a doctor's visit, and she'd only had one. That first one, three months back. Five thousand could get her and her mom and the baby a place with two bedrooms, closer to town and the Shake Shack. But she knew it wasn't just the money. That word, *fiancé*, set off a spark that burned through Sadie's blood and left every nerve raw. And he'd given her a ring. The ring wasn't part of the deal. There was more here, she thought, than the deal.

"I can't chaperone you two," J.T. said, after helping her out of the truck bed. "Wish I could."

Sadie rolled her eyes at him and turned toward Javier, but J.T. gripped her arm. "Let me see your stuff," he said.

"I've got it all, J.T.," she said. "Come on."

He didn't let go. "I want to *see* it. I don't want you getting in there and realizing you haven't got a fucking driver's license and blowing this all to shit."

Sadie unzipped her bag, and pulled out a folder. Her civics folder, which she'd emptied the night before of handouts on the balance of power, which now held her social-security card, her I.D., her birth certificate, and a list she'd printed off the internet called Requirements for Marriage License in Louisiana. Javier had gotten out of the truck, a manila envelope in hand, and was staring up at the courthouse, and Sadie liked that he trusted her, already, to be responsible.

"It's a miracle Jamie kept all this," J.T. said, handing her back the folder.

"She didn't. I had to send away for the social-security card."

"Good girl," he said, and he slapped her ass as she walked toward Javier. That was something J.T. did, when he got drunk, when he caught guys hitting on her at Brenda's. She'd seen J.T.'s girlfriend's eyes seal up and harden, like scabs, watching him with her, and Sadie always wanted to tell her to take a deep breath, that she and J.T. were hinged together by their mothers, by genes, and not much else. But Javier wasn't watching, and Sadie was glad—she didn't want to look cheap to him.

Walking toward the courthouse, their steps were not quite in unison, but close enough. The cypress branches made shadows shift on his face, and in the patches of sunlight his skin was almost as pale as hers, yellow pale, like cake batter. Sadie felt, suddenly, that this was her chance to ask him anything, while they walked, while their eyes could naturally stay on the ground.

"What do you do? At home—in Mexico?" she said.

"I work in a library. In Saltillo." His voice was low and even, and that word *Saltillo* came out sounding like water over something smooth. Sadie wanted to hear him say it again.

"What's it like?"

"It's huge. The size of—" He stopped, and spun slowly in place, taking in the hunched concrete roofs of Main Street, the Atchafalaya that oozed by, brown even in perfect sunlight, the Dunkin' Donuts on the corner, the flashing yellow streetlight. "It's huge," he said, "with columns, and murals. I work on the bottom floor, three levels under-ground. People ask for a book, and I find it in the shelves. I send it up on a tray—it's all mechanized."

"You like it then?" she said, thinking of the Bulah High library, of Ms. Hatcher, who watched a mini TV behind her desk all day and couldn't explain the Dewey Decimal system.

He told her of how it smelled like marble and earth, of how the old books had to be at just the right temperature, of how they couldn't let sunlight in. "That's why," he said, pinching the skin that hung loose on his arm, "I'm so pale." He told her that once he had tried to turn the page of a book from the seventeenth century, and the paper had disintegrated in his hand, flaked away like ash. Normally Sadie would have laughed at someone talking like him, brimming with love, not knowing that it was safer to bury it, but she listened as he spoke. She listened so close that she started to lose track of the individual words. They blurred together, washed over her. Beautiful words, but underneath them she could pick out something raw and keening, something that made her think of her mother, crying, throwing rocks at her boyfriend's car, something like the beginnings of grief.

He was quiet, staring at her. She hadn't noticed when he'd stopped talking. They were almost at the courthouse.

"We should hold hands," she said. "In case anyone's watching." She slid her hand around his. It felt cold, and more, like diving into water that's deep. She thought: This is dangerous, the way everything about him makes me think of something I love.

Javier was quiet for a little while, and she was ready to like that about him too—that he, like her, didn't talk too much—but as they started up the stairs he said, "Are you really pregnant?"

Sadie reached and touched her stomach, like she needed to feel it to be sure, even though there wasn't anything to feel yet. "Yeah," she said, "really pregnant."

"What about the—"

"Danny Makin," she said, not wanting him to say the word *father*.

"Danny?"

"The guy who got me pregnant."

"Are you together?" he asked. His hand twitched in hers.

"Dating?" she said.

He nodded. "You love him?"

Sadie smiled. "No," she said, "I didn't like him much either."

Javier laughed, louder than Sadie thought he'd be able to. He didn't have the belly for a deep laugh, but there it was. Wanting to keep him laughing, she said, "Danny Makin's a retard," but then she worried he might take her literally, so she said, "not a real retard. Just not smart." And Javier laughed again, until the laugh turned to a hack, and he had to take his hand away to cover his mouth. Danny Makin she hadn't cared much about, except once, when he was deep in her and she'd felt suddenly, unbelievably good; and another time, when she'd told him that she'd never met her father, and he'd flipped his eyelids inside out to make her smile.

Inside, Sadie went into the bathroom to put on the ring. It was too small. She could barely get it on her pinky. Her fingers were swollen, her knuckles divots, and the sight of them made her feel invaded, held captive by the baby in a way she hadn't before. Her stomach churned. She bent over the sink and splashed water on her face, then blotted her cheeks with a paper towel. Her hair was damp now, curling at the hairline, but she managed to rake her fingers through it and twist it into a long braid.

"Are you okay?" Javier asked, when she came outside. "We could come back. In a little while." His eyes scanned her face, moved back and forth across it, and she pictured him, in his basement office, neck curved over a book.

"It's just morning sickness," she said. "It comes and goes."

The marriage-license office was a tiny room with walls of pebbled glass at the end of a long corridor. A Xerox machine whirred softly in the corner, and one of the fluorescent lights crackled above them, like the bug zapper Brenda put by the picnic tables when the mosquitoes started laying. Behind the lone desk sat a chubby lady, running an emery board over her nails with long, smooth strokes. Her name plate read *Clarice Gibbons*.

"Can I help you?" she said, without looking up. Her voice was unconcerned, but not unfriendly. She had silver hoops in her ears that grazed her shoulders, and they trembled when she spoke.

Sadie cleared her throat, and Javier said, "We need a fiancé visa. We're engaged." He held Sadie's hand up in his own, and shook their fists, like they were athletes on a podium.

"Well happy day," Clarice said, her voice still flat. "So you're not a citizen."

Javier shook his head. "No," he said, "I'm visiting—a tourist. I've got—" He began opening his manila envelope.

"We'll get to that," Clarice said, then she turned to Sadie, put down the emery board, and looked up. "How old are you, sugar?" she said.

"Sixteen."

"You have a parent or guardian here?" she asked. "You know you've got to have one present."

"No, but I…" She had thought this would be easy, but Clarice was looking at her in this way, with a lot of pity and a little disgust, like she'd seen people look at her mom, like Sadie sometimes caught herself looking at her mom. It was a look Sadie didn't deserve. Her mom had gotten pregnant and lost a man. Sadie was doing it in reverse. "I'm pregnant," she said, keeping her voice high and airy.

She leaned into Javier, and he put his arm around her shoulder. Clarice nodded. She picked the emery board back up. "You have confirmation from a doctor?"

Sadie unzipped her bag and handed her folder to Clarice. Clarice spread the papers across her desk and ran a perfectly curved nail under each line of the doctor's report. Sadie could hear a water fountain dripping in the corridor behind them. The sound echoed a little. Without looking up, Clarice extended a hand toward Javier, and he gave her his envelope.

Javier glanced at Sadie. She could see sweat beading on his temples. She smiled at him, wishing she could mouth the words, *It's okay*, and he'd understand.

"Where'd you meet?" Clarice said.

They'd planned for this, just in case. She and J.T. had sat out on her lawn and listened to the throb of frogs in the marsh and made up a story. They'd told it to each other until the words just ran through their mouths, over their tongues, like a river, deep-set in its course. But the questions weren't supposed to come now. They were supposed to come from Immigration Control, after the fiancé visa.

"Cancún," Sadie said. "Over Christmas."

Javier nodded. "Cancún," he said, and it sounded like a different place. "You fly?"

"What?" Sadie said, then she shook her head. "No, my cousin and I drove."

"That's a long haul," Clarice said.

Sadie nodded. She couldn't read the tone in Clarice's voice and her eyes were still on the papers on the desk. A pain swelled in her stomach. "It is," she said. "It took us two days straight through."

Clarice was looking up at her now, smiling. "I know. I drove out to L.A. once. A long time ago," she paused and her mouth hung open. "God, that was a long time ago," she said.

The pain was spreading, seeping outward. Sadie's palms were clammy, the back of her neck cold. She nodded again, hoping Javier would talk—J.T. had coached him on the story too—but he stayed frozen beside her.

"Here's what we're gonna do," Clarice said.

Sadie breathed in deep, and the air felt barbed. She gripped the edge of the desk. She wanted to buckle over, to fall down. She pushed her knuckles against her teeth, afraid she'd make a noise, afraid of what it would be. Clarice stared at her. Javier's hand tightened on her shoulder, and she shrugged it off. She wrapped her arms around her stomach, pressing hard, pressing herself together, and walked out of the room. Behind her, she could hear Clarice say, "She okay?"

And Javier said, "It's sickness. From the baby."

Her underwear was blotched with blood. The crotch of her shorts too. She sat on the toilet, and pain came in hot waves that left her shivering. Her neck was arched back, the crown of her head against the tiled wall. She held her knees tight together. When she was little, and couldn't sleep, her mom would tell her to think of white paper. Just white paper, not a single word. It hadn't calmed her then, and it didn't now, and Sadie thought, instead, of J.T., and how when she was a month old, J.T. had stolen her from her crib and walked with her, along the highway, halfway to Weeks Bay. "He wanted you all for himself," her aunt Sharon would say whenever she told the story, and Sadie hadn't understood.

She gripped her thighs and dug into them with her nails. The pain was fierce, consuming, but somehow familiar, something she'd imagined for the future. In a hospital bed, she'd seen herself, with Javier's cool hand in hers. Him whispering to her in Spanish, words she didn't have to try to understand, and he would draw the pain from her. She was ripping, something deep and tangled uprooting inside her. Her face was sweat-slick. She felt something inching up her throat—a scream maybe, or a groan, or vomit—and she opened her mouth. "But I want it," she said, and her voice was deep, primitive and strange to her, the voice of a woman grown. "But I want it," she said again, and the deepness was gone. It left her, still pressing her knees together, not sure if there was anything left to save.

The pains were coming slower, like cramps now. Her muscles were unsnarling, and she could inhale and fill her lungs. She stood up, with a hand against the stall door, unzipped her sweatshirt, and wrapped it around her waist. She wasn't sure how long she'd been in the bathroom, whether Javier and Clarice would still be in the office, or whether Clarice had asked Javier a question he couldn't answer.

Javier was waiting for her, leaning against a vending machine across from the bathroom door, smiling. She smiled too, but her skin was tight. Sweat had left salty patches on her face.

"It's okay," he said. "We just have to sign a form. She likes us." He smiled.

She nodded and said, "I think it's gone."

He looked at her. His face was still, except for a muscle that twitched in his cheek. "Dead?" he said. His eyes were light brown, shot through with yellow, and they looked shaken, churned, like muddy water disturbed. He looked at the ground, and Sadie felt a twinge of recognition. It was *that* look—from the picture—and it wasn't wonder, it was fear.

"I think so," she said.

He turned his back to her and put his forehead against the vending machine. The plastic buckled a little under the weight. The water fountain was still dripping and draining, somewhere in the building, and Sadie thought she could hear Clarice, scratching away with the emery board, wearing her nails down to nothing, thinking of that time in L.A.

Javier took off his glasses, and rubbed his thumbs in circles over the bridge of his nose. His elbows poked toward her like twin accusations. "*Me chingaron,*" he said. His voice was a flat line.

She couldn't understand him, and she could tell from his tone that she didn't want to, but she said, "What does that mean?" because she didn't want silence either.

"*Fuck,*" he said, turning. "It means *fuck.*"

Sadie nodded. She didn't feel anything but tired, able to recognize people as simple, skin grown around wants. "I'll still do it," she said.

"I'm sorry," he said. "It's just—"

"It's okay. I still want to." And she did. She wanted, one day, to see that library, in Saltillo.

Sadie thought Clarice would know what had happened to her, smell grief on her instantly, just like she'd thought—each day for the

 58

Glimmer Train Stories

past three months—that her mom might look up from the TV and say, "You're pregnant." But Clarice didn't offer Sadie her chair or ask if she felt better. She made big swooping X's where Sadie needed to sign, and then said, "Okay, folks, immigration will be in touch."

Javier took her hand without her asking and walked her to the car, and she had enough in her to smile at J.T., to say, "It went good," before falling asleep with her head against the passenger window.

"Sadie," J.T. said, and she opened her eyes.

They were at Javier's. The sun was huge and low on the horizon, turning everything violet, like a grand finale, like it knew the show was over. There was a little girl on the stoop, waiting for Javier. When he slid out of the truck bed, she ran across the yard, and he squatted and hugged her. She spoke fast in Spanish, her hair swinging at her waist, silky in the light. An old woman, his grandmother, Sadie guessed, stood at the door, and she nodded at Sadie, then crossed herself.

"Let's go," Sadie said, but Javier stood and tapped on the window. J.T. rolled it down.

"I need the ring back," he said, then he saw her face. "For now," he said. "It's my aunt's."

Sadie nodded, yanking and twisting it off her pinky, somehow more embarrassed by this than by anything else that had happened that day. The little girl was tugging at Javier's arm. From the doorway, the old woman yelled, "*Nelli! Basta ya!*" and the girl grabbed his hand and pulled him toward the house, still talking, pleading for something. Sadie said, "I'll see you next week?" and Javier said, "*Sí,*" but she couldn't tell if he was talking to her or to the little girl.

J.T. floored it on the highway, but didn't talk, and these were the moments when Sadie liked him the most, when he sensed her mood and matched it.

"You want to get some beers?" he said, as they passed the Quik Stop, then he looked at her stomach and said, "Oh."

"Go for it," she said. "I don't have anywhere to be."

There weren't any lights on at home or at the Budreaus'. Most likely, her mom was at J.T.'s house, splitting a pack of Camels and reading horoscopes with her sister. It was dusk, and the two trailers were the color of fog, of no color at all really, and when they pulled in her driveway, Sadie said, "Go turn the lights on," and J.T. didn't say anything back. He hefted the twelve-pack by its cardboard handle, set it on the stoop, and flicked on all the lights. "All right," he said, leaning against the screen door, staring at her.

They put the beers between their beach chairs on the lawn, and J.T. microwaved some mac and cheese, and when he cracked open his first beer, he said, "A hard day's work," and took a swig. Sometimes Sadie thought he was practicing for commercials, the way he made pronouncements with a product in hand.

She leaned back in her chair and propped her feet up on J.T.'s legs. She didn't have a beer—one would have tasted good, cool and salty in her mouth, but she didn't want J.T. to know about the baby.

"Easy work's more like it," he said, "like money for free." He took another swig from his beer. Headlights from the highway swept over his cheekbones, his nose. They dappled the grass.

"For you maybe," she said, thinking of gripping Clarice's desk, of the way Javier's grandmother had stared at her. "You get money for nothing, and Javier gets to move here." She didn't mean this really, and she was talking to Clarice, more than to J.T. He had never pitied her, at least.

"Really, Sadie? You think he wants to move here? That guy's got a job. A legit job. He lives in *Mexico*. On the beach. Where people vacation."

"He doesn't live on the beach. He's in the middle. Saltillo," she tried to say it like Javier had, but her tongue was too heavy to get it right.

"Whatever," he said. "It's still tropical."

"Then why's he doing it, J.T.? If he doesn't want to be here?"

J.T. finished his beer. He scratched at a widening gash on the knee of his jeans. "He got winded getting in the fucking truck, Sadie. I'd bet he doesn't make it to twenty-two." He looked at the grass, and his jaw melted. "I'd say he's here for the meds."

Sadie was quiet. She tried to think of white paper again, but her mind kept shredding it to confetti. Cars flashed by, and each one took the wind out of her a little. J.T. slapped at a mosquito on his arm, and Sadie could see the dark smear of blood it left.

After a while, he said, "You want to practice?"

Sadie shook her head.

"Come on," he said, and she shrugged.

"So you met him in Cancún, over Christmas. We were there together—we drove together—and we were staying at this place. This place right on the beach. I mean you can hear the fucking waves all night long. Daquiris and piña coladas and..."

"Margaritas," she said.

"Margaritas. And we're a little drunk all the time. And mornings, I'm surfing, and you're just sitting on the beach, with a whole bunch of magazines, getting a tan. Then you see this guy, walking along by the waves..."

J.T. kept talking, and Sadie couldn't picture Javier in this story any more, not walking on a beach, not holding a drink with an umbrella and fruit. The story, she realized, was more J.T.'s than theirs, and she looked out at the highway. She could see a truck a mile off, barreling toward them. J.T. was talking about her first date, about the restaurant where Javier had taken her, about the enchiladas that they'd eaten. She could feel the truck now. The ground vibrated, and she braced herself, suddenly afraid that each truck passing snagged a piece of her, a hope, a certain future. They sailed down the low-slung highways, carrying versions of her that could have been. Past town, past marshes, past New Orleans, to wherever, she thought, the road ended. The truck's headlights blinded them, stripped them of color. J.T. raised his hands to block the light, and the driver honked, once. The sound filled the air and left them quiet. 🕴

That's me on the right with my older brother, Jeff, circa 1960.
Chances are I'm dreaming up some kind of mischief.

J. Kevin Shushtari received his MFA from Boston University in May 2010. He lives with his wife, Julie, and their three children in Farmington, Connecticut, where he is at work on a novel. This is his first story accepted for publication. Kevin is also a practicing physician. He is working on his first novel.

THE VAST GARDEN OF STRANGERS

J. Kevin Shushtari

Old Reza finished his noontime prayers and knelt to fold his rug. He put it in the suitcase under his twin bed and went to the window. His son insisted on air conditioning, but he preferred the humid Boston summer, even when it smelled like spoiling feta, as it did today. Old Reza stared at the window of the apartment opposite in the brownstone that shared an entrance and common stairwell with his son's building. He didn't know who lived there; he'd never seen even a shadow cross behind the faded blue curtains. For two weeks he'd been watching the tomato plant on their windowsill, and when he'd woken at five to check on it, he saw that it had fallen over. The plastic container had blown away, and the dirt at the base of the stem was baked into a square flecked with bits of styrofoam. The tomato, not yet fully red, was too heavy for its withering stalk and sat on the ledge as if someone had arranged it there. He could tell it had not been watered; the plant was a foot high with the single tomato at its end, but now the leaves had turned brown, and its two yellow blossoms had dried up and disappeared.

Back home Old Reza would have dug a hole in the dark soil of his garden and positioned the plant carefully in direct sunlight. He would have tied the vine to a stake and watered it after coming home from the oil fields. It looked like the tomato needed another week to ripen—what if it rolled off into the alley? What kind of people would buy a plant and not take care of it? He placed a tiny bitter tablet under his tongue to take away the pressure in his chest.

His son was heating up the *abgusht* from last night's supper. Old Reza had brought dried lemon from Iran to help his American daughter-in-law's cooking.

"Why are *you* cooking?" Old Reza asked.

The son put on yellow oven mitts and took the ceramic pot out of the microwave. "I told you, Baba. She doesn't cook."

"And you don't find this shameful?"

The daughter-in-law had been promoted to vice president of her company. Most weeks she traveled and spent the weekends glued to her computer or her phone. They did not even want a house, and were happy to live in a fourth-floor apartment on Commonwealth Avenue. The son was a musician who wrote jingles for television and radio ads. He worked from home and took important calls with many people at a time, the distant voices rising and overlapping.

The son ladled the chickpeas, potatoes, and lamb into his father's bowl. "I'm going to the grocery store. You don't have to come."

The last time Old Reza had gone with him, the produce manager got upset because he'd popped a grape into his mouth, and then bit into an orange. "Your fruits have no flavor," Old Reza told him. He had been doing all right alone in Ahwaz. When he had agreed to come to America, he thought he would be somewhere like Westwood, where his many friends had settled after fleeing the Revolution. When the daily missile attacks began, Old Reza and his wife once watched a lone Iraqi paratrooper fall from the sky, his chute flapping in the breeze. They decided then that they too would move to Los Angeles. They would shop at the Persian groceries on Westwood Boulevard and eat at the Persian restaurants. Although he considered himself religious, Old Reza had pictured himself walking through vast jeweled department stores and watching the women, without the hijab, spray perfume on their delicate wrists and then hold them out, smiling, for his opinion. He saw himself in the park snacking on roasted watermelon seeds, playing backgammon with men he'd grown up with in Ahwaz. He had heard that people spoke Farsi as much as English in parts of Los Angeles.

But the American government would not issue them visas then, and now Old Reza's wife had been dead for five years, and all his friends had grandchildren. He yearned for little ones to play with, to watch grow. He missed his wife and knew he should be with family, so he finally consented to move. The first thing the daughter-in-law told him was that she didn't want children. "Too much trouble," she said.

"Do you know you have Jews in this building?" Old Reza asked as they ate. He was surprised the American lamb was tender.

"It's a multi-cultural building," his son replied. "That's why we like it."

"Your *abgusht* is missing saffron."

"I took a cooking course. They said I could substitute turmeric."

Old Reza frowned, shaking his head. "I bet the Jews don't have women who refuse to cook." He'd had a friend once who was a Jew, the eunuch who worked for his father, guarding his four wives. Old Reza's mother died of tuberculosis when he was six, and Bijan stepped in to help with her sons for the next five years.

"How old are you?" Reza once asked, stroking Bijan's soft cheeks.

"You know better than to ask a woman her age."

"But you're a man."

"I look ageless, don't I?"

Reza did not understand. He played Elvis on the hi-fi in the front foyer, and Bijan wrapped himself in bright scarves and danced around the fountain, the silk billowing in the breeze from the ceiling fan. Reza was afraid that one of the long scarves would knot itself around his friend's neck and strangle him. Bijan performed traditional Persian dances expertly, tapping his right hand over his mouth the way the women did at weddings, the shrill, high-pitched ululations—*lalalala*—rising above The King's velvety drawl. Reza laughed as the eunuch wiggled his hips like a young girl to "Hound Dog" and "Jailhouse Rock." Bijan taught him to do karate moves to the music because he was not a graceful dancer. "You dance like a stiff old man," Bijan said.

Shortly after Reza's eleventh birthday, he went to the market with his father to buy some Shirazi figs, and there was Bijan, sniffing cantaloupes. He was wearing a yarmulke. Reza's father told Bijan never to return to the house. "As if being Arab is not bad enough," his father said.

Old Reza would not let his son go disgracefully to do the shopping alone. He went to his room to get his *kufi*. He stared at himself in the mirror as he placed the skullcap firmly on his head, and turned side-ways to observe his big belly, visible even under the oversized white short-sleeve shirt he had bought at Filene's Basement. Although his skin was sallow and wrinkled, he was pleased with his full beard and felt it made him look pious.

He checked on the tomato: still there, but he was worried. He could have made it grow; he knew all about gardening from Bijan, who came from the fertile plains of Khuzestan. Bijan's family were Ahwazi Arab Jews. He showed Reza how to stretch soccer nets between poles over the peas. He called his eggplants black beauties and collared each stem with newspaper to ward off cutworms. Sometimes he stood in the long rows, his sandaled feet in the dirt, reading the old news. He sprayed the tomato plants with mint tea and killed the aphids and ants that others fought with chemicals. On the days he sprayed, the air smelled like chewing gum. Bijan placed the tomatoes that had broken off their stems around the basin of the fountain in the courtyard and danced before them. The rhythm would conjure from them a deeper red, he told Reza, a red that would nourish the soul as well as the body. Bijan was sometimes afraid to leave the compound because of the acid attacks, so he asked the maids to stop off at the police barracks to collect manure from the stables for the garden.

After his wife got Alzheimer's, Old Reza tried to take care of her, but she shooed him away with the broom like a stranger. When she wandered off for three days, he knew he needed help just to keep her safe. He had heard from one of his father's widows that Bijan worked as the gardener at the Alborz Home for Aged Sisters, in a converted mansion on the left bank of the Karun River.

He found Bijan stringing poles between the rose bushes behind the Home. The eunuch recognized him before he even spoke, and rushed to embrace him. His gait was slower; his long hair, pulled back in a ponytail, was now completely gray.

"More than fifty years," Bijan said.

"Fifty-three!"

Bijan was wearing mascara, and his skin was as smooth and hairless as Old Reza remembered. "You haven't changed much."

"But *you* have," Bijan said, patting Old Reza's belly.

"I'm sorry my father sent you away."

Bijan lifted his palms and shrugged. He showed his guest the rooms he'd fixed up in the basement of the Home. Most gays and transsexuals tried to assimilate, but some sought refuge in retirement homes. Even though their families paid a higher rent, Bijan used them to help with the chores. But in honor of Old Reza's visit, Bijan gave them the day off. He played Sephardic music from a boom box on the patio and passed out long silk scarves. The old ladies sat at a distance on Persian carpets, leaning back against large satin pillows as the men sang and danced around the fountain. Trellises heavy with honeysuckle blocked the waning sunlight, creating speckled shadows on the mosaic floor. They laughed with Old Reza when he showed them his karate moves. That evening Bijan snuck out and went with his friend to Dolat Park, where they watched the oil-well flares to the north and talked about the old days, the breeze from the river cooling their skin.

Old Reza and his son took the T to Trader Joe's on Boylston, a market in the basement of an old building. Shoppers crashed into each other with their clattering metal carts, but his son said it had the best food. Old Reza thought of the vast open-air markets in Ahwaz. Bijan would not have liked the tomatoes in Boston. They were pale, as if machine made and chemically ripened. Old Reza wished Bijan were here; he would be safe in Boston. There were people right in the store with tattoos on their necks and piercings through their tongues and eyebrows. Nobody cared. Nobody wanted to throw acid in their faces or take them to prison. Nobody paid any attention. Old Reza wondered if Bijan would be able to adjust to this new life, the way he had.

As they walked the kilometer back to Hynes in the ninety-degree heat, Old Reza dragged the plastic grocery bags on the sidewalk. On Newbury Street, people sat on high stools at tables outside, drinking beer and blowing smoke over their shoulders. His son did not seem to know any of them.

"Baba, you're ruining the groceries. Hold up your bags," he said.

The pressure in Old Reza's chest returned. He stopped just long enough to pull the small amber vial from his pants pocket and place one of the tablets under his tongue. His son did not notice; if he did, he would worry. The subway car was packed with people wearing ear buds and texting, their thumbs stabbing at the tiny keypads. The squeaking noise from the train wheels hurt Old Reza's ears, but he couldn't let go of the bags to cover them. He hummed loudly to drown out the racket.

"Hurry up or we'll never make it home," his son said.

Home, Old Reza thought, was back in Ahwaz, where he saw Bijan every day after his wife moved into the Alborz. Within three months, she was down to eighty-three pounds.

"Try this," Old Reza said, spooning the chopped mint leaves from his homemade *mast-o-khiar* onto her rice.

"You don't think I know you're trying to poison me?"

"What about this, my *aziz-delam?*" he asked as he tempted her with *koresht fesenjaan* from the restaurant they liked under the stone arcades on Taleghani Street.

His wife clicked her tongue. "Any fool knows I never liked pome-granates."

Bijan played soothing songs by Azam Ali on the boom box as he helped Old Reza serve her on the terrace. He had prepared a large platter of feta, tomatoes, fried eggplant, grapes, and cucumbers. She stared at her husband as she scooped up bits of everything with pita bread until the plate was clean.

"Get me some more," she said to Bijan. "But don't let this one touch it."

The next day, instead of saying his morning prayers, Old Reza made *chelo kebab*, mincing fresh lamb with onion and grilling it over an open flame. He forked the meat over saffron rice into her favorite ceramic dish, the one with clouds painted in the hollow of the bowl. He would make sure she finished every bite, and he would show her the clouds. Maybe she would remember.

"This she can't resist," he told Bijan, who stood at the front door of the Home, American sunglasses on against the morning glare.

Bijan took off the glasses and folded them carefully. "Reza-Jon, she passed in the night."

"But it's her favorite."

"I know," Bijan said. He pried the dish gently from his friend's hands and set it on the step. Old Reza sagged in Bijan's arms, and the eunuch's body felt softer, more pliant against his than his wife's had in years.

Old Reza left the groceries on the floor of the kitchen and went to his room to check on the tomato. It was the size of an apple, and seemed riper than just a few hours earlier; he thought about cutting into it and serving it in a salad. Bijan would not like it here. The upstairs tenants were so heavy-footed that the ceiling light in his room jingled with each step and he felt the vibrations in his chest. In the hallway, children screamed to each other, and a cell phone rang with the words of a horrible rap song he couldn't understand. In the alley below, the garbage truck whined and roared as it crushed the waste of all the people in the building. He heard muffled voices in the apartment next door. He had smiled at these neighbors the week before when they moved in, but they ignored him. All the men wore yarmulkes, and the short one had sauntered up and down the hall as if he owned the place, barking orders at the movers.

The son came into his room as he was putting on his blue and yellow silk robe. "You shouldn't have the window open. It's a waste of electricity."

"The air conditioning makes my joints stiff."

"I forgot to buy a *Wall Street Journal* and I have a conference call in five minutes."

"Just read it online," Old Reza said, proud that he knew *online*.

"You know how I like a real newspaper."

"You are asking me?"

"Would you mind walking downstairs and picking one up at the corner? The investment banker types always chitchat about stories they read in the *Journal*. It's like the Holy Quran to them."

Old Reza was afraid his son would get angry if he asked exactly what that meant, so he nodded and dressed again. There was no elevator in the brownstone, so he took his time going down the four flights. He heard voices rising, both children and adults, but he couldn't make out the language, only echoes. Suddenly he was face to face with an Indian couple, or maybe Pakistani, followed by little versions of themselves. The whole family stopped and stared at Old Reza. Nobody said a word and they continued upstairs, but the smallest boy turned around to give him one last look. Had he forgotten his *kufi*? He patted his head—no, it was there.

Old Reza leaned against the wall, checking his pockets and trying to figure out if he had enough of the unfamiliar coins to buy a paper. He sat for a while. He was nothing but a stranger here, on his way to buy a newspaper he had never read instead of chatting with friends and sharing the *Iranian Daily* in Dolat Park. Last week, he'd watched an interview on television with the President of Iran, a man he did not support, but he sat through the whole thing just to hear the bits of Farsi the announcer did not drown out. Now, there was no one even to call him to prayers, so he often forgot them.

Finally, he pushed himself off the stairs and made it out into the muggy street and to the corner newsstand. On his way back, Old Reza decided he couldn't face any more strangers, so he walked through the alley to the back door. Something whizzed past his right temple and splattered onto the cement. He cried out: there, at his feet, the tangle of roots exposed, still attached to the stem, the red and green innards. The flesh separated from the skin, and tiny seeds speckled his sandals and the cuffs of his trousers.

He looked up. "Hey, that was a perfectly nice tomato!" He saw no one; only the blue curtains waved from the open window. "You could have cut it up and served it with salt and pepper, some cheese and cucumbers."

In Ahwaz, watching the paratrooper plunge from the sky, Old Reza had prayed to Allah for peace. He ran to where he thought the Iraqi had landed, but he never found him. Maybe the wind had blown the tomato down. Or was it the Indian children? Or the Jews? The old man unfolded the newspaper and placed it carefully on the sidewalk, the breeze fluttering its pages. He took off his sandals and set them on the paper. Slowly, he began to dance in a circle around the spreading stain of juice and pulp, tapping his right hand over his mouth and swaying his hips, ignoring the pressure in his chest, which came and went.

I still clean the kitchen in pretty much the same way.

Robert Schirmer's short-story collection, *Living with Strangers*, won the Bobst Award for Emerging Writers and was published by NYU Press. His stories have appeared in *Epoch*, *New England Review*, *Witness*, *Glimmer Train*, *Fiction*, and many other journals. Several of his stories have been anthologized, including in *Pushcart Prize XXI*, *Prize Stories: The O. Henry Awards*, and *The Best of Witness*. He's also been the recipient of a fellowship from the Chesterfield Writer's Film Project. His screenplays have been optioned by Amblin Entertainment and Warner Brothers.

BLACKOUT

Robert Schirmer (signature)

Robert Schirmer

Only minutes before the lights in the city went out, Sam had been watching a hawk fly overhead, one of those legendary urban hawks that were sometimes spotted near Central Park, swooping down on unsuspecting pigeons or young insurgent rats. *Natural predators*, he thought, although it was uncommon to see a hawk soaring, and rather low at that, over the banks, hotels, and camera shops of Midtown Manhattan. He stared up toward the blazing sky, following the hawk's weightless flight over a breakfast-cereal billboard and out of sight, leaving Sam again to his life, such as it was.

He stopped in a bar for a scotch and water. Although he'd left work early, he was in no hurry to face the crowded subway ride back into Brooklyn. The bartender, distracted by a baseball game playing on the television set chained to the wall, mixed the drink somewhat sloppily and handed it to Sam, who retreated to a corner table beside the window. Now what? He'd only been there for a couple of minutes, alone with his tangled thoughts, staring into the depths of his drink, when there was a brief pulsing sound and the lights went out.

Glimmer Train Stories, Issue 81, Winter 2012
©*2011 Robert Schirmer*

At first the bartender and Sam's fellow barflies glanced at each other with faint and questioning smiles. "Did the lights just crash?" asked a well-heeled woman sitting rather anxiously at the bar.

Sam and the others waited for the electricity to surge back to life. When it did not, the bartender walked over to the television set and smacked one side. "Fucking Con Ed," he said, and flipped the bird at the mute screen.

Sam downed his scotch in two gulps, picked up his briefcase, and wandered back into the street. He glanced up again at the sky, hoping to catch a glimpse of the prowling, shadowy hawk, but he saw nothing but undulating waves of heat.

When Sam was a boy, his grandmother had told him the Holy Ghost was a bird.

He'd walked a block before he realized that the garish lights of the Times Square family restaurants were also off. "Here we go again," Sam heard a mustachioed businessman say to his companion before they stepped into a strip club advertising an Asian smorgasbord of flesh.

"Better get back home," Sam muttered to himself. He walked to a subway stop, and had just started to descend underground when a man with a limp who was climbing up the steps said, "Trains not running, boss."

"None?" Sam asked, but the man had already moved on. Sam went down into the station just to be sure—the surprisingly empty station, unlit, blasted with heat, with only a scattering of perplexed people wandering toward the exit. A man in a uniform was standing in front of the entrance to the train tracks, his brow sopped with sweat and his eyes vague, remote, even as he stared headlong at Sam. *The guardian of the gates*, Sam thought. "No trains," the man said with more volume than was necessary. "Power failure."

"All right," Sam said. Of course trains couldn't run without electricity; why had it taken him so long to recognize that? Yet he stood uncertainly at the subway entrance, reluctant to turn back the way he'd come. But what choice was there? He reclimbed the stairs leading to the street, once again entering the world of loud horns, impatient drivers, and crowded sidewalks, an urban cacophony that seemed today to carry an undertow of confusion, of discernible nervous energy.

Terrorism? He couldn't help but wonder if this was the cause of the citywide blackout; it had been only two years since the towers had fallen. And if the subway lines were down, didn't that mean commuters were trapped in the underground tunnels in the stalled trains with no air conditioning, awaiting rescue while their air grew thin and overheated? If he hadn't stopped for a drink, he might well have been in one of those dark and unventilated cars right now, pressed up against a subway door with the rush hour crowd stirring restively around him.

He tried to call Stacy, but his cell phone didn't work. Sighing, he hesitated on the brink of the sidewalk, trying to figure his next move. Buses inched forward in the snarled traffic, and he could see they were crammed with faceless people standing in the aisles, clutching at the silver overhead bars that were shiny but never clean. Already, long and impatient lines had formed at the bus stops. He could try to hail a cab, but the ones he saw were occupied, even though people dashed into the streets and, out of pure frustration, tried to flag them down.

The only other alternative was to walk home, all the way to downtown Manhattan, and then cross the bridge into Brooklyn.

He turned down Broadway Avenue, resigning himself to the long haul. He removed his suit jacket and slung it over his arm, and unknotted his tie so his collar wouldn't fit quite so snugly. After a couple of blocks, his resignation lifted, and the first surprising flush of adrenaline kicked in, his limbs charged with a sudden exhilarating vigor. So unexpected, this journey...and now people were swelling out of the office buildings, lawyers and businessmen and lightly perspiring secretaries, crowding the streets even more. Police officers had been dispatched at various street corners to direct traffic and answer questions, their presence meant to suggest safety, order, containment. A man pedalled by on a bicycle with a cart attached behind it, and people were scrambling for a ride in even this small two-seat conveyance: could the driver get them downtown, uptown, crosstown, they needed to get *home.*

Sam crossed the street so he could walk with the sun in his face. He didn't care how hot it was. The sun—how easy to forget even the sun. He passed Herald Square and, a few blocks later, walked by a bodega that was selling slightly wilted roses, orchids, and tulips out on the sidewalk. He hurried past with his head bowed. Not for him the sweet funereal stench of flowers.

Once he'd left the flowers behind, his adventuresome spirit returned. His stride was almost jaunty, his briefcase swinging unencumbered in his hand. He hadn't just *walked* in a long, long time. Outside a small electronics store near Union Square, a man had dragged out a bat-tery-operated radio with speakers and set it up out on the sidewalk for people to hear as they passed by. A circle of men and women had gathered around the radio to listen, and Sam joined the impromptu knot of news seekers. He stood beside a muscular and balding older man in a white T-shirt who was holding an open Corona with a festive slice of lime wedged in the mouth of the bottle. The radio broadcaster announced that electricity was out in several eastern states; a faulty power grid was believed the reason for the blackout, not terrorism. "1977 all over again," the muscular man said, shaking his head. "Wel-come back, Son of Sam."

Sam winced at the unfortunate wording. He turned away and moved on, his mouth dry. Of course he'd heard stories of the 1977 New York City blackout—the looting and vandalism, the storefronts destroyed, the neighborhoods torched, the knife fights as looters attacked rival looters. Yet there was something about the energy of the crowd around him, all sharing this same communal inconvenience, that made them seem incapable of such violence. A woman with stylish, short-cropped hair emerged from a street deli, wearing blue ballerina slippers and carrying a single yellow rose that she held to her face. Wistful as she appeared, Sam knew she had the right attitude toward the flower. He followed her for a couple of blocks, determined not to lose sight of her, almost desperate not to…and then he simply did, as if she'd been swallowed up in the displaced crowd, or she'd disappeared in that way dreams do.

He moved with the crowd into the Village, past pubs and arty music stores and a coffeehouse with anti-war posters peeling off a wall. They passed a basketball park where young men were dribbling and shooting and leaping full-throttle into the air, oblivious to—and uncaring about—the city's current drama. The crowd surged past an outdoor café where diners were gathered around iron tables, watching with pleasure as the unending stream of people passed by. A lone woman with a purple streak in her hair held up her wine glass in a silent, commiserative toast. Her eyes seemed to lock on Sam in particular, but before he could know for sure if he'd been singled out, he'd walked past her. Still, he was tempted to stop somewhere for another drink, engage in a little wine debauchery, prolong for a while longer this fleeting euphoria. His one regret was that he had no one at his side to share the experience with. For a few blocks he half-pretended he was in the company of the young tattooed couple in front of him, but when their conversation veered from movie night in Bryant Park to whether God was a sadist or a masochist, Sam lost interest in his charade.

Slow and steady, he reminded himself. By the time the crowd reached Chinatown, walking at a normal pace had become all but impossible. Chinatown was a crowded neighborhood under ordinary circumstances, but today the sidewalks and streets were clogged with inconvenienced pedestrians, with cars and rickety bicycles, with pushcarts of exotic food, with stands selling inexpensive fresh fruit and wilting vegetables. Outside a fish store, an old Chinese woman was sitting on a wooden crate, and two other women were standing around her, dipping their hands into a bucket and patting ice over the old woman's forehead. Another thing he and Stacy had never gotten around to doing was traveling together in China. While Sam had wanted to see the usual Chinese hotspots—the Great Wall in Beijing, the Bund in Shanghai, the Festival of Lights in Hong Kong—Stacy had been most interested in viewing the life-sized pottery replications of Chinese warriors, horses, and chariots in the Terracotta Museum in Xi'an, sculptures that dated back a couple hundred years before Christ. The sculptures had been buried underground for thousands of years before peasant farmers, digging for a well in 1974, first stumbled upon them. Imagine, Stacy said, to witness those petrified figures standing in battle formations in the viewing pits, an imperial army from 2,200 years ago unearthed and come back to life.

But then Stacy had become pregnant, and this had put an end to their plans for China.

A small cloud settled over Sam's good mood. He stared down at his wedding ring. It did no good to kick around the past, he had to keep reminding himself. Up ahead, Sam saw standing on the street corner a young earnest man who was handing out small, palm-sized Bibles. Probably a Jehovah's Witness, judging by the requisite long-sleeve white shirt, the dark tie, the ill-pressed black pants. Sam moved closer. The young man's face was flushed and vigorous with a slightly forced and quiet good cheer that carried at its core a hint of defeat, a gnawing doubt as the crowd trudged past, ignoring him and his offers of salvation for their immortal souls. So when Sam paused in front of him, naturally the young man lit up at seeing an open face amid the sea of indifference. "Take one," he said and offered Sam a Bible.

Normally Sam would have been one of the countless that passed by with a slightly dismissive shake of his head, but at this moment, with reality's brutal shadow creeping up on him again…there was a peculiar flutter in Sam's heart, for what he couldn't have said. Spirit? No, he didn't think so; what he was lacking was even more personal. "Thank you," he said and held out his hand.

The Jehovah's Witness smiled as scripture was exchanged. The New Testament, Sam saw, not the entire Bible, not the Old Testament of blood, thunder, and butchery, of a vengeful God who reduced women to pillars of salt and gloried in the sacrifice of children. The old Yehowah God. "You must be hot," Sam said, although coming from the office himself, he wasn't dressed all that differently.

The young man wiped the back of his hand across his forehead. "It is a little toasty," he agreed with that same modest smile plastered across his face. He had chunky, milk-fed teeth. Now the crowd shouldered a little impatiently past Sam as well, with Sam and the young man the only stationary ones in the ongoing throng of movement. Yet for all of this, Sam still lingered. There was a shock of recognition between him and the young man, as if they could feel the other's loneliness, and this unspoken loneliness bound them. Yet theirs was one of those random, incidental meetings of which nothing could become, for little connected them other than that loneliness neither of them could address, which in fact embarrassed them for revealing itself to the other. And though Sam didn't want to leave, and he could sense the Jehovah's Witness didn't want him to leave, he and the young man could think of nothing else to say to one another that would connect them in any concrete way. "Goodbye," Sam sighed at last and rejoined the crowd of people moving toward the bridge.

For a couple of blocks Sam kept a tight grip on the little Bible. Then, idly, he thumbed through the first pages. A wallet-sized picture of what he assumed was Christ's beneficent face had been inserted into the book, a ceramic, breakable Jesus with a large spacious gold halo hovering above his head. *San Guida Taddeo Apostola* was printed in a child's hand beneath the picture. There was also a folded sheet tucked into the Bible: *You must be born again*, it read. Offended, Sam let the mimeographed sheet drop out of his hand and disappear beneath the crowd's feet. He'd expected more than brimstone-as-usual from the young man, he couldn't be sure why. Yet he continued to page through the Bible, as if compelled, as if his receiving the Bible now must mean something. He couldn't help but hunt for meaning wherever he could find it; the alternative was meaninglessness, the dark swirl of random nothingness. He turned a few more pages. The Book of Matthew. Matthew had been one of the names Sam had tossed around for their son, but Stacy had been partial to Malcolm, after a beloved grandfather, and so Malcolm he had become.

But Matthew was a name that walked, maybe, closer to God. Sam closed the book and placed it in a pocket of the suit jacket he was carrying.

With these thoughts, a permanent pall fell over him. His briefcase, only minutes ago so light in his hand that he'd forgotten about it, now felt heavy, as if packed with a few personal stones. Even the crowd's steady march forward seemed less parade now and more routine, militaristic, all of them soldiers in an advancing army (not petrified, this army!). Or no, not an advancing army, even that missed the mark. They were a *retreating* army; they were refugees being driven out of the city by some mysterious, conquering force. Beware your homes, your family and children, all are in peril. Escape, escape. He shook his head. His mind was straying away from him. He didn't know whether to blame the scotch, the heat, or the young Jehovah's Witness he would never know.

Soon the Brooklyn Bridge rose into view—the magnificent steel cables, the familiar double-arched towers. But once Sam neared the bridge, he grew reluctant to cross over. Too many people, *too many of us*, converged on the bridge at one time, so that pedestrian traffic on the walkway had come to a standstill, like cattle backed up in a chute. Squeezed together shoulder to shoulder with strangers, Sam's childhood claustrophobia came rushing back at him, and yet to reach the other side, he had to cross the bridge. There was no other way.

He was impatient now, when only minutes ago he'd felt elated and nearly happy. The lack of movement was corrupting him. He inched forward with the bottlenecked crowd, stopped, inched forward again. His breath grew shallow and a little piercing. Trapped, cornered, fenced in! Somehow he'd ended up standing inside a group of five kids about thirteen or fourteen years old, loud shouting boys caught up in the whole event the way Sam had been only a short while ago. Their shouting and cursing irritated him, or else what irritated him was how they talked and yelled around him, as if he wasn't really standing there amongst them.

"Fuck this to infinity," the boy in a Mets cap said. Sam was almost sure he'd heard the boy correctly. With one agile jump the boy was standing atop the barrier that divided the pedestrian walkway from the street of incoming traffic below. Spreading his arms wide in a mockery of flight, he leapt down into the street—the jump was only several feet—and started weaving between the stalled cars. His friends shouted and catcalled, and then they, too, clamored over the barricade and dashed among the cars, following their friend, all of them darts of pure energy. Sam watched them go with both relief and an odd poignancy. He wouldn't mind jumping the barrier so he, too, could escape the congestion of people and start hoofing it through the car lanes. Ahead of him, where the barrier rose slightly higher, he saw a young shirtless man with a ponytail hoist a young woman with a darker ponytail onto his shoulders and push her over the barricade. Then he followed her.

And so the leaping of the barricade had begun. Yet Sam was self-conscious about jumping over himself. What if he lost his grip while trying to boost himself over? He was alone, there was no one to spot him from a fall, and he was constrained by his business wear and the suit jacket and briefcase in his hands. On impulse he turned and started pushing his way back in the opposite direction, squeezing himself up against the barricade as best he could, until he'd backtracked to a place where the barrier was a little lower and looked easier to mount. Then he, too, boosted himself over the barricade and jumped down into the traffic.

Sam landed a bit wrong, so there was a jarring in his ankles, but being away from the human traffic jam was worth the minor pain. He joined the growing stream of pedestrian traffic as it slogged among the cars. Somewhere up ahead, he heard the steady beat of an old song, "Baby, baby, can't you hear my heart beat." He mouthed the words to himself until he stopped, thinking better of it.

He'd been walking for a couple of minutes, engaged in his continual march forward, lost once again in his myriad thoughts, when he realized he'd started to tremble. Confused, he paused for a moment, and felt a dizzying vertigo. No, he wasn't shaking. The bridge was, swaying from the weight of the tens of thousands of people and cars passing across at once. His head filled with apocalyptic vision and fire: what if the bridge should collapse from the sheer weight of it all? But no, he knew better. *The bridge may sway but it will not fall*, he remembered from somewhere. Nonetheless, he quickened his pace as best he could.

Yet he could not ignore the bridge and its strange pulsating. It was unmistakable, the constant vibrations. He stared up at the bridge's cables and imagined he could see them quivering, like some giant string instrument fiercely played by air. The bridge was shuddering *alive*, he thought with a headlong rush, an inanimate force rising to life, insisting upon life even under the strain of holding up these thousands of hot and weary people, of whom Sam was only one. Soon he felt the vibrations entering him, pushing down inside him, rattling at his caged soul. Tears leapt into his eyes and he fought them back, but it was too late, the shivering had taken hold now, shaking at his heart. Dizzy and spent, he relented and silently cried out for Malcolm, his dead son.

Once Sam reached the other side of the bridge, pedestrian traffic loosened up as people began to separate in different directions. He was hot, sweaty, emotionally tired, his feet sore. Inside himself he still felt the bridge's quivering, its tragic lament.

He crossed Atlantic Avenue and took his time walking the few remaining blocks to his apartment. He passed a number of women pushing baby carriages. Although the neighborhood had its fair share of the single and hip crowd, the young marrieds were the most visible, in particular the young mothers with their strollers and healthy, exuberant children. The city was filled with reminders.

At last he reached his apartment building. He felt no relief. The bridge had wiped him out. He lingered down at the mailbox, rifling through bills and junk mail and a second notice on an overdue bill from the pediatrician. The door to the downstairs apartment opened and Delia Eastman peeked her head out to say hello. A thin artist's paintbrush held her hair in a bun at the back of her neck. "This city," she sighed. "If it's not one thing, it's another."

Sam nodded, although New York City alone was not to blame. Everywhere infrastructure was crumbling; radios and walkie-talkies were malfunctioning; efforts to find a cure for the common cold were failing; and then, too, children were dying in their cribs. There was no end to it.

"And how is Stacy?" Delia asked a bit cautiously.

"She's fine, she's fine." He glanced down at the suit jacket in his arms, the curious Bible sticking out from the pocket. Already the face of the Jehovah's Witness was fading from his mind—all he had left were blurred features and the milk-fed teeth. Distracted, he missed part of what Delia was saying. From what he could make out, she and her boyfriend had gone to buy food and wine as soon as the electricity shut down. Some of the delis had all but given the food away before it spoiled. Delia was going to lay out a table for anyone from the building who wanted to stop down and share in their "bounty of inconvenience," as she phrased it.

"Or I could bring up some food if you want," Delia offered. "Italian bread, pastrami, cheese, salads. We even bought a few rotisserie chickens."

"No," Sam said, perhaps a little too bluntly. The thought of Delia stepping into their apartment horrified him. "It's very nice of you, though," he added.

Delia didn't seem offended by his brusque tone. She looked at him with a warmth and understanding that was nearly painful. The first couple weeks after Malcolm had died, Delia had brought them up plates of food nearly every night. This had been before Sam and Stacy started closing their door to even their friends. "Well, maybe you two will come down then," Delia said.

Sam envisioned himself smiling more than he felt it.

Upstairs, Sam stood outside his apartment door for a moment, key in hand, listening in vain for the sounds that used to welcome him home—Stacy's rollicking laughter, her hurried footsteps back and forth. Malcolm's crying. But now he heard only silence. He took a breath and unlocked the door.

He was struck first by the stifling, oven-like heat. The lack of ventilation only emphasized the smell of their unwashed dishes, the heap of garbage bags in the kitchen that the both of them had never gotten around to carrying downstairs. Yet the smell was also deeper, more personal. It was the pervasive clinging smell of staleness, of lack of will and energy, of their shut-down lives. Sam closed the door quickly, sealing the smell inside with them. There was also the look of the place, the evidence of their neglect—clothes strewn over the sofa and chairs, piles of newspapers and magazines spread on the coffee table and floor, unvacuumed rugs, empty plastic food containers scattered around. Even the photographs on the shelf by the bookcase were dusty. Sometimes dust just...accumulated. Over the past three months, dust had become its own malevolent force inside the apartment—floating, settling, defiling, leaving a slow and steady grime on most everything they owned. Even breathing in the apartment had become a burden. Air; first must come air. He put down his suit jacket and briefcase on the desk, and stepped over several random newssheets of the *New York Times* to open one of the windows.

Stacy was lying on the sofa on top of a couple of outdated magazines. She was wearing one of his T-shirts as a short dress, and had an arm thrown over her eyes. He figured she was asleep, in fact hoped this was the case, but she stirred and then said, without shifting position on the sofa, "You're home."

"The subways are down," he explained. "I had to walk."

"No cabs?"

"It was easier getting over the Brooklyn Bridge on foot, I think." The bridge had ceased quivering inside him, leaving him feeling empty and unsung. His stomach rumbled. "Are you hungry?" he asked.

"Everything in the refrigerator will spoil." Finally Stacy moved, although all she did was stretch out her arms and sit up. He waited for her to say more but she did not. She had the manner of an invalid these days—listless; not eating; growing thinner; her color pallid, washed out.

Usually he could lighten the apartment's mood, at least somewhat, with music. He went over to the CD player and thumbed through his choices. "Sammy, you can't play music if there's no electricity," she reminded him.

He nodded. Already he'd forgotten. And Sammy. She'd started calling him that a couple of weeks after Malcolm died. He didn't much like it, but this seemed too minor an infraction to object to.

On his way to the bathroom for a shower, he paused outside Malcolm's nursery next to their bedroom. The nursery! It was the one room in the apartment that Stacy would not allow to fall victim to the dust.

There was Malcolm's crib, so resoundingly empty, and his changing table. Sometimes Stacy sat for hours in the chair near the crib, rocking herself back and forth, pensive and waiting for something. When Malcolm had been alive, Stacy had bought a couple of picture books that she'd planned on reading to him when he grew older. Now that he was dead, she would sometimes sit in the rocker with one of the picture books open in her lap, and she would flip through the pages of floppy-eared rabbits, quirky elves, and freckle-faced mischief makers, her lips moving, shaping the words she would never say to Malcolm. Maybe she actually read the books, or maybe was simply mesmerized by the deft and spirited illustrations, or maybe she wanted to digest the untold stories, breathe them in, a kind of nourishment she could no longer draw from food.

When Sam was a boy, his favorite book had been *Harold and the Purple Crayon*. With that simple crayon Harold had drawn himself a moonlit path on which to walk, a boat in which to float over water, a balloon to catch himself when he fell, a picnic to feed himself when he was hungry, a city of houses in which to live. And when Harold was exhausted from his adventures, he had drawn a comfortable bed and a window with the moon shining through it, and he'd climbed into that bed and gone to sleep.

But Malcolm had been too young for crayons.

Next to the crib was a small cot meant for Stacy or Sam to sleep on during those nights when Malcolm had been fretful and needed constant attention. Stacy had slept in Malcolm's room many times during the four months he was alive; Sam had done so only once. Once! But he had to get up in the morning for work—that, at any rate, had been their eternal mantra (how trivial that seemed now, but at the time, so practical). Sam relived that one night over and over again in his mind: feeding Malcolm from the bottle of his mother's breast-pumped milk, rocking him gently, and then holding his son to his shoulder to burp him. He remembered the boy's gentle breathing, his sunny hiccups, his almond smell...

And Stacy. She had been so wiped out from the grief of Malcolm's death that a doctor had sedated her, and even then she had cried for days, knowing that she had not been sleeping in the nursery *that night*. Suppose she had been? Maybe she would have sensed something was the matter, could have lifted him from that deathly crib before it had killed him. Useless for Sam to question the point of such speculation. Eventually Stacy's tears had dried up, and were soon replaced by what Sam considered far more sinister—a brooding depressive silence that settled in around her and, to his horror, devoured her entire personality.

He showered quickly, groping his way in the darkness like a blind man since the bathroom had no window or natural light. When he was finished, he began to towel dry his hair and stepped into the bedroom, which was no cleaner than the living room. The bed was unmade, and the sheets hadn't been changed in some time. Their clothes were strewn around here as well, on the bed and chairs. Books with broken spines were splayed open on the windowsills or lying across the floor like shot-down birds. The clinging pervasive dust had settled on the shelves and the desktops, across the hardwood floor. One of the few things that wasn't coated with dust was the jar Stacy kept on the shelf near the bed. Inside the jar was Malcolm's umbilical cord stump. Maybe it was grotesque that they'd hung on to this. Stacy's younger sister had saved the umbilical cord of her first child, and had convinced Stacy to do the same—*a physical memento of the baby's birth*, she'd said. Although now, of course, the stump took on a more portentous significance, the most potent symbol they had linking them to Malcolm, his existence.

At night the cord stump gleamed darkly inside the jar. Frequently Sam woke and found he was staring at it. The cord was black now, but if light fell through the window at a certain angle, the cord appeared white, just as it had been the morning Malcolm was born, squalling and kicking his legs.

Sometimes Sam dreamed the cord was trying to escape from its absurd jar. Once, in a dream, he had dumped the cord into the toilet and tried to flush it away, but the cord refused to flush, causing the toilet to overflow with its filthy black lava water…

When he'd awoken from that disturbing dream, he was out of bed and stumbling around the room with the jar in his hand. He had no answer for this. He'd put the jar back in its place and returned to the bed, where Stacy was not. That particular night she hadn't been sleeping on the cot in the nursery, but was out on the sofa in front of the television, lolling herself to rest on the detached and hollow noise of the world's misfortunes: Iraq roadside bombings, world markets rising and falling. Since Malcolm's death she rarely spent an entire night in bed with Sam. Apparently his touch disquieted her. He did not take this personally, knowing it was his flesh, his living body and its healthy functioning, that she was turning away from.

He did not take it personally, and yet her behavior troubled him. Sam sat down on the unmade bed, still drying his hair with the towel, remembering nights when he and Stacy had lain together side by side, nude and happy, loving and together and whole, just another couple planning their future with their child. How quickly their bliss had ended. Stacy had been the one who had found Malcolm dead. She'd woken *that night* to the silence of Malcolm not crying for his feeding. The baby monitor had stood mute on the nightstand. Yet she had not suspected a thing as she rose and went to him.

Oh, that warm and treacherous May night, only moments before their lives were to get wrenched out from under them, before loss would cripple them utterly, bringing with it this filth. Sam had been wakened by Stacy's desperate cries. "Honey?" he'd called and sat up in bed with his fists already clenched, fumbling to identify what was happening, sensing already his life in full retreat, away from him.

Because nothing could be done. Malcolm had simply died in his crib, as so many babies before him had died—suddenly, mysteriously, inexplicably.

Babies dead in their sleep all over the world, their small hearts silenced, and the world of reason had no explanation.

At last Sam rose from the bed. He stepped into a pair of jeans and dug around in the dresser for a T-shirt. Only one clean shirt remained and it was not flattering, faded of color and torn insouciantly at one shoulder. Nonetheless, he tossed aside the towel and slipped the T-shirt over his head, returned to the living room, and sat down in a chair across from Stacy. She was holding a sofa cushion in her arms and staring down at it. "Hon?" he said, and she made a small sound to indicate she was listening. She set down the cushion, stood up and walked into the kitchen, then turned around somewhat aimlessly and returned to the sofa. Sam had the strange suspicion she was only making a show of moving around, a half-hearted obligatory gesture of some sort. From the open window he heard the sound of a woman's triumphant laughter, which reminded him. "Delia and a few of the neighbors are going to have a picnic of sorts downstairs," he said.

Stacy picked up an old bank statement wedged between the sofa cushions and began to fan herself. She stared at the windows with loathing. "They're terribly smeared," she said.

"She invited us down to join them," Sam said. "Once the lights went out, she raided the delis, I guess."

Several seconds passed where the only sound was their breathing. "I'm not really hungry," Stacy said. "But you go on ahead."

"I want us both to go."

She shook her head. "I'm sorry, Sammy." She was saying the words too often these days, *I'm sorry, I'm sorry*, as if stuck in a perpetual state of apology. He looked at her a little impatiently. But what words could persuade her, what pleas could bring her back? He couldn't begin to know, stuck in this awful triangle between Stacy and Malcolm and himself, competing with his dead infant son for the heart and soul of the mother. And Sam, with only his love and compassion and puny humanity to offer, was losing the struggle. Only last month he'd suggested Stacy see a doctor, therapist, acupuncturist, someone, *anyone* to help her feel better. There were treatments, medications, homeopathic remedies…he would join her if she wanted…but she clung to her pain stubbornly, unable or unwilling to let it go, to let go of Malcolm. Sam had missed that moment when the grieving over their son had become *hers*, when he'd become excluded from it. Unless he'd excluded himself, at some point refusing to step any further into the darkness with her.

Down in the street a siren passed. There were always sirens. A fly buzzed near Sam's face, landed on the coffee table and flicked its wings. It busily brushed its legs together. The fly seemed almost to challenge him in some way. "All right," Sam said, stood up and walked to the kitchen to root around in the refrigerator. Stacy was right about all the food going to waste—the lean cuts of steak in the freezer, the hamburger and chicken, the frozen grilled vegetables. Pie, why was he hungry for pie? Sam found a piece of string cheese and gnawed on that poor substitute. But he still felt ravenous, so he opened up a container of softening ice cream, and brought the ice cream and a spoon back into the living room. He sat on the floor in front of the sofa, next to Stacy where she could not ignore him. "Have some ice cream with me," he said, daring to hope, even now, that food could reach her, smell and taste, the small sensual pleasures of life. He dug the spoon into the ice cream. "Rocky Road," he added.

She shook her head, a tight fragile smile on her face. Up close, he noticed the faint unwashed smell of her, almost a cloistered smell, a nun shut away in a dungeon. "Come on," he said. "Stace, you have to eat."

"It's *melted*," she said.

"Only partly." Yet his hand began to tremble at her resistance. Drops of the ice cream dribbled to the floor. He set the ice cream aside and impulsively touched her bare arm. And in that moment he felt her frail bones, the heat of her skin, the constrained life of her. He brushed his lips against her cheek and meant to speak her name, but he fumbled and only breathed it.

Stacy pulled away from him, her eyes flooding with outraged tears. Sam was left to stare defeated at the rejected ice cream. He picked up the container and returned to the lounger. Almost, almost he wanted to hurl the ice cream across the room, leave an accusing stain across the wall. But he couldn't deny himself, or wouldn't. He dug the spoon into the slushy ice cream and fed himself until it was gone, then set the empty carton on the coffee table with the other discarded food containers. He felt sweetly sickish yet still hungry. Stacy was starving herself and he was always hungry. Even their hunger divided them. He meant to remind Stacy, someday, that there could be other children, but both he and Stacy were forty years old now, and Stacy was in no emotional place to plan ahead.

"So hot," Stacy muttered as she lay back down on the sofa and closed her eyes. After a moment, Sam leaned his head back against the lounger. Maybe there was no use fighting any of it. Maybe oblivion was good, that lure toward nothingness, if on the other side was Malcolm. Sam's eyes grew heavy. He yielded and closed his eyes, allowing himself to drift, to float off toward some unencumbered place if he could find it, if such peace existed...

Only the damned fly had landed on his face and was moving along his jaw to his mouth. He brushed the fly away and opened his eyes, expecting to see something miraculous. But in the time he'd been daydreaming, the room had simply moved from light to darkness, as happened every night. He forced himself to stand and move through the darkness to one of the kitchen cupboards for a flashlight and some candles. He turned on the flashlight long enough to return to the living room and light a couple of the candles, which he set down on the windowsill. Sam could hear the sound of Delia's party downstairs, the movement and laughter, the pleasure and promise. A woman's voice rose up to him from the apartment's front steps, "So he's really leaving her?"

"Yes," a man answered. "Spreading his wings and reeking of gin."

Sam turned away from the window, lit another candle, and placed it on the bookshelf, mindful of keeping the flame away from the curtains or the accumulated stacks of old *New York Times*. The last thing they needed was a literal burning of the apartment.

After he was finished he sat back on the edge of his chair, across from where Stacy was still asleep on the sofa, illuminated by the flickering candlelight that flung their shadows large against the wall. Or his shadow was there. Stacy's was merged with the sofa.

The bridge—he must cross soon or risk limbo forever. For some time he sat in the uncertain candlelight, staring at Stacy, so distant from him. His heart unclenched, and he, at last, was calm. He stood and placed the large flashlight beside Stacy in case she woke up and needed to find her way. Then, using only a tiny penlight to guide him, he took a breath and walked out of the apartment into the dark hallway that led down to Delia's party, his baptism back into a world where suffering a blackout was the greatest darkness. He did, after all, have to start somewhere.

Botanical gardens, age three.

Joy Wood was born and raised in Michigan. She earned a BA from Vassar College and an MFA from the University of Michigan, where she was recently a Zell Post-graduate Fellow in fiction. She is also the recipient of fellowships from the Santa Fe Art Institute and the MacDowell Colony. She is the managing editor of *Guernica*. "The Man in the Elevator" is her first story accepted for publication.

THE MAN IN THE ELEVATOR

Joy Wood

The first time I saw Uncle Chao, he was standing in the lobby of our apartment building holding a dripping green umbrella. My mother and I were coming home from ordering a cake for my younger sister Nina's fifteenth birthday. My mother made me hold the bakery brochure while she got out her keys. A raindrop rolled off the tip of her nose and into her purse.

"Connie," a man's voice said. My mother and I both turned. A bald man wearing a blue jacket and too-short khakis approached us. His jacket rustled as he walked. A maple leaf was stuck to his left shoe.

"What are you doing here?" my mother asked. I fanned my face with the brochure. Its cover featured a cake topped with glazed strawberries, like bugs trapped in amber.

"I was in the neighborhood," he said, but his laugh suggested that he had traveled far. He used his thumb to smooth a raindrop from the handle of his umbrella. "Aren't you going to introduce us?" he asked.

Her cheeks flushed. "This is my eldest daughter. Anna, this is Uncle Chao," she said, using the respectful title.

I shook Uncle Chao's thick hand. "Your mother's told me all about you," he said. The top of his head, freckled and sweaty, reminded me of a glass paperweight.

"Don't tease her," my mother said, but I didn't care. I just wanted to go inside.

"What about next week?" he asked her.

She ran her thumbnail along the groove of a key. "I'll have to check."

"Yes. Nice to meet you, Anna." He bowed slightly. "Be good to your mother." His shoes squeaked on the tiles.

"Who was that?" I asked as we walked to the elevator.

She pressed the up button. "An old friend."

It took me months to realize that her description was only partially true.

Back then, we lived on 88th Street between First and York, in an apartment that my parents had bought while my mother was pregnant with me. Despite ten years in America and my father's PhD, real-estate brokers eyed my mother's long braid and grapefruit-half belly and said, "Perhaps you'd be more comfortable downtown, Mrs. Tong," while checking the time of their next appointment. Elderly tenants, mummified in cardigans and housecoats, scowled at them from doors cracked open as far as the chain would allow.

"My husband used to shoot people like you in the war," a woman hissed.

In their Chinatown railroad flat, my mother cried on my father's shoulder. "Be patient," he said. "The right place will come." At that point, any place seemed like an improvement. They lived like characters in a children's book, each one of their possessions depending on something else for its existence. The laundry hung on a line above the bathtub, which touched the kitchen counter, where tins of tea—oolong, jasmine, green—balanced like minarets against the backsplash.

One of my father's colleagues at Hunter recommended a broker named Roslyn. My parents went uptown to meet her at an apartment building named The Aegean, which was next to a dry cleaner. As they got out of the cab, the sweet chemical tang of other people's clothes filled their noses.

Roslyn was waiting. "I think you'll love the place," she said.

"When you're pregnant, everyone has an opinion," my mother told me. "Boy. Girl. Don't drink tea. Don't cross your legs when you sit. I just wanted a place to rest." The herbalist on Mott Street, looking her up and down from the doorway of his shop, had told her to eat more mushrooms. Instead, she sent my father out for oranges. She had gotten into the habit of eating two or three in one sitting, until the tartness made her lips tingle.

Riding up to the seventh floor with Roslyn, my parents stared at their reflections in the elevator's mirrored panels, which made the car feel fuller than it was. It was easy for them to imagine their future family in the space.

The kitchen window had a partial view of the East River. Built-in bookshelves lined one wall of the living room.

"Wait," my father said. He took a cat's-eye marble from his pocket and set it down on the floor. The marble scooted toward the window, ricocheting off the baseboard. Roslyn was unfazed. "All old buildings settle," she said.

My mother went into one of the bedrooms. She leaned on the windowsill and imagined watching the sun rise over the East River like an egg yolk, a baby in her arms.

In the living room, Roslyn asked, "Do you know if it's a boy or girl?"

"We want a surprise," my father said. "We buy everything in yellow."

"Looks like a boy to me."

My mother unlocked the window latches, feeling the cool metal fill her palm. She had never lived so high up before.

She walked back into the living room and squeezed my father's hand. "I like this place," she said.

Roslyn opened her briefcase. "Let's see what I can do," she said.

To my parents, 88th Street was the Chinese Park Avenue, a sign that they had made it in the toughest city in *mei guo*, the beautiful country. They now belonged to the city grid, walking on streets that were numbered instead of named. When they wrote their new address down for their friends, the side-by-side eights looked like four eyes, like the beginning of a pattern.

Although my parents never spoke freely about love or sex, they never hesitated to remind us about how lucky we were. My mother knew many Chinese restaurant widows, their husbands toiling sixty hours a week in basement kitchens. My mother's friend Eileen Yip, who had divorced when her son Wilson was a toddler, was an exception, and other women viewed her as suspiciously as a blond hair on the bathroom mirror. Wilson's father, whom I'd never met, lived deep in New Jersey, beyond the reach of PATH and NJ Transit.

Physics had been my father's path out, had allowed his knuckles to heal so that they were no longer swollen and cracked from wielding a cleaver. But the skin had remained dark and tough, like dried jujubes. On her Chinatown shopping excursions, my mother heard about the couples who'd split under the weight of gambling debts or backroom infidelities. She didn't think it would happen to her; she and my father were trying new things. They had Chinese food delivered, entrees that held the shape of the white paper container after being inverted on a plate. My mother bought a pair of Reeboks for her commute. She now used Lipton bags for making tea eggs on Sundays.

Less than a year after I was born, her belly began to swell again. She cut her hair to chin-length, where it would remain for the next two decades. The ends flipped up and off her face like wings.

My father chose my name because he liked how it read the same backward and forward. My mother named my sister Nina because she liked how the two names shared the same final syllable. Our sisterly similarities ended there. Nina was a fussy, restless baby, pawing at her face with her cotton-mittened hands. She still had a faint scar on her right cheek, like the slot in a piggy bank, from scratching herself as an infant.

Even though their apartment was bigger, the neighbors seemed closer. Once, by the mailboxes, a man had grabbed my father's arm and said, "Listen. No menus." The new apartment was quiet, too quiet. My mother had trouble sleeping, and would read at the kitchen table so she wouldn't disturb my father. In their old building, families propped open their apartment doors and let their conversations drift into the halls along with the smell of frying garlic. She dreaded these new evenings, the slam and churn of doors being deadbolted for the night.

"It's like living in a museum," she murmured to my father as she cracked open his beer.

"That's what we're paying for," he replied. He was still teaching intro physics to undergrads, rolling wooden cars up wooden ramps to illustrate the forces of potential and kinetic energy. Tenure seemed like a barricaded avenue. The department chair, Dr. McCarthy, had told my father that he still needed time to develop, that students complained that he was difficult to understand. He smiled and nodded, then appealed to us at the dinner table.

"Lazy kids," he fumed. "They see my face and think I'm not speaking English."

My mother was the office manager for an accounting firm in Midtown. Between the two of them, they had numbers covered.

The uptown life was broad and clean compared to Chinatown, where they had lived among noodle shops and fish markets, where grocery shopping meant jostling with the tired-eyed masses. Not long after she came to New York, my mother saw a man get stabbed on the Bowery. He cried out and fell into the street. Cars honked while blood spread beneath him like a hungry shadow. That kind of chaos seemed unimaginable among the smooth-faced blocks of her new neighborhood. Stores remained open after sunset. At sidewalk cafés, diners dropped empty mussel shells into footed ceramic bowls. Couples lingered over disembodied velvet necks in jewelry-store windows. Joggers stretched their hamstrings, revealing so much thigh that my parents quickly looked away. In the winter, women on Madison Avenue carefully maneuvered their fur coats to prevent different species from touching. There was so much to take in, and still so much more to want.

Every time my mother left the apartment, the city's dangers seemed to multiply. The wail of ambulances up First Avenue served as a constant reminder of what could go wrong. The subway was worse. Junkies lurked at the turnstiles, waiting for the right moment to suck a token from the slot before it dropped, ropy saliva trailing from their mouths like a spider seeking to finish its web.

One evening, my father brought home a gift for her: a Swiss Army knife, the basic model. As he watched, she unfolded all the tools. Both the knife and nail file were shorter than her thumb. She smiled at my father to show her appreciation.

The Swiss Army knife rode heavily in the bottom of her purse, scratching whatever it touched. She still sent my father to buy meat and fish in Chinatown. The big-knuckled butchers at Lok Wing teased him. "Ah, John, special for the uptown man," they said as they slipped in free slices of *char siu* for Nina and me. The butcher's red plastic bags made other riders on the uptown train eye my father, as though they expected the contents to leap out and attack.

Before Uncle Chao, if I had to describe my mother in one word, it would be practical. In China, my mother had been born into a wealthy family. Her father had been a bookkeeper, but during the Cultural Revolution the family fled to Hong Kong, five people in a one-bedroom flat, the toes of their socks on the clothesline pointing in all different directions.

Even my father's appearance suggested economy: my father was tall and thin, his belts pulled to the last hole. His eyebrows grew as straight as dashes, the same thickness all the way through. Practicality had gotten her this far, to the Upper East Side, and she saw no reason to change. She still bargained for bruised and overripe produce. At home, I'd watch her carve out the edible portions with a knife, as delicate as brain surgery, and wonder what she thought she was saving.

Nina was late to her own birthday dinner. Not Chinese late, but full-on American late, 7:17 according to my father's Casio watch, tromping through the door of Evergreen Palace with her boyfriend, Christian, who hadn't been invited. Her wet hair left trails on her pink dress. I gave her a look of warning, to let her know she'd done so many things wrong before even sitting down. The corners of my father's mouth folded down like a staple through paper. I knew he disliked Christian, but I wasn't sure if it was only because he was a boy interested in his daughter. My father had already talked to us about boys. "You do not get a grade in boys," he'd said. "You cannot major in boys."

Christian leaned in to shake my father's hand, and clapped him on the shoulder. "What's up, Mr. Tong?" My father's mouth twitched.

Christian was cute in a disheveled preppy way: he wore his shirts untucked and had dark brown hair, where each curl seemed to float on its own without touching any of the others. At least Christian had dressed up a little, a button-down over a blue T-shirt with some kind of writing on it, the fabric thick enough to obscure the words. My mother pulled a waiter aside to ask for another chair.

Christian and Nina ate shoulder-to-shoulder like they were the only people in the restaurant, dragging the serving spoons roughly, parting the thick sauces to expose the plate beneath. I saw my parents trading glances, and my stomach tightened. It stayed that way through the entire meal. I could barely eat the cake we'd brought, its color and texture reminding me of a kitchen sponge, another thing used to clean up mistakes.

Uncle Chao seemed to be the latest in a string of family mysteries that we were taught to accept without questioning. When I was little and drawing with Nina at the coffee table, my father would slap at the crayon in my left hand and then put it in my right. I didn't know why one hand was better than the other. I didn't know why sometimes my father spent the night in his office.

Growing up, I knew when my father was up for committee review, because the night before he would ask me to help him polish his shoes. We'd go out on our balcony, so narrow that when we were both on it we had to keep our backs to the building. Years ago, my father had showed me how to start a fire with a magnifying glass held over an old newspaper.

"Don't look at the beam," he'd warned. "You'll go blind."

I watched a van try to park on the street below, and then I smelled smoke. A hole was growing on the page, words disappearing into its brown edges.

"That's enough," my father said, and stomped the fire out.

The last time I helped him, I loaded the boar-bristle brush with black polish. The tendons in his wrist played hide-and-seek as he worked the brush over the leather, as if trying to scrub out the cracks. When he was finished, his hands looked like a mechanic's. I told him so and he just laughed.

"I push because I love," he said.

•   •   •

On Saturday mornings, my father would make omelets using the week's leftovers. My mother made jasmine tea, and the four of us would linger at the table until it was time for Nina's flute lesson. After my mother and Nina left, he would read me a riddle from a book that he had brought with him from China, and I would have until they got back to figure out the answer. Because I couldn't read Chinese, I couldn't cheat by peeking. Sometimes when I got frustrated, I would beg him to tell me, but he always refused. "Think about it for a little longer," he'd say.

With the difficult riddles, once I heard the answer I couldn't imagine it any other way, but only one of them made me cry.

"There was a man who lived on the tenth floor of an apartment building," my father read. "When he leaves the building, he takes the elevator down to the first floor and exits. But when he returns, he takes the elevator up to the seventh floor and takes the stairs to the tenth floor. Why?"

"Does he like getting exercise?" I asked.

"No."

"Is he superstitious?"

My father shook his head. "That's not it."

"Does he know people on the seventh floor?"

"No friends." I thought about the old people in our building who smelled like coffee and Ben-Gay. My father closed the book and set it on the table. "You're thinking about this the wrong way," he said. "I'll give you a hint. The man is not normal."

There were other childhood mysteries. Unlike my friends' apartments, which contained framed family trees, heirloom quilts, and communion dresses, the only reminder of the past in our apartment were two blue leather suitcases with darkened handles and no wheels. It seemed like my parents came to New York fully formed. They had met in the subway, standing on opposite platforms of the Astor Place station. She was holding a straw hat, turning its brim between her hands as she waited. After exchanging glances, she watched him turn and head for the exit. The black support columns along the tracks made it look like he was walking out of frame. She scolded herself for thinking she'd shared a moment of connection with a stranger. Then she felt a tap at her elbow. He had crossed over to her side.

Nina and I would ask them about the people in old photos, the ones who stared straight into the lens without smiling, but we never got any names, only descriptions.

"A family friend. She helped raise me and my siblings."

"These were my classmates."

"We are your parents, not your friends," my father said. "Not the American way, but works for us."

In this way, everyone had their secrets. Despite the Upper East Side address, my parents couldn't afford two private-school tuitions. They didn't want to choose between us (and neither of us being boys), so we both went to Hunter College High School.

Our father helped us with our homework when he could. Once, when I was learning about states of matter, he brought over one of my mother's rings with a pear-shaped diamond. He set the ring down on my notebook.

"Look at this," he said. "Nothing is harder than a diamond, but it's just carbon. With extreme pressure and heat, it'll change form, turn into graphite." He tapped the metal band of my pencil. I nodded, but pictured tiny crystals pouring out of my pencil and scattering across the lined pages of my notebook. I liked my way better, the ordinary becoming beautiful.

Two weeks after Nina's birthday, Aunt Mei came to visit on her way back from Tokyo. She was my mother's younger sister, a Delta flight attendant based out of Atlanta. She always brought gifts for us: macadamia nuts, Mickey Mouse ears, smoked salmon in a foil pouch. Her face was full and freckled from layovers spent on foreign beaches. She showed us the brace position under the kitchen table, the glass top cool against our backs.

When Aunt Mei visited, Nina and I had to share the futon in the living room. Mostly I didn't mind, because Aunt Mei sometimes brought a bottle of duty-free Johnnie Walker. She and my mother would stay up late, gasping and giggling as they sipped it from teacups. I liked seeing my mother tipsy, her face bare and relaxed.

I woke up in the middle of the night—Nina had stolen the covers again—and saw the bathroom light on. Aunt Mei was standing in front of the medicine cabinet while my mother sat on the edge of the tub.

Aunt Mei used her index fingers to push her cheeks up. "Do you think I should get a face-lift?"

"Don't be silly," my mother said. "You shouldn't change anything."

She pursed her lips. "How do you like me now?"

The two of them laughed, and then Aunt Mei noticed me in the mirror. "Anna, did we wake you with our crazy old-woman talk?" She began massaging cold cream into her face, a soft smell filling the room. "Do you have a boyfriend?"

"No," my mother answered for me. "Nina has a boy who comes over sometimes, but not Anna." I crossed my right leg over my left to make myself thinner, smaller.

"Your time will come," Aunt Mei said to me. "You know, your mother had so many boys after her that our father kept a broom by the door. It's in your genes."

"Was Uncle Chao one of them?" I said. They were both silent. My mother rubbed her jaw, and I knew I must have said something right.

Despite my father's training, I was terrible at math. I could occasionally luck into the correct answer, but couldn't explain how I did it. In class, if I got called on to finish a problem at the blackboard, sweat rolled down my chest, the elastic band of my bra acting as a dam.

I got a D on my calculus midterm. The test had to be signed by a parent. Nina offered to forge the signature for me, but instead I waited until my father was in the shower and showed my mother. She clucked her tongue. "Let me call Eileen. Maybe Wilson can tutor you."

Although Wilson and I were the same age, he went to Stuyvesant, top of the high-school totem pole. Because Eileen felt guilty for divorcing his father, she let him do whatever he wanted. In elementary school, he put my Barbie in the microwave and I got in trouble for kicking him in the shins.

The next morning, my mother informed me that Wilson was coming over at three forty-five. When I opened the door, I noticed that I was taller than he was in his thick-soled Vans. His hair was dyed dark red and gelled into spikes.

"My mom says I'm supposed to help you." He looked me up and down. "I don't know where to begin."

"Shut up," I said, but moved aside.

He started unpacking his things at the kitchen table. "Does your dad know about this?"

"No," I said, "and you're not going to tell him, either." We were back to acting like the siblings we never were. He leaned back in his chair to look down the hallway.

"Where's Nina?"

I was used to people being more interested in Nina. Even though we had similar features, hers had more space between them. Her face was a face you could talk into. She had a high forehead; I had a widow's peak.

"At her boyfriend's." Christian lived ten blocks away. His parents let her sleep over on the weekends, and Nina told our parents she was staying with a friend. I didn't blame her.

"Do you want anything to drink?" I asked Wilson.

"A Coke."

I took a can from the fridge. "My homework's on the table."

He flipped through the pages. "Where's your boyfriend?" he asked.

Age hadn't made him any less obnoxious. "Where's yours?"

"Changing the subject? I asked you first."

"My mom isn't paying you for etiquette lessons." I opened the can. The carbonation made me sneeze.

"Maybe she should," he said.

My mother was beginning to shine. She came home with bags from Bergdorf Goodman and Henri Bendel. She had a new necklace with a black pearl pendant that looked like the eye of a giant insect.

One morning, I forgot my history notebook. When I went back up to get it, my mother was on the phone, scratching her calf with the big toe of her other foot, her pose like a flamingo at the zoo.

"Anna," she said, putting her hand over the receiver. "What's wrong?"

"Forgot my notebook." We looked at each other for a moment.

I retrieved the notebook from my desk and kissed her goodbye, and then stood out in the hall listening. "That was Anna," I heard her say. "Yes, girls will break your heart, if you let them." She laughed, then said, "No, just you."

I got in the elevator, head pounding. The smell of wet dog and coconut-scented air freshener made it worse. I pressed my forehead to the mirror, which left a mark like a greasy, oversized fingerprint.

Before lunch, I went down to Nina's locker. When the bell rang, she came around the corner by herself, chewing her gum methodically. "I heard Mom talking to someone this morning," I said.

I saw a blue-green flash as Nina shifted her gum to the other side of her mouth. "Maybe it was her doctor."

"I don't think so. She was laughing."

Nina shrugged. "Big deal. She's allowed to laugh."

"I think it was Uncle Chao."

"You're paranoid," Nina said. She checked her watch. "I gotta meet Christian. Later."

As she walked away, I wondered why even though I was older, Nina was better at ignoring things.

That afternoon, when Wilson came over, his hair was different. He hadn't gelled it and it lay flat like rusty steel wool.

"Nice hair," I said.

"I had a bio exam today," he said. "Priorities."

My mother had left out snacks for us: dried mango and a bag of Malaysian beef jerky. I watched Wilson tear open the jerky package and wondered whether the snacks had anything to do with her morning phone call.

"You know," he said, "you'd be prettier if you smiled more." He ate a piece of jerky, then licked the red dust off his fingers.

In February, my father went up to Boston for a conference. I was watching NY1 Saturday morning when I heard the buzzer ring. "We've been invited to dim sum," my mother said as she let Uncle Chao in. "Get your sister."

I woke Nina up. "The guy I was telling you about is here. Mom says he's taking us out for lunch."

She rubbed her eyes. "Dad's gone, and we still have to be on our best behavior?"

We did, our coats sliding against the leather seats of Uncle Chao's Mercedes. A bobbleheaded baby on his dashboard nodded wildly as we turned onto the FDR. Nina took off her shoes and socks and ran her bare feet across the carpet mats.

"Don't be gross," I whispered.

She wiggled her toes. "Don't be a prude," she said.

Through the window, the East River unspooled like cassette tape. Uncle Chao parked the car in a pay lot and led us to a three-floor restaurant on Elizabeth Street, where the hostesses carried walkie-talkies. A woman wearing a burgundy blazer sent us upstairs.

The room we entered was blinding, with flocked red wallpaper and crystal chandeliers. The characters for double happiness hung on the rear wall, ready to provide a wedding backdrop at a moment's notice. As we were being seated, a toddler next to us stood on his chair and shoved the lazy Susan in the center of his family's table, knocking over his mother's water glass. Ice cubes spilled into a dish of fried noodles, floating on top like lenses.

Uncle Chao snapped his fingers at the women pushing the carts, and soon still-steaming dishes crowded the pink tablecloth. He turned to Nina. "What are your hobbies?" he asked. Nina reached for a *loh mai gai*. She unwrapped it and licked grains of sticky rice from her fingers.

"Art." She dropped the lotus leaf on the tablecloth.

"What kind of art?" he pressed.

"Paintings."

"Of what?"

"People and things." With her chopsticks, she picked all the *lap cheong* out of the filling, making a greasy pile on her plate.

"What about you, Anna?" Uncle Chao said. "What's your favorite subject?"

"History."

He laughed. "Just like your mother." The teapot was nearly empty. I flipped the lid up to signal for a refill, while hating the silent codes that Chinese people were supposed to know and understand.

After a waiter brought a fresh pot of tea, I filled everyone's cups. Uncle Chao and my mother laughed at the way the teapot's weight made my hands shake. "You have the hands of a scholar," he said as he squished an egg custard tart into his mouth. He paid for our meal with a hundred-dollar bill.

My mother wanted to buy groceries for Chinese New Year's dinner, so we walked toward Canal. Tourists in parkas were trying on pigtailed hats while local kids threw handfuls of poppers into the street, the tiny explosions kicking up candy wrappers and sunflower-seed shells.

At the fish market, my mother prodded a Dungeness crab with her finger. A rubber-aproned man came over to help. Air bubbles rose from a tub of geoduck clams. A blue crab hoisted itself over the edge of its basket unnoticed and scuttled toward the curb.

My mother bought lotus root, watercress, tangerines. I took a tangerine from her bag and split the skin with my thumbnail as I walked. Nina stopped to sniff sticks of incense as though she were at a perfume counter, finally settling on sandalwood. Uncle Chao carried our shopping bags for us, looping the handles over his wrists like bracelets. Nina and I walked behind them. The buckles of Uncle Chao's shoes winked in the sun.

"Don't you think he's walking kinda close to Mom?" I whispered.

"We *are* in Chinatown," she replied.

My mother and Uncle Chao went into a bakery. Nina and I hung back as they bought curry puffs and custard buns. My mother took out her wallet, but Uncle Chao clamped his hand over it, dwarfing the brown leather. The girl behind the counter started assembling a white box, poking her fingers through the pre-scored flaps.

"I want to go home," I said. "I have a calculus test on Monday."

Uncle Chao smiled. "Good," he said to my mother. "When they study hard, they don't get into trouble."

My mother smiled weakly. "I guess you should take us home, then."

On the ride home, Nina opened the bag of incense and fingered the slender sticks as though they were piano keys.

Uncle Chao double-parked in front of our building. "Nice meeting you girls," he said. Nina kicked my ankle. My mother smoothed her hair and said, "Why don't you take the groceries up?"

Uncle Chao popped the trunk and came around to hand us the bags.

Once we were inside the lobby, Nina said, "Let's watch." Between the branches of a ficus tree, we saw Uncle Chao pulling our mother toward him. She let him kiss her before twisting away, the fringe of her scarf swinging like a beaded curtain.

When my father came home on Sunday, his clothing rumpled from the train ride, my mother kissed him and took the briefcase from his shoulder. He hugged Nina and me. "I missed you. Have you been good?"

"Of course," Nina said, her eyes gleaming. I nodded. My mother wiped her hands on her apron, her eyes touching down on each of us. "Dinner's ready," she said. "I made your favorites."

After dinner, Nina entered our bedroom holding my mother's blue address book.

"What are you doing?" I asked.

Nina thumbed through the tabs. "Looking for Uncle Chao."

"Do you think Mom just keeps his info under A for Affair?" I asked.

Nina rolled her eyes and kept flipping. "Here," she said, "Mr. Terry Chao." The address was in Forest Hills.

"What are you doing after school?" she asked.

"Wilson's coming over."

She copied the address into her notebook. "Call him and cancel. We're going to Queens."

At lunch the next day, I left Wilson a message saying that I forgot that I had volunteered to work at the book fair. After the final bell, Nina and I walked to the subway. The mannequins in store windows were dressed in turtlenecks and corduroys, but I was sweating through my shirt.

The train was filled with other kids our age, no doubt on their way to more productive activities. Across from us, a girl worked her way through a stack of blue flashcards. I spent the ride wondering what we'd say if we saw Uncle Chao. An empty Coke can rolled back and forth across the floor of the train, bumping coldly against my ankle.

"Forest Hills—71st Avenue. Last stop," the conductor announced.

"We need to go south on Continental," Nina said as we exited the train. Nina acted like she knew exactly where she was going, just like our mother had told us to do when we were in an unfamiliar neighborhood. A woman wearing a pink headband jogged past us.

We turned onto Fleet Street. "On the left," Nina said.

Uncle Chao's house was brown and white with a brick chimney. His Mercedes was parked in the driveway. Nina and I slowly walked down to the end of the block before returning on the other side of the street.

"What do we do now?" I asked Nina.

She pulled a map from her backpack. "Pretend we're lost."

A black BMW pulled into Uncle Chao's driveway, and a woman wearing a pinstriped suit got out. She opened the trunk and started carrying groceries into the house, the stripes of her suit warping with the effort.

The woman returned and lined up the bag handles to get them in one grab.

I stepped forward. "We're lost," I said. "Can you tell us how to get to the subway?"

She looked up. She had a mole on her chin. Her dyed hair was growing out. Light brown strands made a herringbone pattern against the black.

"Turn right at the end of the block, then down ten minutes." I saw her wedding ring.

"Thanks," I said. We turned and walked away. Once we had reached the end of the block, Nina said, "She was prettier than I thought she'd be. If his wife was ugly or something, I'd feel better."

"I can't believe you just said that."

She kicked at a coffee-cup lid. "Don't tell me you weren't thinking that, too."

As we walked back to the station, I looked at all the men we passed, searching for Uncle Chao. There were fewer places to hide in this neighborhood. I wondered what steps he and my mother took to be discreet. I wondered whether my mother followed this path back to us, and then I remembered his Mercedes. She didn't need to walk; she was delivered.

After school on Wednesday, I laid out snacks—boiled peanuts and flower-shaped rice crackers—for Wilson. "Thanks," he said. "My mother thinks I eat too much junk food."

"Peanuts are natural," I said diplomatically.

He pinched a peanut shell to open it. "She's such a nag."

Listening to Wilson talk about his mother made me uncomfortable. I opened my textbook. Wilson put his foot up on the chair and retied his shoelaces.

"What's today's lesson?" he asked.

"Shouldn't I be asking you that?"

A pile of peanut shells was forming in front of him. "Let me get these out of your way," I said, sweeping them into my hand. Pulling out the garbage can from under the sink, I froze. A condom wrapper was inside.

"Did you see a rat or something?" Wilson said. I ignored him. Had Uncle Chao been over here while Nina and I were in Queens? I pulled the bag out of the can and took it to the chute to get rid of the evidence.

When Nina came home, I told her about the condom wrapper.

"That's gross," she said.

"Is it yours?"

"We don't do it here," she said. "Christian has his own room." She unzipped her coat. "You think it's Uncle Chao, don't you?"

"I don't know," I said, but saying it out loud only seemed to make it more definite.

When our mother came home, she poured herself a glass of iced tea and took the last two butter cookies from the package. She opened the cupboard to toss the empty container. "Oh, you took out the trash," she said. "Good girl."

Two days later, I was helping my mother put away groceries when Nina emerged from our room to meet friends. My mother dropped a package of chicken thighs to chase after her. "*Aiyaa*," she said. "I can tell you're not wearing a bra."

"So what?" Nina said.

"So what?" my mother echoed. "Go put one on." I crumpled the empty plastic bag in my hand. Somehow having an affair was okay, but leaving the house without a bra was unacceptable.

Nina disappeared into the bedroom and reemerged a minute later. "I'm just going to take it off once I leave."

"Anna, pass me the chicken," my mother said. My thumb sank into the rubbery flesh as I handed it to her. "At least I have one daughter who listens."

Nina slammed the door, making our glasses of water hiccup.

That night, I went to Sherri Taubman's sweet-sixteen party at the River Café. Her parents made sure we weren't served anything stronger than Shirley Temples, so we asked for extra maraschino cherries threaded onto cocktail swords like animal hearts. On the train home, a tall red-haired man with a navy windbreaker got on and sat next to me, though there were plenty of empty seats in the car. When the train started moving again, I noticed his hand moving up and down in his pocket. "You like? You like?" he asked. I got up and moved, but he followed me, yanking on the windbreaker's white zipper.

"Get away from me!" I screamed.

"Beautiful girl," he hissed. "Wanna fuck? I could fuck you now."

No one had ever said anything like that to me before. It made me feel visible.

The sallow light of a station filled the windows, and I ran off the train. I didn't realize I'd been holding my breath until I was back on the street, with what felt like a cold weight pressing against the inside of my forehead.

When I got home, my mother was reading the *Sing Tao Daily*. "Are you okay?" she said when she saw my face.

"Do you still have that Swiss Army knife that Dad got you?" I asked.

"That thing?" she said. "I lost it years ago."

I was disappointed, but didn't think having it would have kept me any safer. There was nowhere in the city I could go to escape that fact.

When I woke up the next morning, my mother had left for Chinatown. Nina had gone upstate with Christian's family, so my father and I were alone. After lunch, it began to pour like the sky had been gutted. From the window, I watched people raid the free-newspaper stands for head coverings. My father pulled his book of riddles from the shelf. "Hey, daydreamer," he said. "Why don't I give you something to think about?"

I shrugged.

He flattened the book's spine. "Here's one. There's a man who either always tells the truth or always lies. He says, 'Everything I say is a lie.' Is he telling the truth?"

I checked my watch. I had my own question for him: if my mother left in Uncle Chao's Mercedes four hours ago, how long would it take for her to return?

"Yes," I said.

"How can you be so sure?"

I wished for my mother to walk through the door. I took a deep breath, giving her a few more seconds to save me. Nothing.

"I just am," I said.

He flipped to the answer. I hadn't even asked. "There's no way to tell."

"How is this important?" I snapped. "Look at everything else that's happening, and you want to ask me questions?"

He closed the book over his finger. "I thought you liked them."

"Well, you're wrong." I went to my bedroom and slammed the door. I could hear him scraping our plates into the garbage. I felt like the only person in the family who cared where everyone else was at all times. I didn't know how to tell him what I knew. Maybe this wasn't even the first time my mother was having an affair. Maybe my father was just playing along, like Dale Fong's father, who didn't tell his family for two months after he'd been laid off from Con Ed, getting dressed as usual each morning and then spending the day in the reading room of the 42nd Street library.

I fell asleep at my desk. When I heard the key in the front door, I went out to the living room. My mother held onto the doorknob as she slipped out of her shoes. "What have you two been doing?" she asked.

I searched her face for any smudge in her makeup, any sign that she'd been careless, but her eyeliner was as black and defined as the vein running through a shrimp. I looked over at my father, who was silently reading the paper. He opened a new section, pinning the cover back on itself.

My mother waited until my father was in the shower before taking her shopping bags to the trash chute. She entered my room and handed me a large paper bag with nylon cord handles. "It's sturdy," she said. "You can use it as an overnight bag."

We both knew I wouldn't. I wondered whether this was who I would always be, a girl who cleaned up the messes and got only leftovers in return.

I took the bag and hid it under my bed. That night, after Nina had fallen asleep, I reached down and ran my fingers back and forth over the thick waxy paper, my thoughts folding in on themselves until I drifted off.

Nina was in a punk phase. She went down to Eighth Street or St. Mark's Place and came back with clothes that were grommeted, studded, or safety-pinned. One night at dinner, my father jokingly ran a horseshoe magnet across her back to see if it would stick. It did. Nina frowned, her brown lip liner a moat around her mouth.

One Monday morning, Nina asked me to apply concealer to her neck. "Hickeys," she said, handing me a tube of Maybelline. I uncapped it and twisted the bottom. The waxy bullet rose between my fingers.

"Don't forget to blend," she said, holding her hair out of the way.

Her neck was covered with purple constellations shot through with blue and yellow, like textbook depictions of the beginning of the universe.

"Oh my god," I said, then wished I could take back how big-sisterly I sounded. I dabbed the concealer on, blowing on it to make it dry faster.

"How does it look?" Nina said.

"Hold on," I said. I added another layer. It didn't look much better.

She looked in the mirror. "I'll wear my hair down. I already tried rubbing them with the back of a spoon."

I nodded like I knew what she was talking about, but I was worried about what would happen to her once we left the apartment, all the people who would see her neck that day and what they would say about it.

In exchange, Nina offered to do my eyes. I didn't normally wear makeup, so I kept blinking as she tried to apply eyeliner. "Look up," she said impatiently as she smudged liner around the outer corner of my eye. "Come on, we're gonna be late."

When I looked in the bathroom mirror at lunch, I saw that the eyeliner had smeared: not in a sexy way, but like the halo around a naked lightbulb.

When my mother went to see Uncle Chao, she left the apartment smelling like perfume and returned hours later with bags of abalone, fat shiitake mushrooms, and dried white fungus. She hummed to herself as she trimmed green beans. As I watched, I wondered what lessons I was supposed to be learning: it was okay to have an affair as long as you were home to make dinner every night? Her cooking got more ambitious. She baked a whole red snapper in sea salt and cracked open the hardened crust with a mallet.

"What's the occasion?" my father asked.

"No reason," she said. "On sale."

One Saturday she brought home lobsters in a damp paper bag. "Can you cut them up for me?" she asked my father. He rolled up his sleeves and pulled a cleaver from the knife block.

He dipped a hand into the bag and felt around. "Big," he said.

My father grabbed a lobster by its head and laid it on the cutting board. The cleaver made a loud crunch and the lobster split in two, antennae waving. My father kept going, stacking the pieces on a plate. When he was finished, the cutting board was littered with bits of shell and broken rubber bands.

My mother stir-fried the lobster with ginger and scallions, using cornstarch to thicken the sauce. At the table, my mother served my father the head of the lobster, his favorite, even though it was bad for you. She gave Nina and me pieces from the tail. For a while, the only sound was the cracking of cartilage and shell. My mother broke the spiny legs to get every last bit of flesh out.

"I didn't know you were going to Chinatown," I said. "I wanted to go there and get some stuff."

"Tell me what you need and I can go back tomorrow," she said.

"It's nice to have someone who buys you things, isn't it?" I said.

My father pushed rice into his mouth. Nina narrowed her eyes at me.

"There was a sale at the market," my mother said.

"Must have been some sale," my father muttered.

After dinner, my father changed into his pajamas and shuffled off to watch TV. I wiped down the table while Nina loaded the dishwasher.

Once the dishwasher started humming, I went out onto the balcony. As I watched cabs collect at the stoplight on First Avenue, I felt dinner tracing up my insides. By eating the lobster, had I promised not to tell? The light changed, and then everything below seemed to expand and contract like a bubble blown from a wand.

I ran to the bathroom, but all that came up was a clear plume. Desperate, I tried my index finger, but my body refused to give up its meal. Aunt Mei's words echoed on the porcelain where I rested my head: *like mother, like daughter.*

To celebrate the first day of spring, Eileen invited us to dinner at her apartment. As we were getting ready, Nina asked me whether I thought her shorts were too short. They looked like another of her St. Marks finds, black with four brass buttons on each hip.

"No, but your legs are too long," I said.

She laughed and pushed me toward the window, the diamond pendant of the necklace that Christian had given her briefly catching air.

It was obvious that Eileen had put a lot of effort into the meal. The steamed soy-sauce chicken had been cut up carefully, even though it was undercooked. Marrow showed in the cross section of bones like a reddened eye. I took the smallest piece I could find.

"Wait," Eileen said, "let me get a serving spoon."

Nina leaned back to get out of the way, and the neckline of her shirt slipped down. "That's a beautiful necklace, Nina," Eileen said.

My father looked up. "You're too young for a gift like that," he said.

"They're not that serious," I said, trying to help.

"Shut up," Nina said. I could feel Wilson trying to make eye contact, but I kept my head down.

"Men give diamonds to women they think they can own," my father said. I couldn't believe he was doing this here.

My mother looked over at Eileen and laughed nervously. "This isn't good dinner talk."

Nina was squeezing her wrists, alternating right and left.

"A boyfriend should be the last thing on your mind," my father said.

Nina hooked two fingers around her necklace. My father pointed his chopsticks at her. Grains of rice skidded greasily across his placemat.

"Wilson," Eileen said brightly, "tell Mr. and Mrs. Tong about your summer internship."

Wilson was happy to discuss the free soda in the employee kitchen. Eileen kept interrupting him to say things like "satellite offices" or "market share." My father finished his Tsingtao. Eileen set a new bottle down in front of him. My father kept eating, but it was obvious he wasn't listening. He shoveled rice into his mouth, the tips of his chopsticks clinking against the bowl like an egg timer.

My mother took a piece of chicken that was still pink near the bone. I sipped my water, too fast, and spilled some on my shirt.

My father looked up at me. "What's your hurry? Do you have somewhere else to be, too?"

I shook my head.

"It's getting late," my mother said.

"Not until I finish my beer," my father said. He pushed his napkin off his lap, but didn't reach to pick it up. I realized that something was about to happen.

"Do you have to wear a suit?" I asked Wilson.

"The VP doesn't even tuck in his shirt."

The adults all frowned. I prayed for my father to finish his beer so we could leave, but he was staring into his rice bowl as though searching for dirt. Nina sat back in her chair, arms folded.

"You must be tired," my mother said to Eileen.

"Of course not," Eileen said, refusing to take the opening offered. "I had Wilson's help."

I finished my glass of water. With all eyes on him, my father tipped his head back and drained the bottle.

My mother stood and made a silent clapping motion.

Eileen went to get our jackets. We put them on, zipping and buttoning and snapping, our fingers making four different sign languages. She and Wilson filled the doorway to watch us leave.

On the street, my father hailed a cab and sat up front. "Nice weather we're having," the driver said, but my father didn't respond. I lowered the window and let my hand drift out. My mother yanked it back in and kept it hers, as though the city were an electrical outlet I hadn't yet learned to avoid.

When we got home, we followed my father into the building, letting him set the pace. Someone had shoved a wad of gum between the elevator panels.

In the narrow hallway of our apartment, my father hung up his jacket, then turned to Nina. "What do you need a diamond necklace for, anyway? To impress your classmates?"

Nina closed her hand around the pendant. "It was a gift," she said.

My father looked at my mother. "A gift. What did she do for that necklace? What else will she do?"

"Are you calling me a slut?" Nina said.

"Watch your mouth," my mother said. "This isn't about you."

Nina went into our bedroom, the rest of us close behind. I sat on her pillow. My mother reached out to comfort her, but my father stepped between them, shaking his finger at Nina's face.

"Who taught you this?" he said. "Who taught you?"

Nina started to cry. "No one taught me," she said. "I did it myself."

I didn't even know what we were talking about anymore.

My mother put a hand on my father's shoulder and said his name. She never called him by his name.

"Look at me," he said to Nina. "This is a house of liars. And I'm sick of it."

"Not everyone," I said, but my words fell to the floor like powder.

He grabbed Nina's necklace and yanked. Nina screamed and reached up, but too late, her fingers reaching bare skin. Blood filled the rut where the chain had been. A drop loosened and ran down the back of her neck. I pressed my tongue to the roof of my mouth to keep from choking. It felt like the only part of my body I could control.

"Get out," my mother yelled. The words slicked her teeth.

"Women stick together," he laughed. "I don't need this. I don't need you." The necklace curled in his palm like hair in a drain, its ends swinging as he left the room. The toothbrush holder in the bathroom rang out as he removed his. He got a suitcase from the hall closet and unbuckled its straps, pinning it against the wall with his knee so it wouldn't tip over.

When people we love leave us, we're supposed to divine meaning from the objects not taken: holey socks, old scientific journals, a tin of Tiger Balm rubbed down to silver in the center. My father left a handful of neckties draped over the closet rail, and they sat there untouched for months afterward, like prayer flags.

In college, I briefly dated a guy who was on the wrestling team. In his sleep, he would pull me to him and kiss the back of my neck.

I rolled over. "Don't do that," I said.

"You must be the only girl who doesn't like her neck kissed," he mumbled.

"Just don't," I said.

While visiting home a couple of years later, I found the book of riddles at the bottom of a basket of magazines. I brought it over to my mother and asked her to read to me.

"Where did you find this?" she asked.

I picked at my nail polish as she put on her glasses.

The man in the elevator was abnormally short. He could only reach as high as the button for the seventh floor.

It still didn't feel like an answer.

None of us saw my father leave. My mother went to get the first-aid kit, and I helped her press squares of gauze to Nina's neck. As Nina sobbed, the squares slipped down, but I didn't move, afraid of what was underneath. I kept waiting for the front door to slam, but instead my father turned the knob slowly behind him, a burglar in reverse. I heard the lock reset, the elevator chime, and then there was silence, a swallowing with no end.

My parent's house, circa 1969, with my siblings Rick, Deirdre, Maura, and Kerin. Two more—Michael and Jennifer—were still to come. I'm the one in the middle—eating a cookie or a binkie? My brother and I still like to break out the matching striped overalls for holidays now and then.

Sean Padraic McCarthy's short stories have been recently published or are forthcoming in *Water~Stone Review, Hayden's Ferry Review, Confrontation,* the *Sewanee Review, The Art from Art Anthology, Bayou Magazine, Salit Magazine, Red Cedar Review, Glimmer Train,* and *Another Chicago Magazine,* among others. He earned his MA in writing at the University of San Francisco, and he lives in Mansfield, Massachusetts, with his wife, children, and a very big Great Pyrenees. He recently completed work on a novel.

THE PIPER

Sean Padraic McCarthy

Jack McAlary didn't want to go into the church. They had already conducted a séance in the cemetery and then done some acrobatic stunts on the iron rail of the train bridge—Mason had heard that Jack sometimes hopped across it on one foot, and he wanted to outdo him—and now Mason wanted to go into the church. He knew that Jack wouldn't want to, that Jack worked on the grounds sometimes doing odd jobs for the priest, and Jack figured that was the reason he was pushing it.

Mason had crooked bangs and pointy ears that made him look like an elf. He didn't like to be called an elf, though—he liked to tell people he was the Devil. He had *Ozzy* written across the four knuckles of his left hand, and he said it was a tattoo, but Jack suspected he just retraced it each day with a pen; some days it was darker than others. Mason wore dirty white socks that had lost their elastic and hung loose around his ankles, and his pants were bell-bottom floods. Bright orange-and-blue running sneakers. Keds. His eyelids were bright red, and he liked to tell people he could make his eyes bleed.

The train tracks ran between Mason's house and the church. Mason lived with his brother and mother in an old white Georgian-style house. Mason said they owned the whole house, but it was divided into four apartments and they rented out three. Mason's apartment wasn't very big, but during the day he was usually there, and almost never in school. His mother worked long hours, and each morning Mason would wander out to the small stone bridge that crossed the stream that ran through the cemetery, and he'd look for people to skip with him. He made a lot of money selling pot—rolling thirty to forty joints to a half ounce, skin-tight pinheads—and he always had some on hand. He would lure followers with promises of his chocolate-milk bong, plenty of music—Pink Floyd and Led Zeppelin, and Ozzy, of course—ice cream and chocolate sauce and whipped cream and nuts, and sometimes a video. Mason had a porno called *Taboo* about some guy who has sex with his mother—who was kind of hot—and it was 1983 and pretty hard to come by a porno at fourteen or fifteen, so that was always a draw. Sometimes he would break it out, and sometimes he wouldn't; it all depended on whether he felt like watching or not. Once you were in Mason's house, he called all the shots, and it didn't matter what he had promised before you had agreed to go.

"I'm sadistic," he would say with a giggle, and if a kid didn't know what that meant—and most of them didn't—Mason would just shrug. "Look it up in the dictionary."

Mason considered himself an intellectual and a scholar, and he liked to tell people he was going to go to law school. Whenever he said this, Jack liked to remind him that you had to finish high school first, and in order to finish high school, you had to actually go once in a while. Sometimes it burned Mason's ass when Jack said this, and other times he just shrugged it off. "I plan on finishing, but if I don't, I'll just get my G.E.D.," he said. "It's no big deal, it's the same thing." Jack had never liked Mason much, but the skipping-school thing with him had gotten personal, because Mason had begun luring Jack's best friend Danny back to the house on a daily basis. Jack and Danny had been inseparable since the first grade. They played football together, basketball and street hockey, and Danny's house was so crowded that for years he spent nearly all his time at Jack's. Jack's house was crowded, too, but Danny said it was different. And if Jack ever asked how, Danny would just shrug. "Normal," he would say. They were both in the honors program, but now more often than not, Danny wasn't there. He was over at Mason's.

Today they had the day off, though—it was Veteran's Day. Jack and Danny had been shooting baskets up at the school, rebounding balls off the brick wall that served as the backboard, when Mason came up over the hill. Jack felt his heart sink at the sight of him. It was the first time in a while that Mason hadn't been around, and he had been praying it would stay that way. At least for the day. Mason had sparked a joint within a minute of arriving. He had two other kids with him— one they called the Outlaw, and a skinny little kid named Fred, who they usually just called Pumpkin Head because he did so much acid. Fred was weathered so bad—stringy hair, stringy limbs, and rotten teeth—that he might as well have already been in his nineties. But he was only fourteen.

The sky today was low and gray and smothering, looking like it might rain, but Mason's mother was home so they couldn't go inside. Jack didn't mind, though, because he hated going in there, hated feeling like he was trapped, and he hated following Mason's rules. They had sat on a hill above the cemetery for a while, smoking some joints and watching the old men in VFW caps drive by, stopping to plant small American flags at several of the graves—"They're trying to grow more Americans," Mason had said, and Jack watched the old men without saying a word. It didn't seem possible that they could ever have been soldiers, had ever been that young. Jack kept a box of toy soldiers under his bed at home, and sometimes when alone, when his older brother was out, he would still take them out and line them up, imagining the battles, their lives. Their bravery and heroics, saving their buddies at whatever the cost. Up until a couple years before, Danny had still played with them with him, but now Jack would never tell Danny that he still had them. Not at fourteen.

After the veterans had cleared out, the landscape again quiet, they had started down the railroad tracks. The tracks were old, only used by the occasional freight train, and the ties had all begun to splinter with time, coming to pieces. Mason pulled a rusty spike up from the tracks and began chasing Fred around, saying he was going to carve the pumpkin. Fred, though small in stature, had long gangly limbs, and he ran with his knees going high like something out of a cartoon. Mason was getting awfully close to him with the spike, though, and then the next thing Jack knew, Fred was sliding down the embankment, off the tracks, and back into the cemetery, rambling over the hills of dying brown grass. Mason stopped, catching his breath, and yelled out for Fred to come back, but Fred was gone and having none of it. "One down," Mason said, looking at Jack.

They climbed off the tracks and started across the church parking lot, passing the school, the convent, and the small pink function hall. Jack had just helped fix the steps of the function hall—mortar and brick—and there was still a large pile of leaves in the far corner of the parking lot that he had to get rid of. Father McDonough wanted to burn them, but the town told him he couldn't; you could only burn in the spring. Now Jack scanned the landscape, but the old priest was nowhere in sight. That much was good. The quicker he got through without being seen with Mason, the better. Mason watched his eyes. "Looking for somebody, Jack?" he asked, but Jack just shook his head.

There was a side door to the church, opposite the rectory, and that was where Mason wanted to go in. The door was always open unless it was dark, so that wasn't the problem. The problem was that if the old priest saw them going in there, he would know they weren't going in to pray. Jack didn't exactly know what they were going in for either, and he didn't think he wanted to.

"Life is full of surprises, Jack," Mason said. "That's what makes it interesting."

He opened the door, the silence pouring out into the afternoon as he did. Pouring out and sucking in. The silence in an empty church was different than anywhere else. It wasn't just a matter of lack of sound. It was a presence. It struck all five senses, and toyed with the sixth. You could feel it hovering all around you, and turning your head quickly—to the ceiling, the altar, or the balcony—you almost expected to see it. See something. The eyes of God are quite powerful in the church, the old priest had told Jack once, puffing on his pipe. They're powerful everywhere, of course—don't think there is ever a time where he can't see you—but in the church they're magnified a thousand times over.

Danny and the Outlaw shuffled inside, and then Mason stood there, holding the door open and waiting for Jack. Jack had heard the stories before. Stories about Mason when he was younger, sneaking into the church and scribbling obscene messages about Jesus and the Blessed Mother on the wall behind the altar. Drawing pictures. Jesus with horns on his head and his penis in his hand. Mason never confirmed this, but he never denied it, either—he would usually just giggle—but even just thinking about Mason doing it made Jack feel guilty. Trying to picture it himself, even just to understand it, seemed its own kind of sacrilege.

Now Mason raised his eyebrows. "Are you coming in?"

The breeze picked up, and a scattering of leaves scurried by at Jack's feet. Brown and dry and dead, some hitting the open door and others disappearing down the walkway. Jack almost expected to see the old priest turning the corner and holding the rake, calling to him. And at this point it would almost be good to see him. He hadn't done anything yet, and he could pretend he was here to see him. The old priest could save him.

But the priest wasn't in sight; no one was in sight. The whole day seemed empty. There weren't even any cars on the road.

"Come on, Jack," Mason said. "Step inside." He twisted his lips into a theatrical frown. "My toes are getting cold."

Despite the silence, everything inside was instantly familiar. Almost as much as home. Jack had helped clean in the church before—washing floors and stained glass—and he had even helped paint the window trim once. His mother came daily to attend Mass, and Jack came at least every Sunday, walking when he couldn't get a ride. The stained glass was dark today with the absence of the sun, but Jack knew it was St. Brigid, Jesus, and St. Patrick looming in the three enormous windows above the altar. When the sun was out, they all looked like royalty. Scepters and crowns, and magnificent robes of reds and greens and purples, only Brigid in blue. But now the images only gave the impression of eyes watching from the shadows. Jack had, for a long time, thought Brigid was Mary and Patrick was God the Father, but the old priest had corrected him on that.

"Brigid *was* called 'Mary of the Gael,' though," he said, "so you weren't too far off. She and Patrick are the patron saints of Erin. You know what Erin is, don't you?"

Jack shook his head.

"Ireland. That's the trouble with kids these days, you know nothing about your heritage. They teach you nothing. At least not in the public schools."

Now, Mason and Danny and the Outlaw were running toward the balcony. It was dark in the balcony. The balcony was mainly used for the choir—black metal music stands, and pages of sheet music scattered all about the floor—but there were also six rows of pews on either side for when the church got too crowded. The old priest sometimes sectioned the stairs off so people couldn't get up there. It was important to have people close together, close to the altar, he told Jack, close to God. The balcony gave people too much room to daydream. Most people who sat in the balcony didn't bother listening, he said. There was an enormous pipe organ up there, too, and behind the organ a steel ladder bolted to the wall. The ladder ran all the way to the ceiling, to a hatch door that led to the attic. And that was where Mason was going.

Danny had told him about going up there before with Mason, gone over the whole routine—the candles and pot and bribes for kids to make fools of themselves—but Jack had said nothing. Preaching to Danny sometimes just seemed to make things worse, and he didn't want to lose him. But he knew what was happening. Leaving him feeling helpless. He just didn't know how to stop it.

Mason pushed open the hatch, the Outlaw just behind him, and Danny turned to Jack. "Don't worry about it," he said. "He'll get bored soon, and then we'll be out of here."

Jack tested the steel, pulling hard, but it didn't move from the wall, not even a little. He was looking at the bottom of Danny's sneakers. Torn black high-tops. Converse. They had come from his brother, who had owned them seven years earlier. Captain of the varsity basketball team. As far as Jack knew, Danny didn't own any clothes that had actually been bought for him; everything was hand-me-downs.

Danny's house itself looked to be leaning a little at an angle, and Danny had told him once it was about to fall over. And once it does, good riddance, he said. Now he disappeared into the black square in the ceiling, and Jack began to climb.

The hatch door was still open, but the voices were muffled coming from inside. Jack looked out once over his shoulder, the statue of Jesus just to the left of the altar, robes pulled open to expose his heart, and then a hand came down through the hatchway, latching onto Jack's and pulling him up. They were all sitting cross-legged, Indian style, in a circle, and Mason had a big candle lit in the middle. The rest of the attic was lost to darkness. Jack could taste the dust on his tongue, and everything about them felt dry and old. He wondered if anyone else ever came up here, and couldn't imagine why they would. The old priest would never climb the ladder, probably wouldn't be able to even if he knew they were up here, so in some ways it was safer than being in the church.

Mason pulled out a bag of joints, and lit one with his plastic Marlboro Man lighter. He held the joint in one hand and the lighter, orange-and-blue flame so bright in the darkness, in the other, a good eight inches away. Everything was a ritual with Mason. A game and a test, thinking he was the funniest guy in the world.

"Seventy-six trombones led the big parade, Jack," he said.

"I'm not singing it," Jack said.

"Do you want to partake or not?"

"I don't care," Jack said. "I'm already stoned enough."

"No such thing," said Mason. He was still holding the lighter lit, his thumb on the wheel, and Jack imagined it must be getting hot.

"Last week he made me sing 'C is for Cookie,'" said the Outlaw.

Mason giggled. "Five times fast. And no tripping on the words."

"I didn't even know what that song was," said the Outlaw. The Outlaw was around Jack's age, but he had stayed back at least twice, so now he wasn't even in high school. He was called the Outlaw because he had been arrested shoplifting candy at least two or three times. His mother cut his hair, a bowl cut, the bangs going across the front at a choppy angle, and it seemed he was never dressed for the weather. Today he was wearing a red pocket T-shirt, biceps bulging in the short sleeves, and he had been complaining all afternoon about being cold. It was November, but that didn't seem to have sunk in yet with the Outlaw. Not much did. He almost always either looked angry or confused, or some combination of the two.

"It's from *Sesame Street*," said Mason. "You don't watch enough *Sesame Street*."

"I stopped watching that show about eighteen years ago," said the Outlaw. "It's gay."

"It's not gay," said Mason. "It's educational. Where else can you learn to do 'The Pigeon'? You know how to do 'The Pigeon,' Jack, don't you?"

"Every day," said Jack.

"That's right," said Mason. "Every day. You look like Bert, you know that? Now, are you going to sing or not?"

"Nope."

"Party pooper. No pot for you." He turned to Danny. "How about you?

Danny lit a cigarette, let the smoke seep through his lips. "I don't know that one."

"I'll sing it first," said Mason. "Then you repeat after me. Then we can sing it together. Just like Harold Hill. *Seventy-six trombones led the big parade...*"

Danny started to smile. "Seventy-six trombones led the big parade," he said.

"No," said Mason, "you have to sing. If you don't sing, no pot for you."

"*Seventy-six trombones led the big parade,*" sang Danny.

"*With a hundred and ten cornets close at hand,*" sang Mason.

Danny opened his mouth, paused a moment. "*With a hundred and ten cornets close at hand.*"

Mason began to swing his fist with the lighter in the air in the manner of a band leader's baton. "*They were followed by rows and rows of the finest virtuosos, the cream of ev'ry famous band.* You like that part, Jack? The cream of every famous band?"

"Fuck off," said Jack.

"I don't even know what a trombone is," said the Outlaw. "Is that one of those big white things, with the real big horn that the guy wraps around his body? I've seen one of those things before."

"That's a sousaphone." Mason smacked his open palm against the floor between him and the Outlaw. "Get your horns straight or no pot for you!"

"Well, I bet they're like the same thing," said the Outlaw.

Mason grimaced. "No, they're not! Seventy-six sousaphones can't lead the big parade! Can they, Jack?"

"I don't know," said Jack. "You seem like you know more about it than I do."

"But you play the saxophone, don't you?"

"So?"

"So, you're in the band." He pointed at him with the unlit joint. "You're Harold Hill."

"Maybe you can lead the band with the saxophone," said the Outlaw.

Mason smacked the floor again. "Trombone!"

"Yeah," said the Outlaw, "but if nobody has a trombone, and they need somebody to lead it, it might as well be a saxophone. I saw a guy in a rock video once play a saxophone, and he wasn't even gay. At least I don't think he was. It's hard to tell."

"He didn't lead the big parade though, did he?" said Mason.

"Maybe when he was younger," said the Outlaw. "How should I know?"

They heard some noise down below, then. Somewhere in the church. A door, and footsteps. It was amazing how everything echoed in the quiet. Jack wondered if it might be the old priest. Or it could be the guy they had come in and help out. Billy. Or maybe someone coming in to pray.

Mason giggled. Put a finger to his lips. "Shh.… They're going to think there is something in the attic. Something evil. Did you ever see *The Exorcist*? And that old guy, the butler? 'See? No rats.'"

"We should go," said the Outlaw. "I don't want to get arrested again. Remember that time you had us all break into the bowling alley? We all got arrested."

"Yeah," said Mason, "but not until we had already bowled two strings."

"That didn't matter," said the Outlaw. "My parents were pissed. I almost got grounded."

"My parents didn't even find out," said Danny. "My sister bailed me out, and then she took me to court." He blew one last smoke ring, and then snubbed his cigarette out on the floor. It didn't surprise Jack that Danny's parents didn't find out. They never knew where he was half the time these days. He sometimes stayed out all night, and they didn't even notice him gone. He came from a family of twelve kids. Seven still at home. The others had either graduated high school, or got knocked up and quit. Jack had been recruited on the day of the bowling-alley heist, but he had refused, gone to school. He had tried to talk Danny out of it, told him the whole thing was asinine, anyone could see they were going to get caught. He told him a lot of the kids didn't have much of a future, but he had a future. Why ruin it? he asked him, pleaded, but Danny just laughed a little. "Asinine," he said, eyes small and red. "I like that word. Asinine."

Mason had the team meet at the bridge that morning. Eleven kids. It amazed Jack how Mason could get eleven different kids to do something so stupid. Mason was a Piper. He had lookouts up on the roof on all four corners of the building, while inside they bowled and raided bottles of booze from the lounge, but the lookouts all climbed down and scattered when the cops pulled in. At least three of them did. The fourth was the Outlaw, and only he was stupid enough to hold his post, signaling with the agreed-upon bird call. Over and over.

Somehow Mason had gotten away—carrying a case of booze with him as he ran—but most of them had not. And even thinking about it now still made Jack angry.

"I didn't get to bowl," the Outlaw said now. "Not one string."

"Next time we have to plan it out a little better, that's all," said Mason.

"We have to plan it so if one gets caught, everybody gets caught," said the Outlaw. "That's only fair."

"Fair only counts in tennis," said Mason.

"Well, he's got a point," said Danny. "The person whose idea it is should get arrested, too."

"Not necessarily," said Mason. "The person who came up with the idea is probably the smart one to begin with, so it only makes sense that he wouldn't get caught."

"Anyone with half a brain wouldn't want to do it to begin with," said Jack.

Mason grimaced again. "You're just no fun. All work and no play makes Jack a dull boy."

"A dull boy without a record," said Jack.

Mason waved his hand in the air. "Seventy-six trombones led the big parade."

The church was soon quiet below them, and they started back down the ladder. Mason was trying to get Danny to tell him how far he had gotten with his girlfriend, but Danny kept changing the subject. Even Jack didn't know, so he was going to be pissed if Danny told Mason. Danny's girlfriend was a year behind them in school, but looked like she was four years ahead. Pretty, with brown eyes, and what Danny said was a D cup. Jack wasn't sure what that meant, but Danny explained. "You can have A, B, C, or D. If they're bigger than a D, then it's a double D, and if they're bigger than that, forget it. They wouldn't be able to walk."

"Where did you learn this stuff?" Jack had asked.

"My old man told me," Danny said.

Mason leapt from the last rung of the ladder onto one of the chairs they used for the choir. He landed on one foot, balancing like that for a moment, and was then off and leaping again. Right over the balcony rail.

"Oh, Christ," Danny said. "He probably broke his neck." Danny dropped to the floor, Jack behind him, and they ran to the rail. Mason was right there below them, atop the confessional booth, crouched as if once again ready to spring, pinkies, index fingers, and thumbs of both hands projecting out, the sign of the *Ozzy*. "Did I flip you out?"

"You're an idiot," said Danny, his eyes alive and laughing.

"No. I'm a genius."

"Man," Danny said, putting his hand to his heart. "I thought you killed yourself. You scared the shit out of me."

"I would never kill myself," said Mason. "Not in a church. That is like…sacrilege. Now," he said, hanging down from the side of the box and dropping to the floor. "Let's go get some wafers." He looked up and smiled again. "We can make peanut butter sandwiches."

Mason ran toward the altar, but everything suddenly seemed to be slowing down for Jack. He had smoked too much, and where sometimes, right after smoking, everything seemed more vivid and clear, his senses heightened, now, time having passed, it was all becoming foggy. Even though Mason probably hadn't been to Mass in years, if ever, he knew right where to go to look for the Host. Mason was instinctive that way. He could smell anyone, anything, out. He went to the tabernacle, and hit the button to open the folding doors. Yelling "Open sesame!" as he did. None of it seemed real to Jack anymore. Coming into the church to get high was one thing, bad enough, but now he was moving to desecrate the Host. Probably about the worst thing they could do. If the Host was in the tabernacle, it had been blessed, and to desecrate it was to desecrate Christ. The Host once blessed *was* Christ, not just a representation. One in the same. How many times had the old priest told Jack that?

Mason had his hand inside searching, and Jack's heart began to pound, hoping it would be empty. Even if he found a box of the wafers out back in the Sacristy and messed with those, they wouldn't be blessed. It wouldn't be as bad. Jack wasn't sure how long he had been searching. Time seemed to have stopped, seemed distorted, it could have only been a matter of seconds, but it seemed like an hour, and then he turned to face them, the chalice held high in front of him. "Bingo!" he yelled. "Let's go, gentlemen!"

Jack turned to Danny. "Don't worry," Danny said, "He's just being an idiot."

"So what are we then?" Jack asked.

"Idiots," said Danny. "Come on, don't make a big deal out of it. The bigger the deal you make, the longer he'll drag it on. He just wants to get under your skin. Let's just let him get it over with, and then we can get out of here."

"Let's just go," Jack said.

"Nah," said Danny. "If we don't do it, he won't leave, and then we'll get caught. He's that stubborn. Let's just get it over with and we can go. I promise."

Jack looked, listened, for the Outlaw, but he was gone from the balcony. He must have slipped off down the stairs. He would do that sometimes. There one minute, gone the next. It was easier for him that way. Would probably be easier for everybody. But for Jack to go, it would mean leaving Danny. And what would that make him? How could he leave him? In the church. With Mason. Danny didn't know any better, somewhere inside him Jack was sure of that, so how could you be held responsible if you didn't know any better? So why did Jack? Why did he have to? Life was easier without knowing. If you didn't know, you couldn't care, and Jack was tired of caring. He didn't want to care about anything.

Danny was down there now, walking up the aisle, and Mason was sitting atop the altar, the marble sheep with the golden sword piercing its side below him. The sheep, head raised, looked to be still alive, though. Wounded but unhurt, at peace. "There's not many left!" Mason shouted out. "What's wrong with these people?!" He banged the chalice on the altar. "Where's a man supposed to get a decent meal around here?!"

The church felt to be growing then, the ceiling rising, and Mason was becoming more distant. They were just small specks, moving about below. Mason chewed the Host, and he gave one to Danny, first telling him to drop to his knees. And Danny did. Of course he did. He did everything Mason told him to. Jack could feel the eyes on them, on him. St. Patrick and the Christ. The Christ was everywhere. All twelve stations of the cross, opening his heart to the right of the altar, outlined in stained glass above, and on numerous prayer cards and drawings in the missal. Everywhere. Eyes.

Jack came down from the balcony, barely feeling the steps beneath his feet, and by the time he started up the aisle, Mason had walked down to the foot of the altar, the chalice in one hand and the Host in the other. Tight between the tips of his fingers. Jack stopped within ten feet of the altar, and then he shook his head. Mason smiled. "Body of Christ, Jack?"

•   •   •

They had just come down the ramp on the side of the church when the old priest pulled up in his driveway. Black topcoat and black bowler, driving his big black car. Jack froze on the walkway. The priest stepped out and looked at them. His glasses were thick, nearly opaque. Mason waved to him and yelled, "Good afternoon, Father!" and the priest studied him for a moment longer before slowly raising his hand. He called Jack over. His voice raspy and soft today, sounding as if he were fighting a cold. The sky looked heavier now, lower, and the wind had picked up. Everything gray.

"You spending your time with him?" the old priest asked.

Jack turned. Mason and Danny had started back toward the railroad tracks. Jack felt a sudden flare of panic. He wanted to run after them, to leave the priest standing there alone. Left without an answer. But Danny wasn't looking back. He was saying something to Mason, and Mason was laughing.

Jack's heart began to slow, something sinking inside him. Flashes of memory. He swallowed his breath. His insides all felt hollow.

"Not much, Father," he said. "Once in a while."

Mason and Danny were climbing the embankment, up to the tracks, getting smaller and smaller. Their voices carried on the breeze. The priest glanced at Jack from the corners of his eyes. "And you brought him to the church?"

Jack's eyes were beginning to burn, water, his nose running. He wiped it with the back of his hand. "He brought me, Father."

The priest seemed to think about this for a moment, and then he tapped the back door of his car. "I have a fruit basket in there I won at the VFW. Do me a favor and bring it inside."

Jack took the basket from the backseat of the car and followed the priest up the walkway. The priest stopped to pick up a piece of paper that had blown against the steps of the rectory. A flyer for Kmart, the paper thin and colors faded. He moved very slowly, reaching the ground, but once he had the paper in hand, he crumpled it quick. The side entrance of the rectory had a gray metal storm door that never stayed open on its own. The priest wedged himself between it and the door inside and turned his key in the lock, shaking it hard when at first it didn't move. He was talking about lunch at the VFW. Spa-ghetti. The worst spaghetti he had ever eaten, he said. Jack could hear a television going somewhere as they stepped into the kitchen, and he wondered if Father Dolan was home. Father Dolan was the only other priest. Probably in his forties, with greasy hair and flaky skin, dandruff covering his black shoulders. His face was flat, and his eyes were shallow; he liked to look at you, to stare, but when he did, it was impossible to tell if he was ever really thinking anything. Jack didn't see him interact much with the old priest, and when the old one said something to him, Father Dolan usually just nodded without looking his way. Moving by with slouched shoulders and eyes on the floor.

"Hold your head up, for crying out loud," Jack had heard the old priest mutter once. "You're supposed to set an example. Be a leader."

The rectory was large, but empty except for the two priests. Jack could picture the old priest down here in the kitchen at night, the lights dim, eating sardines and crackers—he was always saying he loved sardines and crackers—the crumbs tumbling from his lips, and Father Dolan moving about upstairs like a ghost.

The old priest took off his coat, and hung his bowler on top of the coat rack. "You want any fruit?" he asked. "You want to bring some home to your mother?"

"I don't want to take it off you, Father," Jack said.

The priest shrugged. "It will just go to waste around here. I wouldn't even have taken it, but they insisted. And they're all drunk over there, so there isn't any point in arguing. There's the parade in the morning, and then they're drunk by noon, and by then I'm done with them. Some are forgetting, I suppose, and some just like to pretend that's what they're doing."

"Were you a chaplain in the service, Father?" Jack asked. He didn't want to talk, didn't feel like talking, but if he didn't the priest would wonder why that was. Ask more questions. Jack wondered if he still looked stoned. There was something about being outside—the fresh, cold air—that made you feel as if you didn't necessarily look like you had been smoking. But once inside—the warmth, the confinement—you suddenly felt it again, and it was hard to imagine that wasn't how you looked. He cared, and he didn't. He was trying to picture tomorrow, but it looked grayer than today. Everything stagnant and stale. More bleak.

"No," the priest said. "I was a soldier in the service. I didn't enter the seminary until after I got out. I saw enough of the absence of God over there, that it made me curious enough to want to look for Him elsewhere."

Jack tried to picture the old man as a soldier. Couldn't. He couldn't even picture him young, with a full head of hair. Never mind carrying a gun. Maybe shooting people. He wondered if he had ever shot anyone.

There was a den just down the hall from the kitchen. The light in the hallway was always off, the hallway always dark. Dust and shadows. The priest went to the den, Jack following, and clicked on the lamp. He took a seat in his chair, removing his shoes before he put his feet up on the hassock.

"You want to get the fire going?" he asked. "There's already some wood in there." He pointed. "And there's a box of paper beside the mantel."

Jack nodded. There was a box of long matches on top of the mantel, and Jack removed three after he had crumpled balls of paper beneath the wood. The wood was cut even, all the same size, and Jack figured the old priest had bought it at a gas station or something.

There was only one picture of Jesus in the room. A flat Jesus, with almond-brown eyes. Flat little angels with halos like yellow dinner plates flying all about his head. A picture from medieval times. Jack sometimes liked the medieval pictures better because they were so flat and didn't look real. The images just something from stories. Fairy tales. Not beings that were aware of where you were. Watching you. No one who had ever really walked the earth.

Jack struck one of the matches, the flame blue and red, and nearly immediately getting smaller. Jack watched the flame for a moment, and then touched the edge of the crumpled paper. It hissed for a moment, and then began to spread, the spreading turning gray and then black, smoking, before actually igniting. He and Danny used to have a fireplace in the woods. A circle of heavy rocks, one piled upon the other.

It was before they met Mason. The fireplace was on a pond where they used to skate, and after a while they would take off their skates and warm their feet before putting on their boots. Sitting on milk crates they had stolen from outside the convenience store. They would talk about girls—the pretty and the not so fortunate—and the Celtics and the Red Sox. Danny had decided back then that he could play for both, just waiting for basketball to end before starting baseball, since the seasons overlapped. He would've played for the Patriots, too, he said, but the Patriots stunk. Jack liked to listen, and he believed Danny could do it—he was that good—but he didn't have any designs on being a professional athlete himself. He liked to play, but he had never been good. He was much better at drawing and playing his horn, and back then, Danny said that was fine. He wished he could draw, he said. As long as you were good at something. That was the only way you made it in life—if you were good at something. He used to say that.

Now Jack could smell a different smoke, and realized that the old priest behind him had lit his pipe.

"We had about seven people at Mass this morning," he said. "Imagine that? A day like Veteran's Day, a wonderful day to pray for the dead, and only seven people. Your mother was there."

"My mother is always there," said Jack.

"Quite a bit," said the priest. "She sets a good example. What does she think of Mason Finneran?"

Jack hesitated. His mother was always on him about Mason. Mason always looked high, she said. And he had burned Jack's little brother once with a cigarette. Under his chin. He said it was an accident. Mason and a couple other kids were holding Jack's little brother and his friend captive—all in fun—and he had the cigarette under his chin so the little boy wouldn't move. And then he moved.

"I don't know," Jack said.

Jack could feel the priest smiling. "Maybe you should tell her you're trying to get the boy to go to church," he said. The rest of the paper had caught, as had the loose splinters of wood. Jack stood up and backed away. He didn't turn to look at the priest, and he knew the man wouldn't be looking at him. He never was when smoking, when telling him a story, or a memory of some sort. His eyes were always averted.

"Is that what you were doing, Jack?" he asked at last. "Trying to get him to go to church? Him and your friend there. What's your friend's name?" Jack could tell by the old priest's voice that he was at least a little amused, and he didn't necessarily think Jack would answer, but there was no point in not answering.

"Danny," he said.

"Danny," said the priest. He was quiet a moment. "I had a brother named Danny. He died a few years ago. He used to raise chickens, and unfortunately for him, he wasn't any smarter than they were. It didn't matter much. It doesn't take a great deal of brains to raise chickens. You just need to know how to feed them, keep them warm, and then when the time comes, raise an axe. It used to send his children into fits every time he did. They would always get attached to them, and he would always promise he wouldn't kill them—just to keep them quiet—but of course he still did. And that just made it worse. It's hard when you're young, I suppose. You trust much easier, and it takes a while to become jaded enough to know better. I learned that in the war."

Jack turned and looked at him. "You don't trust people, Father?"

"In general? Well, you know, we're all just human. People make mistakes. I forgive them, and that's the important thing."

Jack thought about telling him what they were doing, what Mason did. Tell him all of it. Confess it. As terrible as it was, the priest would forgive him, he believed. He would be disappointed—he might never look at him the same—but he would forgive him. That was his job. But to implicate himself and Mason was to implicate Danny; he didn't want to implicate Danny, to have the priest think poorly of him. He didn't want anyone to think poorly of him.

"But you don't trust them," Jack said.

The priest did look at him now. His eyes wide behind his glasses. "I trust God, Jack."

He asked Jack to take the trash out to the dumpster before he left. Jack was halfway across the parking lot when he realized he had forgotten to take any fruit. The dumpster was used for the school, the hall, the convent, the church, and the rectory, and it was starting to overflow. Jack had to heave the bag high to get it on top—he could picture the priest, still in his chair, eyes closed as he smoked and he prayed, aging and shrinking and surrendering to time—and then he walked across the parking lot and back up to the railroad tracks. It had started to rain—the sky spitting. Jack could see far down the tracks, and there was no one else on them. That was the good thing about traveling on the tracks—you could always see people in the distance, people coming, people going. It was a long walk home, at least two miles, but he didn't mind. The tracks were removed from everything else, the rest of the town, always quiet, and sometimes he liked that. He was thinking about soldiers.

My brother and I, hopefully on Halloween. I am the magician, and though it's hard to make out, he is a rabbit in a giant top hat. There are times when I think that at this moment I was as cool as I will ever be.

Nick Yribar received his BA from the University of Michigan in 2010. He lives, writes, and works in Ann Arbor, Michigan. "The Getaway Driver" is his first published story.

THE GETAWAY DRIVER

Nick Yribar

Eli called me around ten in the morning the day before he was supposed to go to jail, and told me to come over to his apartment. When I got there, he was smiling like an idiot and smoking a cigarette, sprawled out on his couch. He was a big guy, though he managed to conceal his girth with expensive button-downs that he spent most of his money on. His mop of curly, light brown hair seemed to inflate and deflate along with his disposition; when I found him that morning his hair was standing on end, as if it were trying to leap off his head. Eli had high cheekbones that, on a thinner guy, would have made him look effeminate. I could tell he was stoned—his face was red and swollen—but I didn't know on what. "Check it out," he said, pointing at the wall just beyond the coffee table I'd lent him a year ago. His apartment wasn't much; the living room barely held his white leather couch and the coffee table and a Panasonic TV sitting on top of a pedestal. It was literally a pedestal: a hollowed-out, Roman-looking cylinder with ridges that Eli had found in an alleyway and dragged home. I don't know what the pedestal had been used for originally, or why it had been in that alleyway, but Eli had the sharpest sense of fashionable irony of anybody you've ever met, and he knew the effect the pedestal would have in that shithole. "Look at the floor," he said.

Following where he was pointing, I kneeled. There was a burn mark in the floor about the size of a nickel, right at the edge of the carpet where the floor met the wall. I thought I could smell the smoke, but given the range of odors in the apartment, that seems unlikely. "What is this?" I asked. "Is that from a cigarette?"

"Nope!" Eli laughed. From the coffee table, he picked up a revolver that I hadn't even noticed was there and pointed it at me. "Kah blaow!"

I put my hands on my head and ran toward the doorway. In my mind, when I imagine myself in heroic situations that involve guns being pointed at me, I always see myself performing some kind of disarming maneuver that tips the scales in my favor. Some piece of jujitsu I'd intuitively realize. It seems to me the last thing a thug would be expecting is someone so fearless, and that my fearlessness alone would frazzle him. In his panic, I would be saved and be able to save whatever beautiful woman I was with. But there were no beautiful women in Eli's apartment (nor had there ever been, as far as I knew) so I covered my head with my hands and, screeching a little, ran for the door.

"Jesus Christ, no!" Eli said, though, for some reason, he followed me with the barrel of the gun. "Don't freak out. It's not loaded anymore."

"Don't fucking do that!" I yelled at him, still pawing at the deadbolt.

"I know, sorry. Jesus Christ."

"Don't point fucking guns at people!" My voice was up three octaves.

"I know, okay. Okay, that was dumb." Eli started giggling. He looked at the revolver in his hand and realized he was still pointing it at me. He looked as surprised as if it were being pointed at him and set the gun down on his lap. "That was dumb. I'm a little shaken up, and I'm not thinking so good. Sorry."

I took a long look at the door and considered leaving. I'd just woken up, for Christ's sake. If it had been any other day, when Eli wasn't being sent to jail within twenty-four hours, I'd like to think I would've left and spared myself his bullshit. Instead, I took out a cigarette of my own from my jacket, walked over to the table, and lit it with a match from a box of Kitchen Strike-Anywheres sitting half-open on the couch. "Is that why you called me over here? To point guns at somebody?"

"Did you think I was going to shoot you?" he asked with interest. Eli was a natural mouth breather; his default facial expression was a slack jaw and wide eyes. He knew how unappealing this expression was, and so, for the most part, he made an effort at controlling his face and his mouth, especially in front of others. He slipped and breathed loudly and obviously through his open mouth when he smoked, which was often, or when he was fascinated by something or other, or captivated, or when he was drunk. He was smiling at me now with his weird, gaping grin. "Did you think I would do that?"

I took a drag off my cigarette. I was actually still catching my breath. "Quit grinning at me and breathe with your goddamn nose. What happened to your carpet?"

"You need to get ahold of yourself, you know? You can't panic like that. That's why you'll never make a decent getaway driver. It's vitally important that you *keep* your *cool*."

"What happened to your carpet?"

"I shot it with this gun," he said, and brandished the revolver again.

I had no response to that. Maybe it was embarrassment over pan-icking and squealing at having a gun pointed at me, but I didn't want to be the square who pointed out how monumentally bad it was that he'd shot off a gun inside an apartment complex before noon on a Wednesday. That's the effect Eli had on me—I felt, somehow, less cool or worldly because I *hadn't* endangered anyone's life today and I wasn't going to jail tomorrow. I looked at the gun, which he'd set back down in his lap, and thought I could see the barrel glowing red hot. I almost told him not to burn himself, but caught myself in time.

I'd known Eli since we were in junior high school, but I didn't have much use for him then. He had a weird arrogance that rubbed everyone the wrong way, and even then he had an amazing talent for winding up mired in bullshit. Eli lived in the same neighborhood as my best friend Dolph, and the two of them had known each other since they were very young. It was through Dolph that I met Eli. Dolph was a restless guy, and he always wanted to climb something or fight some-body. We became friends over comic books and kung-fu movies, and the first time I went over to his house he insisted we climb on top of the Westgate shopping center to see if we could do backflips off the roof. I agreed that it sounded like a good idea and, without say-ing anything, Dolph had us out of his house into his neighborhood.

We walked for a block or two until we came to a long driveway that curved off from the road, obscuring the house that it led to. There wasn't another driveway like it that I had seen in that neighborhood—it was like the suburban equivalent of a private drive. The rest of the neighborhood was made up of cheap, one-story houses, the kind of thing you'd expect from an area sitting across from an Interstate exit.

Eli's house was easily the nicest in the neighborhood. It rested against a small lake, with a wooden dock leading out from the yard into the water. I found out later that his parents were both psychologists with private practices. The house, where I'd come to spend some time in over the next decade, was a two-story behemoth with a finished basement. It was a house of dens, with two or three rooms that served no purpose other than watching TV or playing foosball, the most impressive of which was a loft that overlooked a massive living room. But all I could see when Dolph and I walked up was the outside—brick, covered in ivy. "This is a nice house. Whose is it?" I asked, after walking down the driveway for what seemed like a long time.

"His parents are Jewish," Dolph replied, and left it at that.

Eli answered the door, his mouth hanging wide open. He hadn't gained a sense of embarrassment over this feature yet. "Good morrow, sirs," he said. I immediately disliked him. We were thirteen and thus had no etiquette when it came to introductions, so the two of us just eyed each other for a second or two before we both turned our attention to Dolph.

"Let's go, let's get up on that roof." Apparently the two of them had discussed this idea before, because Eli knew instantly what Dolph was getting at and he turned green. "Come on, let's do it, quick quick quick."

Eli looked at something behind him in the vast compound that was his house—maybe his television, with its promise of safety. Then he looked back at Dolph. Dolph was a hard guy to say no to, as numerous frustrated women would later attest. The problem was, as Dolph knew full well, Eli's weight. When Eli and I would reconnect years later, you'd have called him stocky, bordering on chubby. But, at this point, he was a full-on Fat Kid, and years of forced schoolyard athletics had instilled in him a natural fear of activity. But there were worse things than being sweaty and out of breath: the unblinking Dolph, for instance, staring and waiting expectantly at Eli's front door. "Indeed," Eli conceded with a sigh.

We walked about a mile to the shopping center, stopping first in a toy store that featured educational novelty crap. The clerk recognized Dolph and Eli immediately and eyed them terribly. Dolph nudged me. "Go talk to that ass-head," he whispered. "Ask him about the matinee puzzles."

I did. The clerk became animated and started showing me pictures out of a catalog of seals and porpoises. While he did, Dolph and Eli darted around the shop for a few minutes before quickly walking out the door. I let the clerk run out of steam and told him that I didn't know, that I'd think about it. When I walked outside, I saw the two of them turning a corner of the parking lot toward the rear of the shopping center.

I ran to catch up. Dolph had snatched a fistful of marbles and a small snow globe with the letter *B* frosted in fake snow inside. Eli had one of those green army men with their feet attached to a molded plank and a plastic parachute fixed to its back. "I'm going to toss this from the roof," he said with a grin. "See how she flies!"

"That's pretty gay," Dolph said. Eli shrugged.

The back of the shopping center was all pallets and dumpsters. The doors were all the same tan color, and some of them didn't have door-knobs since they were only to be accessed from the inside. We spotted a pile of milk crates behind the drugstore, and Dolph ran toward it. He had one leg on the crates, and in an instant he was pulling himself up onto the roof and looking down at us. He wasn't that high up—maybe twelve or fifteen feet—but the distance seemed like a lot. Dolph had shoulder-length blond hair, and standing up there with the sun behind him, he looked very impressive. "He looks a little like a god," Eli muttered. I had never heard anybody talk that way before. I kind of liked it, since the phrase reminded me of something somebody would say in a Bruce Coville novel, but I recognized that it was unusual and that, combined with the first impression Eli had made on me as a fat, spoiled mouth breather, turned me sour. Turning toward him with a shitty look on my face, I saw that he was already regretting saying anything.

I walked toward the crates and climbed them. I didn't have Dolph's grace, but I made it up. I asked Dolph, "Still wanna do a backflip off?"

Dolph grinned. "It's pretty high, ain't it?"

Eli walked over to the crates and put a hand on them. I saw he was shaking. He fumbled up on the pile and grabbed the ledge of the roof with both hands. Beneath him, the crates wobbled and tipped over, and we had to pull him up by his arms. He lay panting on the roof, clutching the paratrooper that he had fished out of his pocket.

The clatter of the crates falling over and Eli kicking at the wall trying to get up must have been louder than we thought. A man in a white dress shirt and a tie came out of a doorknob-less exit with three other guys. Their uniforms were from the drugstore—apparently what we were on top of. "Get off the roof, *now*," said the guy with a tie who I assumed was the manager.

Dolph relished the opportunity. He ran down the roof a ways until he was just over a dumpster. The lid was closed and Dolph jumped down on top of it. There was a hell of a noise. Then he hopped down to the pavement and took off, not looking back. This was his way: sudden, drastic action without consultation or regard for his accomplices. This scene would repeat itself with subtle variations for years to come. Sometimes I'd follow him and we'd outrun whoever was chasing us (or whoever we assumed was chasing us), and sometimes I'd stay behind and try to talk my way out of the situation. I usually failed, and I'd take my scolding, and sooner or later they'd turn me loose. Eventually I learned that you always run, because they never wanted you bad enough to seriously try to catch you, not when you're fourteen or fifteen or sixteen, and you were just on their roof or stole something stupid or were generally being a minor pain in the ass. They almost never called the cops, and when they did, we'd get yelled at and that would be that. Eli always stayed, and he always got caught. He didn't trust his body enough to carry him out of trouble. As a result, he became very, very good at talking his way out of bullshit. He cut his teeth for bullshit on the fire escapes of downtown Ann Arbor and in the back rooms of small businesses too numerous to count. Over the years, as Eli grew into himself, he had to rely on this skill more and more often, and the stakes grew higher with each successive encounter. This time, on this roof, my first, I stayed because I didn't know any better, and Eli stayed because he did.

The pharmacy people watched Dolph's escape with awe. One of them whistled and said, "Jesus Christ, look at that little shit run." I couldn't believe I'd been abandoned. And left with Eli, no less, who sat on the roof cross-legged. He didn't seem surprised by what was going on.

The manager watched Dolph run for a moment, then fixed his attention back on us. "Both of you get down right now, or I'm calling the cops."

"You don't have to!" I yelled, a little louder than necessary. I felt a panic rising. "We're coming down! We're sorry!" I walked over to where Dolph had jumped down over the dumpster and lowered myself onto the top of the lid, which buckled and collapsed as soon as I landed. I fell into the dumpster, which was mercifully full of closed, secured trash bags. I climbed out and put my hands up, for some reason.

Eli was still cross-legged on the roof. The manager yelled up, "Now you, tubby."

Eli shook his head. "I don't think I'll be doing that, no."

"I'm not playing around with you. I'll call the fucking cops."

"Nevertheless, I'm not jumping down. I could very well break my ankle or tear my ACL."

One of the lesser pharmacists made a hissing noise with his teeth, as if he had just stubbed his toe. "Shit, he's totally right. If he gets hurt we are fucked. His parents could sue."

"His parents are psychologists," I offered.

"What does that have to do with anything? I think we better call the cops or something and let them deal with these idiots."

And that's how, an hour later, Eli finally got off the roof. The Ann Arbor Fire Department parked a fire truck behind the Westgate shopping center and raised a cherry picker and a fireman to the roof to get him down. They blocked off either side of the building with cop cars and brought an ambulance along for good measure. It was nearing dusk, and the lights from the emergency vehicles must have been visible from the highway. Passersby probably thought someone had taken hostages or robbed a bank. The cops and paramedics and extra firemen stood looking up at Eli, shaking their heads, disgusted. One of the firemen shouted, "What were you even *doing* up there, kid?" Eli took out the little paratrooper and carefully unfolded his parachute. Without saying a word, he tossed the figure into the air and we, all of us, watched silently as the toy rose, its plastic parachute expanded, and the paratrooper wafted gently to the ground. The little man even landed on his feet.

Eli and I walked along the outer wall of his apartment building trying to locate the exit hole. "I'm certain, *quite* certain, that the angle I fired from would have made the bullet leave the building." Eli straightened his arm in an imaginary trajectory.

I craned my neck to see better along the white siding. The building was a duplex, and Eli lived in the upstairs unit. "You are quite certain of fuck-all."

"Don't be that way."

"What if you shot into somebody else's apartment? What if you shot your downstairs neighbors?"

"Impossible. You saw that hole. It was along the wall. Nobody was in any danger. You need to keep a positive attitude. That's why I called you: I need positive support right now."

We walked around the building for another half-hour before deciding that if there was a bullet hole, we couldn't find it. Eli explained that he was preparing his guns for storage in anticipation of getting locked up. He was cleaning them, something he'd never done before, or even knew how to do. This one happened to be an antique and he must've been distracted, he said, because he'd inadvertently left a round in the chamber.

"It might be lodged in the wall. Maybe it hit a stud," I said.

"That's unlikely. That is a huge gun. If it couldn't go through a few pieces of wood I would be very disappointed in the gentleman who sold it to me."

"Well, shit, Eli. I don't see a hole. And your neighbors must be at work because they definitely would have called the cops. I think it may be your lucky day."

We walked around to the front of the building and sat on the roof of his car, a beige '89 Ford Escort I'd sold him a year earlier. "What would they do to me?" Eli said, not looking at me. "Throw me in jail twice?"

I could see he was being morose, but I couldn't resist correcting him, then or ever. "They could throw more charges on top of it. They could keep you in longer."

"I know that, man. I was kidding. Jesus." Eli pulled out his wallet and flipped through the cash. All twenties from what I could see. "We probably oughta leave, though. Just to be safe."

"I agree."

"Okay, I'll buy you some breakfast. For being such a little ray of sunshine. But you drive, though, yeah? I've had a few beers." He was not concerned with my safety; the Escort was equipped with a breathalyzer attached to the ignition that prevented the driver from starting the car if his blood-alcohol content registered above a certain point. Not only that, the information was stored in a database that'd be analyzed later by Eli's probation officer. He told me once that *that* was what disturbed him the most: some bureaucrat from the future, spying on him, judging him. So I drove whenever we were together, not only because I was generally sober in the middle of the day, but also because of the device itself. To get the breathalyzer to read accurately, you had to breathe into it with a certain amount of force while humming at the same time. The resulting noise sounded like a kazoo when performed correctly. I don't know why you had to hum, why just breathing wasn't enough. Eli said otherwise you could fake out the machine with an air compressor or a fan, but I wasn't sure. At any rate, Eli was incapable of making the sound in front of an audience, and so when we were together, he asked me to drive. I breathed into the tube, waited for the congratulatory three beeps, which meant that you were sober enough to drive according to the State of Michigan, and started the car.

"Let's make one stop before we grab food." Eli said. He was fussing with the glove compartment, and I thought I saw a glint of black metal before he latched the little door.

The three of us, Eli, Dolph, and I, got into the local "open" high school together, where students had to apply to get in and then were selected by lottery. The premise behind the school was progressive; students called their teachers by the first names, the entire city was designated as the "campus," and the administrators generally emphasized non-traditional education. What happened in practice was that some students, a minority of self-motivating go-getters, were able to "take hold of their education" and create a curriculum in conjunction with school administrators that made college admissions officers go cross-eyed with pleasure. These students then wrote their own tickets and eventually became the leaders of the free world, the movers and shakers; well rounded, interesting people who never told lies and were, one assumes, amazing lovers to boot. The rest of us smoked pot.

Eli took to marijuana naturally, gracefully. Perhaps the only graceful transition of his life. While the rest of us went through an awkward period when we were first introduced to pot—a general discomfort with the new sensation, the strangeness of the first high, the reconciliation one had to make with the anti-drug espousals from teachers and celebrities that we had been subject to our entire lives, the adjustment to secrets kept from your parents, the shift in seeing "the system" go from something you never thought about at all to a looming, threatening force that wanted to stop you from having fun—Eli didn't miss a beat. It was as if he'd been unconsciously waiting for marijuana his whole life. His neuroses dulled, his speech became less pretentious, and he became generally more relaxed around others. And his immediate adjustment to the pot culture into which we were all initiating ourselves made him somehow superior, like some kind of slacker guru. Here was someone who took being high in stride; Eli enjoyed smoking, but he wasn't ostentatious, displaying brand-new pipes and paraphernalia every week like some did, or reminding everyone how high he got when he smoked. He functioned; he mastered the careful art of attending class stoned, which was crucial to that all-important practice of speaking with authority while stoned. Eli gained confidence, lost weight, learned to breathe through his nose, and I started to like him.

I was one of those for whom the drugs would have been better put off. Pot was everywhere; smoking a joint was as casual as drinking a glass of water in our high school. I smoked for the most after-school-special reason of all reasons: everyone was doing it. Instead of meeting girls or developing interests or taking any steps whatsoever to better myself when I was in high school, I smoked pot. The ubiquity of smoking had me fooled into thinking that getting high was a substitute for having a social life, though I wouldn't realize that until well after I'd graduated.

I began to live vicariously through Eli and Dolph, even though I was right alongside them. I tagged along on their escapades, climbed more roofs, stole more shit that I didn't need or want, wondering what made them so fearless and increasingly wanting to show them that I, too, didn't give a fuck.

I don't mean to say Eli turned into Frank Sinatra overnight. On the contrary, for those who didn't know him, he developed a preternatural ability during high school to rub people the wrong way for the smallest offenses. For looking at a girl's leg (her name was Sasha and she was wearing a miniskirt, sitting on a bar stool at a local diner, and we were all staring at her legs), Eli was forced to lick her boyfriend's shoe as punishment. It was an ugly episode, a moment in my life I'm not proud of. Here was my friend—regardless of what I might've thought of Eli, we were childhood friends—on his hands and knees in the parking lot of a real-estate agency, nearly enclosed by a sickle of high-school seniors, one of whom, Romeo, a dark-skinned, black-haired, mustachioed bad-ass, had taken offense at Eli for staring at his gorgeous, exhibitionist girlfriend and her world-class legs.

Dolph and I watched as Eli tried to talk his way out of the shoe-licking as he had talked his way out of so many ass-beatings for similar offenses, looking over at us while his face was inches away from Romeo's size-twelve Nikes.

"I just think it's possible," Eli said, on his hands and knees, supplicating before the cross-trainer, "it is *possible,* that she mistook me checking my watch for something else. Which is *completely* an honest mistake. I'm looking down—you know, at my wrist—her legs are down there… that *completely* makes sense, right? I would make that mistake, absolutely. If I was her, you know?"

"You need to shut the fuck up and lick this shoe, man." Romeo spoke loudly, for the benefit of his crew, who frequently hooted and hollered their encouragement.

"Okay, but what does that get you?" Eli asked, looking up at Romeo. "I lick your shoe and *then* where are we? Sure, everyone's gonna see me lick your shoe and that's really humiliating and everything, but at the end of the day, who really wins?"

"I win, motherfucker."

"Of *course* you win, no one is disputing that. But wouldn't you rather walk away with something? Wouldn't you rather win…a prize?"

I couldn't believe my ears. What in the fuck is he talking about? Did he just say a "prize"?

Dolph and I looked at each other. Dolph was barely suppressing a giggle. Romeo and his friends laughed. "What's my prize, bitch?" Romeo asked.

Eli smiled. For a second I thought he might walk away from the whole thing. "That's the beauty of it, Romeo! Whatever you want, man! Let's make it happen! A mistake was made, not her fault, certainly not my fault, and now we can forget this whole thing with some kind of…prize."

Romeo was almost buying it. "What you got, man? What you got for me?"

"Okay, all right. Now we're talking, right? I've got like…" Eli paused and did some calculations. "Forty-some dollars in my wallet right now."

Romeo's smile fell away. Everyone was quiet and I felt the air grow tense. Dolph folded his arms and took a step backward. One of Romeo's crew whistled and said, "Romeo, he tryin' a *buy* you, dawg."

Romeo glared down at Eli without saying anything for what seemed like hours. Then he said, quietly, almost in a whisper, "You tryin' a *buy* me, motherfucker?"

I wanted to shout from the sidelines: That's what a prize is! What did you think he was offering! It's a motherfucking prize! But I was a coward and I stayed silent. The reversal seemed so unfair to me, to dangle the promise of escape in front of Eli's nose only to snatch it away, to use the offer as an excuse for aggravation. Only later did I realize that the whole shoe-licking was theater: there was no right answer, there was no restitution, just the delicate dance with fragile, teenage egos and unfledged notions of respect and manhood. Eli was attempting reason in an unreasonable situation, and I admired him for it.

So the negotiations fell apart. This was the compromise; Eli would lick Romeo's shoe instead of receiving an ass-beating for disrespecting Romeo's woman and his honor as a man. Eli licked that shoe, and the sight of it made everyone watching sick to their stomach, including the crowd of seniors supporting Romeo, all of whom stopped laughing and watched in silence and disgust as Eli put his tongue to the white laces, his eyes wide open. The crowd dispersed, leaving Eli and Dolph and me in the parking lot. I reasoned with myself that there was nothing I could do, that there were too many of them for Dolph and me to get involved, but I felt deeply ashamed of my inaction. Dolph hardly waited for the assailants to leave before laughing his ass off.

"You licked a fucking shoe!"

"I know I did."

"You *never* lick a shoe! Didn't you know that? Didn't your mother ever tell you that?"

Eli smiled, but he wouldn't look at us. "I guess I'm just a rebel, you know? They say don't lick shoes, and I can't help but buck 'em."

I couldn't tell if Dolph was trying to make light of what'd happened to ease the tension, to get us laughing to ease the awkwardness, to ease his own guilt that must have mirrored mine, or if Dolph was laughing because he genuinely thought seeing his friend devastated and humiliated in front of a crowd of people was hilarious.

Eli began selling pot not long after that, and eventually he started carrying a weapon around, ostensibly to protect himself from would-be thieves. And he made a point of letting everyone know; never missing an opportunity to flash the gun or to tell about some scrape he narrowly avoided with would-be thieves.

•　•　•

Eli was arrested one night about a year before he shot the hole in his apartment. He'd met one of his usual customers behind the shopping center where he'd launched that paratrooper nearly ten years earlier. Eli walked up to the driver's-side window with an eighth of an ounce of pot in a sandwich bag, and this guy snatched the bag with "baffling" speed, still sitting in the driver's seat with the seatbelt buckled. Eli instinctively reached into the car to grab the bag back, but the guy pulled a boning knife that'd been lying on the passenger seat and slashed Eli across the belly. Eli backed away, and the guy took off.

I found all of this out much later. I was living alone in an apartment near downtown, a place I'd had for nearly six months. I hadn't seen Eli for a while—we'd gotten into an argument over a girl I was seeing whose legs I felt Eli had been taking too serious an interest in. After floundering for some time after high school, I'd enrolled in a community college and found that the change suited me pretty well. The time I spent with Eli and Dolph and the time I spent doing homework and going to class seemed to relate inversely, and eventually I discovered I wasn't seeing either one of them much at all. When we did get together, I found myself using words I hadn't said since high school, like "grip," as in, "Yeah, I'm tryin' to score a grip of dope for this weekend," or, "That motherfucker's in a grip of trouble if I catch him."

I'd been at home sleeping when, around four thirty in the morning, I got a call from a mutual friend who said she'd seen Eli get into a fight with some guy on First Street, right downtown. I hung up the phone, and even as I was assuring myself this wasn't my problem, I found myself pulling on a pair of jeans, grabbing my car keys, and walking out the door to my car. I drove downtown and, as I pulled onto First, I spotted the Escort parked in the middle of the street, pointing the wrong direction for the one-way street. A tow-truck driver was hooking the Escort to his rig. I parked my car quickly and ran up to the driver.

"You don't have to tow it," I said, out of breath. "I can take it with me in just a second. I just have to get the keys."

"It's hooked up. Too late," said the tow-guy without looking at me.

"It'll take two seconds."

"It's being impounded. Talk to the cop. They found some bullshit in it."

I looked further up the street at the cop car, whose rear was facing me, lights blazing, and I remembered the fire trucks behind Westgate. I walked up to the cop car with my hands raised, just as I had when I'd approached the pharmacists when I was twelve years old. I approached the driver's side and yelled, "Excuse me, officer!"

The cop was a middle-aged woman with a full face, exhausted looking. She was writing something on a pad of paper while I stood alongside her car. She rolled down her window with a nonchalance that suggested nothing more could surprise her tonight.

"Hi, officer."

"What can I do for you?"

I looked in the backseat and saw Eli. His shirt was covered in blood, and he was swaying back and forth. He looked drunk, and his mouth was hanging wide open. I pointed at him. "I know him. He's a friend of mine."

"Well, that's fantastic."

"What'd he do?"

The cop glanced back at Eli in her rearview mirror for a second before focusing back on her pad of paper. "I was called to respond to drunk and disorderly conduct about a half hour ago. Your friend...," she checked her notes, "...Elijah, pulled his car down this one-way here and exited his vehicle to assault a pedestrian."

I looked back at Eli and mouthed, "What the fuck?" Eli rolled his eyes.

"Elijah and the young man were having a confrontation, and Elijah pulled out a... some kind of kitchen knife?" She glanced at her notes. "The other party took off when I arrived. I asked Elijah to show me his identification and he pointed a knife at me instead."

While she was talking, I saw a second cop car pull up behind us. "Can I do anything? Is there anything I can do for him?" I asked.

"He'll be detained until tomorrow morning."

"What does that mean?"

"Elijah's going to have to sleep it off with us tonight, and he'll be arraigned before too long. You can bail him out at the clerk's office on Fifth Avenue."

"Hey, buddy! It's my getaway driver!" Eli shouted from the backseat.

His hands were cuffed but he was trying to point his shoulder at me. "Where were *you* when I needed you?"

"How much is that…what does that cost?"

"You gonna have to take that up with the clerk's office."

"Hey! Getaway driver! You gonna bail out old Eli? You gonna bail out your *old buddy?*" Eli had his forehead pressed up against the window. "You want some money? Take my debit card. That fucking cop's got my wallet and my debit card."

"Is that all right?" I asked. "Can you give me his debit card so that I can bail him out?"

The cop looked tired and bored. God knows how many times she had repeated this exact scene with some drunken asshole. She was going through the motions and she seemed to be able to foresee every possible outcome to this situation. She picked up Eli's wallet from the center console between her seat and the passenger's and plucked out his yellow TCF Bank debit card and handed it to me. "Makes no difference to me. One way or the other, he's spending the night with us, so."

"Thanks. Can I talk to him for a second?"

She reached behind her head and opened a small, sliding window in the plexiglas that served as a barrier between the front and back seats of the patrol car. She went back to her notepad.

Eli inched his way to the opening. There was still a steel grate in the gap she had created in the plexiglas and Eli pushed his forehead against it now instead of the side window. "How'd you find me here, old friend?"

"Somebody saw you get arrested. What's the PIN on the card?"

"Use that card. It's got a grip of cash on it. I just made a deposit so we're *goodago.*"

"I will use it—I can't afford to bail you out. Unless you want me to call your parents."

Eli stopped grinning. "Don't do that. Uh, for real, though, just use that card. There's cash on it like a motherfucker."

"What is the *PIN*, goddamn it? Give me the PIN number, and I'll go bail you out."

"Well, I'd tell you, but I don't *trust this crooked-ass cop any further than*

I can fucking throw her! This corrupt-ass, crooked-ass PO-lice!" His voice rose to a yell and he started banging his head against the metal grate.

Before he'd finished speaking the cop reached behind her head, without looking up from her notepad, and slammed the window shut. Eli shouted at the top of his lungs, his voice muffled by the glass and metal and alcohol, *"Hey! Hey, man! Six! Nine! Four! Three! Six! Nine! Four! Three!"*

Eli spent the next year in a battle of wills with the Ann Arbor Police Department and the State of Michigan Probation Board. The police had found two unloaded, unregistered pistols in the Escort as well as an ounce of pot with "Humboldt County" written on it in thin, black Sharpie lines. That, combined with the knife he'd "pulled" on the lady cop, the drunk and disorderly conduct, and the assault on some guy walking down the street in the middle of the night, made for a hefty court case and the threat of years in prison. Eli's parents hired a lawyer who specialized in drug-related offenses, but the lawyer quit after two meetings with Eli. Eli represented himself at the hearings. I've been told since that this is unheard of in a criminal trial, so rare that it is almost a legend in the legal world. I asked Eli if I could attend, but he said no. "I need to be in top form," he told me. "You'd make me nervous."

From what I gathered, Eli's performance was staggering. I have no idea exactly what he said, but he was evidently able to establish that the unloaded pistols in his car were antique family heirlooms that he kept in tribute to his grandfather, who'd presented them as a legacy before his passing. The pistols were tokens of remembrance, nothing more, and Eli had never even fired them—he wasn't even sure they would fire. The scuffle he'd had with the guy on First Street was a non-issue since the guy had taken off and could not be located. As for the knife he'd held in full, menacing view of a police officer—that Eli chalked up to the unfortunate effects of alcohol. He acknowledged that he did, indeed, have a problem with drinking, one he'd been wrestling with all his life, and he'd welcome any assistance that the State might offer him in the form of substance-abuse counseling.

The intoxication and the pot could not be gotten around. Another hearing was set to address the latter issue since the quantity indicated intent to distribute, but in the meantime Eli was released on the condition that his car be equipped with a breathalyzer and that he attend AA meetings for six months. The presence of his wealthy, concerned parents at the hearing no doubt contributed to the judge's leniency, as did the fact that Eli was white, well-spoken, and apparently sincere and full of regret.

Eli went as far as having the breathalyzer installed in his car, attending one AA meeting, and one meeting with a probation officer. After that he stopped going. He never said why, but he'd occasionally mumble that he found the whole business humiliating and unnecessary. A bench warrant was issued for his arrest, and eventually they picked him up. His parents bailed him out that second time after he was found guilty of violating the terms of his probation.

After he got arrested, Eli and I started to hang out more. In the early days of his "recovery," when he thought he might make an honest go at sobriety, he needed new people who didn't encourage his old habits. I wasn't a new person, but we'd been out of touch for a while, and I'd cut out the smoking when I enrolled in college. Even when his attempts failed, we kept up the friendship because I missed him and Eli needed somebody to start his breathalyzer-restricted ignition.

I drove Eli's Escort through town the day before his sentencing, which he told me he planned to attend. The car reeked of cigarettes and filth; the ashtray was filled to the brim with crushed butts and the ends of joints. I could tell Eli's nerves were shot. He kept fiddling with his hands. Eli watched the city roll by, his forehead leaning against the window. I thought this might be the last time I'd see him. Who knows what jail does to somebody like Eli? What would he be like when he was released? Would he be cut with muscles, hardened in body and mind, vicious? Would he be broken? Everybody'd seen the movies, including Eli. What would happen to him in there?

I looked over at him. He was quiet, staring out the window, speaking only to tell me where to turn. I obliged him, willing to take him anywhere he needed to go. "Eli?"

"Yes, sir?"

"Are you really gonna go to the sentencing?"

Eli sat up. His mouth was closed, and his profile looked strong, resolute. It was clearly a ruse. "I am scheduled to appear, yes."

"And you're gonna go?"

He shrugged, and was silent for minute. "Time to face the music, motherfucker," he finally said.

"Why now? You didn't go to any of that other bullshit."

"It's no way to live. It's such a bother. Always in the back of one's mind." He grinned. "Why? You think I should skip it? You wanna skip town with me?"

I shook my head. "No, I think you should go. I thought you should've done all of that other bullshit. Gone to the meetings. I told you that. Get it over with and put it behind you."

"I know. You said that before. I don't know. Take a left up here." He put his head up against the window.

"Tell me again about that night you got picked up."

"What about it?"

"Tell me about that guy you got out of the car for."

"Didn't I tell you about this?" Eli sat up again and pulled a cigarette from his jacket.

"Tell me again."

Eli lit his cigarette, taking a little too long to do it. Building suspense. He loved to tell his crime stories. He was suppressing a smile. "So I was just back from getting stabbed," he said, and took a long drag for further effect. "He got me, but it wasn't too bad. You saw it. The cut was shallow, no big deal. But I was fired up. I went home and patched it all up and started pounding rum."

"Why rum?"

"It was all I had in the house. So, anyway, I'm all fired up and I get hammered, like, *hammered*. Then I get it into my head that I'm going to go find Romeo. You remember Romeo? From high school?"

"You never told me that."

"I could have sworn I told you that. Yeah, I remember thinking, I'm gonna go find that fucker. Somebody told me they'd seen him around that club on First Street, so I saddle up and I go down there. But I got all mixed up and took a wrong turn, and I was going the wrong way on motherfucking First Street. And this guy, some guy I didn't know, starts yellin' at me, '*Wrong way, asshole!*' I stopped the car, and I still had that knife that I got slashed with. That one dude threw it at me before he took off." He paused for a moment, considering. "Maybe it was my knife. Yeah, yeah it was definitely my knife. That one I kept in the glove compartment. So, anyway, I got out of the car with the knife—turn right here—and I told that guy I could cut his balls off if I wanted to. He was with some chick and I guess she called the cops. We were all yelling at each other in the street for a minute."

"Do you think you would have?"

"What? Cut his balls off?"

"Yeah."

"Fuck, no, man. I'm not cutting anybody's balls off. I was just drunk and pissed off, and this guy was just…I don't know. I mean, I *was* going the wrong way down First Street. I probably would have yelled at somebody, too. Anyway, the cop showed up at some point, and there you go. We're here."

We were in a neighborhood I recognized. I'd been driving absentmindedly, listening to Eli, thinking about Eli, and I just turned whenever he told me to. I realized we were in his old neighborhood. I saw Dolph's house coming up on the right. "You going to Dolph's? I haven't seen him in years." Eli didn't say anything. "Does he still live here?"

"Pull over. I'm going to jump out."

I brought the car up to the curb and put it into park. Eli reached into the glove compartment and pulled the revolver out. My muscles tensed as I stared at the gun.

Eli saw me staring at it. "Relax, buddy."

I looked at him and saw he wasn't smiling. Suddenly, I was walking out of a toy store in the Westgate shopping center, watching Eli and Dolph saunter toward another crime. And I was behind them, having taken too long making nice with the counter-guy. I was in high school, watching Eli lick a shoe, too scared to do anything about it and feeling complicit, as if it were my shoe. I'm in Eli's apartment, the straight guy, the one you call to hear what the sensible thing to do is when you've fired a gun by accident before noon on a weekday. The guy you show off to, tell your stories to, because he's just a mark, a square, outside looking in. "What's the plan?" I ask, and all of a sudden I feel ready.

Eli laughed. "What do you mean?"

I gripped the steering wheel with both hands. "What's the plan? What are you gonna do? You're gonna go get Dolph?"

"Go get him?"

"What are you going to do? Are you gonna rob him? Has he got a bunch of pot? What is it?" My stomach turned over and my hands went a little cold. I kept my face as solemn as I could make it. I set my jaw, I stared right at Eli.

"Relax."

"I'm just saying, tell me what the plan is. Dolph was such...he was a huge asshole when we were kids, and if you need to...I'm just saying do what you need to do and then we'll roll out and I'll sit here. It doesn't matter what's going down, I'm just saying, let's *do this.* I'm at the wheel. I've got the engine running." My adrenaline was pumping and my eyes were wide. I craned my neck to look at Dolph's house—a small, ranch style with a covered porch. I squinted and tried to see if I could see anyone through the windows, but the drapes were drawn on all of them.

Eli took another drag off his cigarette. "You've got to be shitting me," he said. "Grow up."

He opened his door and left the car, and me sitting in it. He leaned down and motioned for me to roll down the window. I did. "I'll see you around. Take the car to my parents at some point, will you?"

"What about your hearing? Are you going?"

Eli leaned forward, resting on his arms. "Yeah, I don't know. Might be better to dip on out."

"Like Dolph used to do? Like at Westgate when they called the fire trucks?"

"Yeah, this motherfucker knows how to dip on out," Eli said, smiling.

"Where are you guys going to go?"

Eli backed away from the car. "Don't worry about it. Thanks for giving me a drive. And thanks for coming over this morning. That shit freaked me out."

"Call me in a while," I said. "Call me up and I'll swoop you up. Take you back home."

"Yeah, man. All right," Eli said, but he wouldn't look me in the eye.

He turned and walked toward the house, shoving the gun into the back of his jeans and pulling his coat over it. As he walked toward the house, Dolph came to the front door in a ribbed undershirt and long, black shorts. He'd become a man since I'd last seen him, but he still had long blond hair and a mean look. Dolph had a duffel bag in one hand. He motioned toward the street and raised his hand in a wave when he saw me, but Eli walked past him and said something that I couldn't make out. Dolph's smile dropped and he lowered his hand. He turned and went back into the house, shutting the door behind him.

I thought about following him in. I'd knock on the door and Dolph would answer. His house would smell like marijuana and cheap incense. We'd shake hands and hug and he would grin the way he always did, and the three of us, Eli, Dolph, and I, would plot our next move. We could pool our cash and buy some guns and hit the road. We'd have to get out of town, out of Michigan, hole up for a little while. But before too long we'd start a crime spree, the likes of which haven't been seen since the days of Dillinger and Pretty Boy Floyd. We could rob banks and knock over trucks. We'd live like kings in between each score, and soon we'd become legends. I wouldn't have to sit through another composition class, and Eli wouldn't have to go to jail. They might catch up with us at some point, but Dolph could keep us running for a long, long time. When they finally caught us, when they'd back us into a corner with no way out, there'd be a blaze of glory that none of us could attain on our own; not me in some community-college classroom, not Dolph doing God knows what, not Eli faking it through another AA meeting. The three of us, on rooftops, forever.

Instead I sat in the car, both hands on the wheel, staring at the door to Dolph's house. I wondered about the hole in Eli's apartment and the bullet we couldn't find. I wanted to start the car and go look for that bullet again, give the grass outside the building another once-over. Was the bullet stuck somewhere in the wall? Did it escape from the apartment, from Eli's gun, out into the world? These questions, and the urge to go search Eli's old apartment, strike me sometimes for no particular reason, usually when I'm driving, and I linger on them longer than I should before pushing the thoughts from my mind and refocusing on the road, on the task at hand.

SILENCED VOICES:
Irina Khalip

by Cathal Sheerin

Irina Khalip's first taste of the dangers of reporting in Belarus came in 1997, when she was covering a demonstration against the country's proposed unification with Russia. Although the thousands of protesters that had turned out were demonstrating peacefully, the police—as so often is the case in Belarus—turned violent. Khalip was clubbed to the ground and dragged through the street by her hair. Her father, an elderly documentary filmmaker who was also there covering the rally, was beaten unconscious. "It was the worst day of my life,"

Irina Khalip

Khalip would say years later. It was also a formative experience that would drive her to campaign, through her journalism, for "the victory of freedom over the stagnant, ugly, abrasive dictatorship" in Belarus.

As this is being written, Khalip is under strict house arrest and faces at least fifteen years in prison on the politically motivated charge of "organizing mass disorder." She was arrested on December 19, 2010 while reporting on a political rally protesting the results of the 2010 presidential election. She has two KGB agents living with her (in Belarus the security services are *still* called the KGB), who ensure that Khalip cannot access the telephone, internet, or newspapers, and who deprive her of all contact with the outside world, except for tightly regulated visits from her three-year-old son, Danil, and her mother. Before being placed under house arrest, Khalip was held for a month in one of the KGB's notorious isolation units. Her husband, presidential candidate Andrei Sannikov, with whom she has had no contact since her arrest, remains in detention. Khalip's greatest concern, however, is the state's targeting of the more vulnerable members of her family: in recent weeks, the authorities have threatened to remove Danil—her only child—from the family, and place him in permanent state custody.

Winner of the 2002 Courage in Journalism prize and declared a Hero of Europe by *Time* magazine, forty-three-year-old Irina Khalip is the Minsk-based correspondent for the independent Russian newspaper *Novaya Gazeta*. In the fifteen years that she has been working as a journalist, she has been the subject of death threats, intimidation, all-night interrogations, and beatings at the hands of the police and the KGB. In 2008, after investigating a series of corrupt relationships between Russian billionaires, the KGB, and international diplomats stationed in Minsk, Khalip received a chilling warning that she would soon "meet with Anna Politkovskaya." The message was clear: Politkovskaya, renowned for her reports on the Russian-Chechen wars and unpopular with both Russian and Chechen authorities, wrote for the same newspaper as Khalip, and was murdered in 2006. Khalip knew the threat was serious. She also knows that she has been under surveillance almost constantly over the last ten years, and that exposing the misdeeds of the rich and powerful in Belarus—especially the misdeeds of the KGB—rarely goes unpunished.

Belarus is often referred to as Europe's last dictatorship. Through a combination of violent repression and corrupt elections, President Alyaksandr Lukashenko has held on to power there for the last sixteen years. On December 19, 2010, he was returned to office for the fourth time with an incredible eighty percent of the vote. International observers declared the election flawed, but it was not an unexpected result.

Cathal Sheerin

NGOs had predicted before voting began that Lukashenko would do anything in order to retain power; the crackdown on the opposition and independent media had begun long before the election.

In Belarus, opposition politicians and journalists like Khalip put their lives at risk on a daily basis. During Lukashenko's presidency, three opposition politicians have "disappeared," and around four thousand people have been imprisoned on political charges. For writing negatively about the government, countless journalists have been arrested, beaten, or worse: on September 3, 2010, Aleh Byabenin, a noted journalist with close links to Irina Khalip, was found dead, hanging by his neck. The authorities were quick to declare the death a suicide, but family and colleagues suspect the KGB: Byabenin had been openly critical of the Lukashenko regime and a vocal supporter of presidential candidate Sannikov.

On December 19, 2010, shortly after the Electoral Commission announced the results that would return Lukashenko to power, thousands of angry demonstrators swarmed onto Minsk's snowy streets. It was cold—winter temperatures in Belarus can fall as low as -13° Fahrenheit—but the protesters braved the chill and congregated in the capital's Independence Square. There, they were met with extreme force by the security services, who threw stun grenades into the crowd. Riot police then launched themselves at the protesters, turning a peaceful demonstration into a mass beating. In the hours that followed, over six hundred people were arrested, including twenty journalists and six of the nine opposition presidential candidates. Hundreds were badly injured. Khalip and her husband were also there and were pulled from their car by the police. Khalip, who had been giving a telephone interview to a Russian radio station, was beaten up and arrested. Her husband was battered so badly that his leg was broken. The couple was then separated and taken to a KGB detention center.

Khalip was placed in isolation. She was denied visitors, medical treatment, and proper access to her lawyer. Her home was ransacked by KGB agents, who were busy tearing apart newspaper offices and journalists' homes all over Minsk. The KBG took all of Khalip's reporting materials and computer equipment. They even took her son Danil's toys.

A week after Khalip's arrest, her punishment took a particularly vindictive turn—even by Belarusian standards—when the state threatened to take away her son. Danil had been living with his grandmother, Lyutsina, since the arrest of his parents. The authorities descended on the elderly woman's home and announced that they were concerned about Danil's well being. They forced Lyutsina to undergo a series of invasive medical and psychological tests, which they said would assess her fitness as a caretaker for her grandson. They also forced Danil to undergo testing for sexually transmitted diseases, such as HIV and syphilis. It is difficult to know if this was a genuine attempt to take away the little boy, or whether it was an unusually nasty scare tactic, but both Lyutsina and Danil passed their tests, and, for now at least, the child is still with his grandmother.

Khalip, however, remains under an extreme version of house arrest, where her every movement is strictly controlled. In the words of her sister-in-law, Irina Bogdanova, "She is not even allowed to approach her windows because she might see people outside who are supporting her."

Khalip's voice might have been silenced for now, but she is strong; she doesn't crumble easily. As she said in an interview in 2009, "Once you have been beaten, you become an activist, you become a fighter."

Messages calling for the release of Irina Khalip, for the dismissal of the charges against her, and for an end to the persecution and repression of opposition politicians and journalists in Belarus may be sent to:

President of the Republic of Belarus
Alyaksandr G. Lukashenko
Karl Marx Str. 38
220016 g. Minsk, Belarus
Fax: 011 + 375 172 26 06 10 or +375 172 22 38 72
Email: pres@presidenty.gov.by

Cathal Sheerin has worked as a journalist in the UK and in Chile. He currently works on the Europe Program of the Writers in Prison Committee at PEN International, London.

My great-grandmother and me, Denver, Colorado, Thanksgiving, 1982.

Kathryne Young is a JD/PhD candidate in sociology and law at Stanford University, and holds an MFA in creative writing from Oregon State University. She is working on several short stories and finishing a novel set in California's San Joaquin Valley, told from four points of view. Young lives with her rescue dog, Scout, in the California redwoods. "Roadrunner" is her first published story. www.kathryneyoung.com.

ROADRUNNER

Kathryne Young

There's a lousy little diner in Portland, Oregon that I love called Yosef's Espresso. Yosef chain-smokes Camels in the back while he flips eggs and pours coffee. He can do this because technically he's made the diner a bar. Arbor Mist is listed on the menu for two hundred dollars a bottle, right below the biscuits and gravy. Everything else is stock: splits and gashes mark the booths' upholstery, the coffee is muddy and sour, and everything fried tastes faintly of Teflon.

I am twenty-eight years and two days old, and considering quitting grad school. I started a literature PhD because I love reading, which now seems like a poor motivation. We don't *read* books. We dismantle them. It's like taking down a house. Someone hands you a crowbar and you start stripping off the drywall. You pull up the carpet, pry out the plumbing. Maybe you learn something about how it was built, maybe not. Either way, it's not a house anymore. You can never put things back together the same way you took them apart.

Tonight Yosef is playing Ella Fitzgerald. The song takes me a minute to recognize. I've never heard a rendition of "They Can't Take That Away from Me" besides the one my grandmother used to play on her organ, and this new version sounds artificial, like a movie that tries too hard to make people seem like they're falling in love. There's humming in the background and too much piano. I close my eyes and the stillness of the Mojave Desert replaces the sweet, stale effusion of smoke and espresso grinds. I remember the rattlesnake my grandmother and I fended off together. I think of my grandmother's boxy feet and wrinkled nylons. Sometimes when I dream, I see her just the way I found her, lying next to her Hammond organ with her respirator cord coiled like a serpent at her feet.

Half the song passes before I realize the humming is not part of the recording, and I turn to the booth behind me to see a man with thin hair and thin limbs who stops humming when I look at him.

"Don't stop," I say.

He's at least a decade older than me and looks like he probably hosts Marxist cell meetings in his basement. Dark edges around his brow, a drastic, plunging jaw line, tinted glasses. The skin just below his eyes is almost gossamer, and he's oddly handsome. A lot of guys might assume there's something wrong with a woman who goes out alone in the middle of the night. Not this guy, though. He gets up with his coffee and stands next to my booth.

"Have a seat," I say, stubbing out my cigarette.

"I come here because the music keeps me awake."

"Most people sleep at night."

He smiles a little. "Yeah, well. Not you."

"Not you, either."

"Not tonight."

Suddenly, I am glad for the company. We look at each other. I have a thing for older men. Sidra says it's because my stepdad was such a wreck. But really, they're easier to get along with—better in bed and unconcerned about pleasing you outside of it.

His name is Harris, and I notice his shirt has come untucked from his Levis, and also that his Asics are dirty. I wonder what his skin tastes like. Sidra says that I'm the horniest woman she knows. I've only slept with fourteen men, but compared to her, that's downright slutty.

"Been to that Asian Film Festival yet?" he asks.

I have never been to a film festival in my life. "I've been wanting to check it out," I say to let him know I'm interested. Which is another great thing about older men—they don't need to be told twice.

•   •   •

The following night, I'm Yosef's only customer. Little Walter is wailing on the harmonica at low volume and I'm smoking and eating burned eggs. There's a book open in front of me, and I'm turning pages and looking at words, but I'm too distracted to retain anything. Last night's music is unyielding in my head.

My grandmother's house floated like a wayward sailboat on an ocean of fine-grained dirt, scrub brush, and yucca trees. Crisp desert mornings, we sat outside eating cottage cheese and frozen peaches in ancient white bowls with ancient silverware, talking about men and families and what happens to women when they grow old. A miniature silver roadrunner adorned her neck on a thick chain. Tiny turquoise stones were glued in for the eyes, and its feathers stood out in silver spikes. We'd spend hours on her back porch, looking out at cacti, jaundiced brittlebush shooting from the sand like coral, mounds of ants with bulging red abdomens. I'd walk to her house when my mom and stepdad fought, or my stepdad was in a bad mood and I was scared of what he'd do to me.

At night, we played cards and sipped hot chocolate with cinnamon. Her respirator would hiss, then make a clicking sound like a kid tapping a toy drum. She'd play her Hammond sometimes, an enormous instrument poised like a throne in the center of her living room, with three rows of keys and hundreds of black and white levers. I loved pulling them out in patterns when the organ was off, all the white ones out and the black ones in, or every other lever, or all of them partway out, in staircase gradations. She'd smile at my arrangement, then turn the machine on and push the levers back into place while it warmed up. Vibrations thrummed through the carpet. I'd fish through the sheet music for Ella Fitzgerald or Chet Baker, or one of our other favorites, and then she'd prop up the pages and play.

The organ thundered through the house, and I'd imagine the sounds sluicing across the sand, startling lizards and centipedes. As the sound churned, her limbs would seem to grow, her five-foot figure plunging to press pedals and reaching to pull levers. She dipped and bobbed to work the organ, and together we crooned blissful melodies into the desert.

If she had been *my* mother, I would have taken her to a real specialist, not some baby-faced twentysomething GP from Kaiser. They
would have caught the cancer earlier. Maybe there would have been
less pain. Maybe she'd still be alive.
Or maybe it wouldn't have mattered.
I blink. Smoke curls around the edges of the booth, like fingers.

On the way to see my advisor, I'm in a good mood because I'm
thinking about my first date with Harris. But just as I'm replaying the
part where he laughs, touching his hand to mine and then squeezing it
for a second, an asthma attack hits me, a bad one. I hyperventilate like
a crazy person, then I slip into the bathroom and puff on my inhaler
until my lungs relax. When I finally go into my advisor's office, I'm
fifteen minutes late. "I had an asthma attack," I tell her, but it sounds
stupid when I say it out loud. Asthma is a kids' disease, like chicken
pox. She nods but says nothing.
The English and Rhetoric Department smells like a government
building: wet concrete, dank stairwells. My advisor adds decaying food
to the mix. Her trash can bears two unfinished bananas, a half-eaten
apple, and part of a granola bar. I once read that the average American
throws away thirteen hundred calories a day. She asks if I have any ideas
for a dissertation topic. I fiddle with my grandmother's roadrunner
necklace in the pocket of my jeans.
For the most part, the other students in my department have parents
who are lawyers, or work for publishing companies, or are college
professors. It took me a couple months to realize I must have been
a token of socioeconomic diversity. My mom did manicures, my
stepdad was a trucker, and I did my undergrad at Cal State Bakersfield. For these reasons, my advisor wants to think I am intriguing
and smart, but she seems to find this increasingly difficult. We're like
an arranged marriage that almost works. I say I'm working on some
new ideas and we schedule another meeting, which always makes us
feel optimistic.
Outside the building, I light a Pall Mall and think about the different ways to die. You can do it yourself: reckless driving or a gun to the

temple. Or you can wait for something, or someone, to do it to you. Smoking is somewhere in the middle.

Some people from my cohort are walking over from the main quad and I stub out my cigarette, stuff the rest of it back in the pack, and head home.

The first time Harris stays over, we order in Thai and eat it from the containers, sitting on my hardwood floor. He says it makes him feel like a student again, then looks to see if I'm offended. I stare intelligently at the building next door. Yosef's, Taqueria del Toro, and Soo's Bakery are all on the adjacent block, smashed together like some monument to falling nations. After our first date, I'd halted us at my door when his warm hand snaked beneath my sweatshirt. I didn't want him all at once. I wanted to kiss like high schoolers and grope at clothing.

"How long have you lived here?" he asks me.

"Three months." A year ago, I started lying about this. The truth is, I unpacked a few things the first year of grad school, and then the semester started and I grew accustomed to stepping over boxes and living without whatever was inside.

"It always takes a while to unpack."

I nod and change the subject. "You told me you're a water-quality expert, but what do you actually do all day?"

He scratches his ear. "Well, I go to dams, canals, all kinds of water sources. I collect samples, then test them to see if the water's good enough for drinking, swimming, ranching trout, or whatever. There's different standards for different water uses."

"Ever find anything weird?"

"In the water? Sure."

"Like what?"

"Guess."

I think on this a minute. "Decapitated Barbies?" I guess. "Dildos? Cans of soup?"

I like the way his eyes start laughing before the rest of his face joins in.

"Mostly shoes," he says.

"What else?"

"Baseballs. Golf balls."

"What's the weirdest thing you've ever found?

"Skeletons."

"*People* skeletons?"

He shakes his head. "Nah. Well, once. Mainly it's raccoons. Sometimes cats."

I shudder, thinking about the corpse in the water. "So our tap water is filled with decaying skin cells and fur?"

"Well." He shrugs. "Animals are mostly minerals and water, anyway."

The sun has sunk beyond the next building and it is black outside, which makes me think of the Mojave, the way the night drew us into it, the lantern on my grandmother's porch beckoning winged dragon-insects that don't exist north of Barstow. Desert nights are coal black, with heavenly bodies piercing the sky like scars, or pearls. In Portland, the night is muted, city lights blotting out the constellations.

He pushes a box out of the way with his foot and sits next to me on the floor. "What do you work on, exactly? In school, I mean."

"I told you already."

"Barely. I don't even know your dissertation topic."

"Me either."

He smiles and takes a bite of pad thai. A small piece of chicken falls onto his shirt.

"The whole goal is to pick critical race theory or queer theory or whatever, then apply its specific, myopic conventions to a genre or author no one has thought of yet."

"So why'd you go in the first place?"

I shrugged. "I love books. I thought it would let me read all day long."

"Which it does, I guess."

"Sort of. Sometimes in class I think of this kid, Roddy Dutro, I knew in elementary school. He was kicked by a horse and it bashed in his skull. It had to be reconstructed by a specialist from Los Angeles. Before the specialist got there, you could visit Roddy in the hospital but weren't allowed to touch him. The top of his skull was gone, and the skin just laid over his brain. It looked like a grapefruit sitting in a bowl with a towel over it."

"Jesus," Harris says.

"I know. I can't believe they let us visit. I remember when I saw it, I said something like, 'Oh my God, Roddy.' And Roddy, perfectly calm, goes, 'Yeah, in my size all they had were girls' pajamas.' I looked at his pajamas for the first time, and they had little pink tulips all over them."

Harris finally notices the piece of chicken on his shirt. He picks it off with his fingers and puts it in his mouth.

"That's what my lit classes remind me of. There's a brain sitting there in the bowl, but everyone's talking about the fucking pajamas."

Usually I don't smoke inside my apartment, but talking about school makes me nervy, so I open a window and light up. I offer the pack to Harris and he declines, watching me. I can tell he's thinking how he's seen me use an inhaler and he's deciding whether to mention the smoking.

"How'd you get to liking reading in the first place?" I like the cadence of this, *get to liking reading*, and I want him to repeat it, but know that if I ask him to, he'll be self-conscious.

"My grandmother," I answer.

"Was she a teacher?"

I shake my head. "Nope, a cleaning lady," I say, a little proudly.

He gets up to pour us another glass of wine, then asks if he can use my stereo, and starts fiddling with it. I finish my cigarette, then go to the sink and wash my hands. I imagine skin cells, pus, infection, running in rivulets over my fingers.

I recognize it in an instant: "They Can't Take That Away from Me," but some other version, not the one from Yosef's. He must have brought it with him, which admittedly is pretty romantic. A few minutes later his mouth is on me and he's lifting my shirt, his teeth making tiny dents on my areola. He is purposeful, fierce, flattens my back against the hardwood floor. I like to make men figure out what I want, but Harris, in the darkness, seems to know me already. The crescendos slide over us, and I decide that this version of our song contains a certain violence—a reservation. Something deliberately held back.

When I meet Sidra for coffee, she knows immediately.

"Is this one married?"

I roll my eyes. Sidra has a way of making me act like a fourteen-year-old. "Divorced."

"How long ago?"

"A couple years."

"How old is he?"

"Forty-two."

"Slept with him yet?"

I grin.

"Slut."

"It was very hot," I say, matter-of-factly. "We did it on the floor."

"Did what?" she asks, all wide-eyed mock innocence, and then cracks up. Sidra's husband landing a job in Portland was the luckiest thing that's happened to me in a long time. We've known each other since she was fourteen and I was eleven. She rescued me from three girls trying to beat me up in the bathroom, and I started helping her with math. We've been friends ever since.

"Screw you," I say.

"You have hardwood. Ouch."

"Better than carpet burns."

She pretends to consider this. "Well," she says at last. "At least this one is single."

I frown. "That's unfair."

"I still say you're getting back at your stepfather."

I sigh. This is one of those conversations we have so often that we're just reciting lines. "Why are you so protective of every guy I deign to fuck?"

"It's not them. It's their families."

"That's their commitment, not mine."

"Even so."

"Even so, what?" I ask, but Sidra has lost interest in the conversation. Her perfect nails glisten against the white porcelain. The café is playing a saxophone version of "More Than Words Can Say," and she's tapping her cup to the rhythm.

"You realize this is the worst remake ever done of the worst song ever written," I say.

She sticks her tongue out at me and flags down the waitress for a refill. When it comes, she tears open three packets of sugar and dumps them in. The liquid matches the rich brown of her skin, and I add so much milk that my coffee matches the sickly pallor of my own. "So you gonna keep this guy?"

"Who knows."

"Here's your problem, Lori: you've got to live life as if you expect it to last."

He does not, it turns out, like to be called Harry, which is a relief. Back at my apartment we open a Chianti and sit on the floor.

"I like the whole urban-chic thing you've got going here," he says.

"City lofts, grainy peasant-loaves of bread. Soon no one will be able to tell the very rich from the very poor."

He takes this in, and I wonder what he's thinking. He keeps a lot to himself, which I like. He even reads some of the same stuff I do, though I had to pry this out of him. He says talking about books makes him worry that he didn't really understand them.

"I'd like to go to work with you sometime," I tell him.

"Why?"

There's something satisfying about seeing a man at work. Something about the familiarity, the ease of movement, the swift completion of rote tasks. I shrug. "I've never dated a water-quality expert."

"Sure. We'll go on a site day. Lab days are boring."

I smile and pull him onto me, hiding my nose in the place where you can tell what a man smells like, under the crook of his chin, just below his ear. His hand slips beneath my sweater.

After we finish he does everything right: lets me dress with the light off, kisses me, asks if he can spend the night. At three in the morning I find myself staring at the ceiling next to a water-quality expert whose breaths have grown long into my pillow.

In the morning he wants to walk me to class. I have an old blue Chevy, but I leave it in long-term parking because I don't know how many miles it has left, and I don't want to waste them. We stop for coffee at Yosef's, which is becoming our place—meaning it's no longer mine. When we get to the English Department he kisses me roughly and I actually blush.

"What do you want to do tonight?" he asks.

"I can't help noticing that you haven't taken me to the Asian Film Festival yet."

"The old bait-and-switch," he says, scratching his nose. "Let's go tonight."

"I'm busy."

"Tomorrow night?"

I pause. "I'll call you," I say, and leave him on the steps.

There is no good reason for being up at four a.m. except fishing or sex, and I am engaged in neither. I don't want to go to Yosef's because Harris might be there and I want to be alone, so when I start to feel stir crazy in my apartment, I take a walk. It's amazing what you can smell in the early morning. Hot dogs, coffee grinds, sickly sweet pot smoke wafting from an open window. Sewage, fried batter, decomposing fruit.

I hear a sound, a bang-clang, bang-clang. Edging around the skeleton of a fixed-rent housing project, I am suddenly facing a whiskery homeless man in a stained Blazers cap. One hand grips an oil can, the other a broken Louisville Slugger. He strikes the bat against the can, then the can against his knee. Bang-clang. Catching me watching, he freezes. I have strange effects on homeless people, particularly the crazy ones. They look at me like I'm one of them in disguise, like the wall that separates us is thin as tissue. I half-expect him to say, "You know what your problem is, Lori?" Instead he begins laughing like a maniac, so hard he's practically doubling over. I walk on and he's still laughing. His eyes burn a hole in my back, and after a minute the bang-clang starts again.

"Write your advisor's wet dream. Just as a mental exercise. Über lit-crit, over the top."

"Why?"

"So you see how it feels," Harris says. "Then you'll know the worst it can get, and you can decide whether to go on anyway."

176   *Glimmer Train Stories*

Harris rents a flat, not an apartment, and the distinction seems important. Apartments are where college students live. Flats belong to retired foreign servicemen and characters in British plays. Blueprints line his floor, topographic maps of canals and rivers throughout the western U.S. Color codes mark depth, purity, chemical composition. I trace the maps with my fingers. "Okay," I say.

He looks at me, surprised. "You'll do it?"

"I'll do it for *you*," I say, fluttering my eyelids, mawkishly romantic.

He smiles. "You always do that."

"What?"

"Pretend to be sappy. Because you don't want to have a real, tender moment."

He's caught me dead-on.

"It's okay," he tells me. He takes my hand and kisses it, then kisses my forearm, my elbow, my shoulder, and then my lips. I still don't know what to say, and he gets up and goes into the kitchen, then comes out with two bottles of Anchor Steam. We listen to his records and split the six-pack over the next two hours. My mind assumes an optimistic fuzz.

Eventually I tell Harris about how each time my stepdad beat me up, my grandmother took care of me afterward, pressing packs of frozen corn on my forehead or collarbone. I pull *I Get a Kick Out of You: Cole Porter Songbook Vol. 2*, from my bag. "I brought this," I say. I try to sound casual, but I've never shown anyone besides Sidra. I tell him how I was only allowed to save one small box of my grandmother's stuff, and how I filled it with her favorite sheet music.

"Your grandma never did anything?" he asks after a minute.

"What do you mean?"

"She knew what was going on with your stepfather. But she let it happen."

All at once I'm sorry I brought the songbook over, sorry I'd told him anything. "What the fuck was she supposed to do?" I demand. "She was seventy years old."

He holds up a hand. "Don't get mad."

I light a cigarette. "It wasn't her fault."

I almost tell him about finding her next to the Hammond. "Lori—

love you," her note said, and that was it. It was months, maybe, before the cancer would have taken her. When the person you love most in the world doesn't protect you, what does that mean about you?

"Please don't smoke in here."

After I don't say anything for a while, he gets up and returns with a jar lid for me to use as an ashtray. "You've got asthma."

"So what?" I ask, and he doesn't answer.

By my next meeting with my advisor, I've given her thirty single-spaced pages in which she is cited, repeatedly, in the footnotes. When I arrive, she's holding the pages and tossing out a half-eaten d'Anjou pear. There's another on her desk and she offers it to me. I accept.

"This is very well-written," she says. "But I'm not sure what the thesis is."

She's right, of course. There isn't one. I just threw theoried jargon at Audrey Lorde to see what stuck.

"There are lots of good ideas in here, though." She pats the stack of papers. "It's really original."

"I've grown fiercely autonomous," I say. "I'm bursting with daring."

She smiles. "Good for you. Seems like you're starting to get your footing."

I nod. If this is as bad as it gets, maybe I can handle it. There are worse jobs, after all, than writing things you don't quite believe.

More and more of my lonely evenings are replaced by Harris's moans in my ears, the grainy whisper of my hand through his hair. We see each other often, and he doesn't complain on the nights I slip from his side and pull on a sweatshirt at three or four in the morning to go for a walk or to sit at Yosef's. I feel him stir when I leave, then again when I return, but he says nothing. I start to love him for it.

Two months after our first date, Harris takes me to a jobsite on the county border. There are more than three hundred canals in Oregon, he told me, and this one holds irrigation water. He's up to his waist in the murk, holding a test tube and frowning into the wind. He takes a reading and pulls off his gloves. "Whatcha thinking?" he asks.

"It's nice out here."

"Mm. We should go on a vacation, don't you think?"

"Where?"

"Santa something. Cruz, Barbara, Fe—your choice."

"Maybe." I reach into my pocket to make sure my roadrunner is there. It's warm, pokey against my skin. What am I afraid of? "That sounds nice," I say.

He shows me how the test kit works, and I pretend to understand. I lean in from the bank but can't reach to the bottom, and he tells me to wade in, which I do, muddying my khakis. He puts an arm around my waist.

"Get a dropperful and put it on this."

"What is it?"

"pH paper. Seven is drinkable, not too basic or acidic. That's the first test."

I'm suddenly delighted to be playing in the canal, like something forbidden. I reach in with the dropper, and the water soaks my shirt, rendering my white blouse nearly translucent. Harris looks at me hungrily and my limbs stir with excitement. He's going to have me right here, in this semi-potable water, and I intend to let him. Then something touches my calf and I scream.

"What?"

"There's something in here."

"It's okay. There's no frogs or anything. The bottom is concrete."

"Shit, shit, shit," I say. I feel skin, nails, and I know what it is. I think of the bodies in the drinking water. Decomposing skin, human hair.

"Reach in and pull it out."

The water's too murky to see to the bottom and I can't move.

"Where is it?" he asks.

I point to the surface where I felt the thing. I can't tell if it's a foot or a hand, and as Harris reaches into the water a few feet below where I've pointed, the thing presses harder against me and I imagine a skeleton's fingers closing around my leg. I scream and lose my footing. My head goes underwater for a second and I try to get to my feet but the concrete is slippery and the current drags me along the bottom. For two or three seconds, I'm lost in that brown water, me and the corpse drifting toward some farmer's field in the middle of Oregon. And I think of my grandmother. How she should have taken me with her. How great it would be if she came back and took me now.

Harris grabs my arm and my face touches air again. Once he helps me to my feet, the current seems weaker. I can't believe it's the same water that submerged me a few seconds ago.

We crawl up onto the bank together and he wraps me in a towel, then sits with his arms around me and his legs stretched on either side of mine, rocking. I'm suddenly crying a little, which makes me feel pathetic.

"You had quite a scare," Harris says.

I crawl out of his embrace, coughing, and grab my Pall Malls.

"It was a just tree branch. See, part of it's poking out of the water now."

"Fuck," I choke out, because my lighter was in my pocket and it's drenched, and then I feel again for my roadrunner, and it's missing. "Fuck—my roadrunner." I double check, but it's not in my other pockets, either.

"It's okay," he says. "I'll buy you another necklace."

"No," I say, feeling hurt and stupidly childish. I check my pockets a third time and it's still not there.

Harris puts his arms around me. "I'm sorry," he says. "It was your grandmother's, right? That was stupid of me."

"No," I say.

"We'll find it," he says, suddenly determined, my old prince. It's a little romantic and a little ridiculous. For the first time, I wonder if I love him. How can I? What's the threshold for knowing someone well enough to love them?

"She killed herself," I say. It is the first time I have said this out loud, and it sounds to me like I'm just reciting dialogue, like it happened to someone else.

"I thought she died of cancer."

"She killed herself first."

I can tell he's thinking of the story I made up about how I was at her bedside in the hospital when she took her last breath. How she said, "Lori—love you," then died.

"I'm sorry," Harris says.

I look at him, and I'm helpless. I wish I'd never come here.

"I'm so sorry," Harris says.

A week later I stand outside Yosef's and peek in. Harris's back faces me, shoulders bent over his coffee. The taste of his neck fills my mouth. He rubs the top of his head and I think of his hands on me. I think I could love him forever. It's been a week since the canal and I haven't answered his calls. I press my cheek to the glass but can't hear whatever music Yosef is playing.

I stare at the street. Then I turn and walk toward the parking garage. My car is already packed. Five changes of clean clothes, three books, cash, CDs for the drive. The garage door whirr-clicks open, spears of orange metal and corrugated iron, and a red Jeep drives out. A car alarm sounds somewhere beyond the buildings.

When I reach Redding I phone Sidra. She wants to know whether I'm with Harris. I say I'm not.

"Where are you?"

I tell her.

"Jesus." She sighs. "When will you be back?"

"I don't know," I say, which is true.

"Want to catch a movie on Saturday?" she asks.

"I won't be back by Saturday."

We talk for a few minutes, and then I hang up, buy a Coke from a vending machine, and drive some more, stopping once for the bathroom and once more for fries. I only have enough money for a week of motels, but for now I'm pretending I'm going back for good, that she'll be there, waiting on the back porch. I think about all the things we could have done for each other, how she could have taken me away from my stepdad, or how I could have loved her enough that she wouldn't have killed herself.

Not long after Bakersfield, the trees get shorter, thinning as the mountains recede. Five miles outside Barstow, everything is replaced by sand-colored dirt sprouting creosote bushes, bladderpod, datura. Half an hour later I see the first yucca. I think about calling Harris.

I imagine what it would be like to return in a week, to love him, to see him grow old. Then I imagine what it will be like if I never go back—what we'd say, someday, when I finally dialed his number, if he'd remember me. "I'm living in Hesperia now," I'd tell him. Or Adelando, or Victorville. Maybe I'd invite him down.

Soon the mountains grow tall again, craggier. Yuccas sprout in the valleys and I think of turquoise stones, of jackrabbits. I grab a blanket from the backseat and wrap it around my shoulders. It's almost night, and most of the cars streaming toward me have their headlights on. I wonder what they're going to, or leaving.

Thirty minutes later, I pull over at a rest stop, breathing hard. My grandmother is just over those hills, I think. Something of her. Just past Victorville. In the dark, the mountains look like an ocean. Maybe I'll turn the car around. I could head north and be back before morning.

There are no other cars at the stop. I roll down the windows. Water is running somewhere nearby. One of the streetlights in the parking lot is busted, and the other is right above me, shining yellow-orange, turning the Chevy's blue paint black. If it was cleaner, the light would have bounced off the hood, but I haven't washed it in years, so the coating of dirt absorbs the light, just sucks it all in.

Sitting there, I suspect that someday I'll look back at my late twenties with a wistful nostalgia, forgetting some things and misremembering others, yearning romantically for my tiny apartment, for a simpler time when grad school was all I worried about.

This will turn out not to be true.

But right now I don't know that. I can't picture becoming lovers, briefly, with Yosef, nor using a year's worth of fellowship money to visit Alaska, nor meeting the tall carpenter who will convince me to move to Corvallis and open a bookstore. I don't know about my DUI, my vegetarian lasagna recipe, the three-legged terrier I'll adopt with the carpenter, or the scars I'll get from biking in the nature preserve near my house.

I turn off the ignition and let go of the steering wheel. I'm alone, completely alone, more than ever before. The wind whistles through the car like music, and I'm suddenly angry. My hands clench into fists the size of peaches and I begin beating the steering wheel, just beating and beating it, and in a minute there's a red smudge on the leather, blood from one of my knuckles, and I don't care. I can barely feel my hands and tears stream down my face and my breath catches in my throat. I cough and gag but I don't stop crying. I catch a slanted glimpse of myself in the rearview mirror, a woman in her late twenties, still a kid, really, beating the shit out of her car, out of her own hands, hair going crazy in the wind, missing her grandmother for all the world, and wondering if it will always be like this, if it has to be like this, and if it was ever like this for her.

One of the first fishing trips I took with my dad. I think I'm ten years old.

Dennis Bock's books include *Olympia*, *The Ash Garden*, and *The Communist's Daughter*. His work has been short-listed for the International IMPAC Dublin Literary Award and the Kiriyama Prize and won the English Society of Authors Betty Trask Award. He lives in Toronto with his wife Andrea and their two children.

IMPROVISED EXPLOSIVE DEVICE

Dennis Bock

Dennis Bock

Zack was barely twenty-four years old and still walked without the aid of a cane when he got the journalism fellowship at Columbia University. He'd never travelled much before then or heard the sound of live gunfire. He'd certainly never written a love poem. But he knew by heart the names and dates of all the presidents of the United States, the eighteen provinces of Angola, and had once on a dare at a Jewish Defense League gathering recited Section One of motion 497 of the United Nations Security Council. He was, and he knew it, a well-informed shit disturber, the perfect journalist in the making. He breezed through the inaugural year of the MA program and, to no one's amazement back home—at least those who worked at the *Niagara Falls Review*, where Zack interned in high school before getting serious about journalism—won the J. Anthony Lukas Works in Progress Award for the eighty-seven (double spaced) pages he'd written in three frenzied weeks on the African land-mine problem.

In mid-May of 2005, only weeks after graduating at the top of his class, he flew up to Ottawa, where a job was waiting for him at the *Citizen*. For the next year, when he wasn't commenting in print on the shenanigans up on Parliament Hill, he labored on his land-mine book. It tormented him. He still had the ear of a certain New York editor he'd flirted with at the J. Anthony Lukas ceremony. Her name was Bethany. She sent occasional notes to his Ottawa home address now, usually handwritten and always professionally flattering, and included the odd *Publishers Weekly* clipping that spoke to the interest in the industry regarding his area of expertise. *The world needs someone to tell this story*, was a typical Bethany sentiment. He knew the land-mine issue wasn't going anywhere anytime soon, but he was stalled and, worse yet, he was bored. So bored he wished at times he'd chosen some other grave injustice in the world to write about. The truth was, after all the concise prose and towering stacks of statistics, he didn't know what the hell he was talking about. He felt like a fraud. The book was pushing two hundred pages and had, at some unidentifiable juncture, begun to read like a UN report warmed over by an eager creative-writing undergrad. He was despondent, hardly an inch away from abandoning the project, when the opportunity for a six-week tour in Afghanistan came up.

He jumped at it. When he left the editor's office, grinning, after receiving word that afternoon, he fist-bumped his way back to his cubicle, where he quickly composed an email to Audrey, with whom he would soon share a brief romantic blunder, and victory-punched the air between his knees. He hit *send*. This was the moment in his professional life he was waiting for. He figured, apart from the real reporting he'd be doing, the book would finally come alive. He had to frame the thing with some real-time tension, definitely first-person present. It would all fall together now. Next he emailed Bethany about the positive development. She herself had hinted that the manuscript was missing something. (She'd read the latest draft almost three months ago.) A personal edge, maybe. We all want stories these days, she said. Not just history, and not just facts. She was right. She wasn't in the business for nothing.

It wouldn't be fun or pleasant, he knew, but that's not why he was in this game. It was the truth he was after. He needed to know the rattle of automatic-weapons fire and the smell of cordite lifting through the air. There were too many realities he knew nothing about to be writing the sort of book he wanted to write, which was real and urgent and gritty. He'd never even seen a dead body before. He mentally prepared himself (as far as you can prepare yourself for something like that), but seven weeks later, on the December morning the armored vehicle he was riding in blew up on the Kandahar Road, killing the four Canadian soldiers he was embedded with, he saw his first cadaver when he came to in the middle of the gravel highway, and then he saw his second, draped over his lap like a steaming rag doll, and Zackary Tessler, winner of the inaugural J. Anthony Lukas Work-in-Progress Award, knew now that he and not his land-mine book was the real work in progress.

How or how much he would change, though (and even then it took some time to sink in), he didn't understand until the afternoon five days later when he pulled a pad of paper out of the bedside-table drawer in room 225 of Building 10 at the Military Base Hospital at Ramstein, Germany, and tried to write a letter to the girl he thought might be his girlfriend. He still wasn't sure about where she stood. But that bomb had changed something in him. If he'd had any doubt before, he didn't now. His younger brother, Rick, who'd flown over from Vancouver two days after he got word of the Kandahar Road incident, had just left the room to return to the hotel in town. Rick was a florist and ran his own shop down in Granville Island. Zack had thanked his brother, again, for coming all this way, and told him he was going to close his eyes for a bit. But Zack just wanted to be alone to think. He wanted to file a story. He wanted to write his damn book. There were large bouquets of flowers in the four corners of the room, courtesy of his brother, of course, and the *Ottawa Citizen*, and Bethany in New York, etc., but none had arrived yet from Audrey. Her name was printed on the card attached to the large bouquet of roses the newspaper had sent over. But none yet had arrived from her alone.

His left leg was gripped by a throbbing pain. The oxycodone helped, but the pounding was always there. There was still a high-pitched ringing in his ears. The faces of the soldiers he'd ridden with flashed before his eyes at the strangest of times. He'd spoken to people back home—colleagues, his mom and dad, the CBC, even CNN—about his ordeal. He was, for a few days, a cause célèbre. This gave him no pleasure. He didn't trust television. He was a print man. He was often forced to close his eyes and grip the sides of the bed when the subject of one of those interviews came up. A number of mornings he'd woken up crying; and certain foods he'd once enjoyed now nauseated him. He'd only known those four men for less than three days, but each of their faces haunted him. Writing something, anything, he decided, might help get the monkey off his back.

So as his brother rode the small European elevator up to the fourth floor of the guesthouse in the historic center of Ramstein, Zack, fighting his fifth wave of nausea of the day, started in on a letter—his first since arriving at the hospital—to the girl he'd begun seeing just weeks before leaving for Afghanistan. Of course he'd already spoken to Audrey from his hospital bed. But the connection had been cluttered with static and she'd seemed only politely concerned. The emotional distance in her voice had terrified him. She was a University of Ottawa journalism undergrad, an intern at the paper, twenty-three, leggy in a way that positively redefined the adjective, and wrote sentences equal to his own. This last fact, in and of itself, startled him. She drank pints with the old pros at the Highlander Pub across the street from the paper. They'd spent one night together, the one night before he'd left, during which, due to nerves, he'd failed to fire.

It was surprising then that the first thing to come off the tip of his pen that afternoon, only days after being blown up, was a love poem. He hadn't written a poem in fifteen years, and, he thought, casting back, had certainly never attempted a love poem. It just wasn't in him. And why should it be? In his undergrad years at the University of Toronto, back in the late nineties, he'd penned some inspired Ferlinghetti rip-offs. Two had even appeared in the English department rag. But love poems, not a chance.

He read over the poem, confused. In fact it looked like a sonnet.

He stared out the window at the gray German sky and thought about those four dead kids he'd ridden with. His age, more or less, but he could call them kids now because it was right to heighten the tragedy. One, the Sergeant, had a three-year-old daughter named Colby. The things he remembered, and the detail with which he remembered them, troubled him. He stared at his left foot, raised in suspension and wrapped in heavy plaster.

He set the poem aside and began to write his letter to Audrey.

But now a second poem came. Even faster this time. This one was a sonnet about the things he wanted to unremember.

He wrote three sonnets that afternoon with hardly any effort before he slid down against his pillow and permitted his exhausted brain to be poured into a long oxycodone-inspired sleep.

When he woke up the next morning he found his brother sitting in the chair beside his bed with the blue notepad in his lap.

"Since when are you the poet, bro?" he said.

His hot mid-day meal was delivered four hours later by the freckled redhead from Iowa. Her name was Karen. He tucked his papers beneath his pillow—he'd written another one, a good one by his reckoning—and watched a rerun of *American Idol* as he ate.

Three days later, startled by his output, he asked Karen if she'd ever think about doing something with her life other than nursing.

"I'd like to have babies one day."

"I mean for a profession."

"Well, anything's possible," she said. "I'd like to think we're not set in stone. Not yet anyway."

He reached for his pad of paper after she left the room and rifled off a sonnet that described, in perfect detail, the young nurse's tunic pressing her lovely breasts together, shy as two alert doves, and the chilled German sky into which they flew after his trembling fingers released them from their cage.

After nineteen months of part-timing at his brother's flower shop back in Vancouver, trying to get his life up to speed again, Zack tracked Audrey down in New York City. She was living with a chiselled Latin-looking boy, probably about twenty-five himself, like her, and also, if the textbooks he carried and the buildings he dipped into on campus were any indication, a master's in journalism candidate. Every morning the boy left their apartment just before ten. Zackary witnessed this five mornings in a row (enough to feel comfortable that this was a reliable pattern) as he sat at the coffee shop on Malcolm X Boulevard, stirring his double/double with heavy clumps of blueberry muffin. Audrey would appear at the door soon after, her right arm slipped to the shoulder through the yellow frame of her mountain bike, and pedal west on 117th over to the Morningside Heights campus. She usually wore a backpack. She was to him now, in the summer of 2008, even more beautiful than she had been on the night he'd failed to make love to her. Even more beautiful than she had been on the night she'd allowed him to see her, socially, away from work, after he got back to Ottawa from his foreshortened tour before he quit the paper and headed west. It had been a swift and uncomfortable meeting. She'd listened to his entreaties, told him she was off to New York soon anyway, no hard feelings, and wished him the best of luck.

On the sixth morning of his reconnaissance he drank down the last lumpy gulp of his coffee, anachronistically tipped his baseball cap to the Sri Lankan cashier, who smiled shyly, and caned his way out into the bright Manhattan sunshine.

It was a pleasant feeling to be back, because it had all, in some broad sense, started here, another lifetime ago. He'd returned because he wasn't done with this town yet. That's why he was here now. To convince for a second time those whom he'd convinced already once. He carried the manuscript under his arm. It called in at a whopping 647 pages. It was no longer a work in progress. From start to finish he knew it was a book of immeasurable importance. He could hardly contain his smile when he thought of the impact it would have. Its effect would be felt first at the trade-magazine level and then, like a tidal wave, move outward until it eventually swamped all shores. Even TV was possible. He didn't doubt for a moment that the book stood a chance of making its mark on a cultural level as wide as that. He'd tied—over and over to the point of assuring himself the motif—the making of land mines to the most mundane of levels. Nobody was exempt. Wasn't that the point, wasn't that the kicker? Everything we did, everything, could be linked back to that dark practice, the manufacture of those hidden bombs that surround us. The metaphor was starkly poignant. We were all, he knew, responsible for the blind boy in Sri Lanka. The dead children of Beirut. And with a cred like his, he thought, he who struggled every day with the burden of that left leg, the world would be his again.

He smiled, tapping his way along Malcolm X, and with a Charlie Chaplin flair, waddled left on West 112th to where four years before he'd liked to sit in the window of the Shawmra House and eat a cheap lunch while he watched the crowds. He recognized the man who served at the counter. He still wore the green apron with the palm trees embroidered into the chest. His moustache was grayer now, but the place felt as reassuringly derelict as it always had. It was a real student dive. Some things don't change, he thought. A ceiling fan pushed the stale air about; day-old newspaper, trampled to a brown smudge, layered the floor. He ordered the Number 3 and ate it slowly as he observed the street. The brick of a manuscript rested safely on the seat next to him, out of view, as if it were a vulnerable child he'd promised to keep out of harm's way. Today was the day, he'd decided. Bethany's card, tattered, worn thin as a wafer but still legible, was pressed between the damp skins of his wallet. He took it out and examined it, finished his meal, and headed for the door.

Bethany emerged from her office with arms outstretched. After two kisses she said that all her emails to him, at least half a dozen, had bounced back over the past year or so. "Where on earth has this prize-winner been hiding!" The junior editors, publicists, and interns at Willis & Sacks emerged blinking from their cubicles to get a look at the unknown writer with the mangled foot. It was weirdly twisted, pointing forever eastward to his nose-tip's northern orientation. He leaned on that cane in his best impersonation of a smiling Rimbaud just back from Abyssinia. When he handed over the brick of pages he blushed theatrically, coughed twice for emphasis, and told Bethany that in his opinion this would prove to be the book of the decade.

"I don't doubt it," she said, "not for a minute."

It was the kind of chutzpah Bethany heard most days of her professional life and, on a good afternoon, a bravado she appreciated. She found it difficult to believe in someone unless he was capable of this sort of impertinence. He looked a little worse for wear, she noticed, leaner, altogether a more drastic version of the boy she'd met years before. She liked the change, apart from that monstrous foot. She noticed the light scar on his chin and the hummingbird quivering in his right hand. There was something about him now, something smouldering. She promised to read his manuscript over the weekend.

He took a cab from there up to the campus, where he spotted Audrey locking her bike to a tree.

"Holy smokes," he said.

"Hey. Wow." She straightened her frame.

"What are you doing here?"

"I go here."

"Right on," he said.

"You're back in New York?"

"I'm in Vancouver these days. I'm just here visiting some people." She glanced at his leg.

"Looks weird, doesn't it?" he said.

"Not really. I mean, something's definitely going on down there, but..." She drew a strand of hair back behind her ear. "You have time for a coffee or something?"

He looked at his watch. "Half an hour maybe. Sure."

She wanted to know all about it now. Every last detail. Maybe enough time had passed since the kiss-off up in Ottawa. He told her everything but the most relevant parts. He told her that he woke up every morning, if he'd been able to sleep at all, with the pain still digging into his left thigh and foot, the fucked-up knee and the haunted nightmares that visited him, and the little girl named Colby who sat at the edge of his bed sometime between two and four in the morning and asked about her dad. He told her about everything except the knife blade that ripped into his heart whenever he thought about Audrey. He told her about the things he'd seen over there—you could never really believe it until you woke up covered in some guy's guts, thinking the man who buried the IED that just blew you up was jogging up behind you now to finish the job, you just lying there waiting for him to put a hole in the back of your head. He smiled a smile of bottomless surrender.

She placed her hand in his and told him how unbelievably awesome it was that they'd crossed paths again.

Five days later he found the note from Bethany taped to his hotel-room door. It said, simply, *Call me. Now.* He walked down to the booth on the corner, dropped a couple of quarters into the slot, and waited for her to pick up. It was the last phone call he ever made from a booth. The next week, after he went in to sign the deal, he got himself a cell phone and a plan.

Eleven months later, *Colby* was published to strong reviews and weak sales. The comparisons to Vikram Seth and Alexander Pushkin had been made, but hadn't helped move the product. They were justified, of course, these parallels (he'd studied both once he knew what he was getting into), though Zack believed his rhyming tetrameter sonnets were technically more accomplished and slipped from the tongue with greater ease than Seth's, and they were certainly more realistic than the Johnston translation of Pushkin. He did not bat down the compliments, however. In fact he played on them. They were all he had. How else would he sell the book? His publisher, after three weeks of barely perceptible enthusiasm, had all but let the project sink into oblivion. This was only months after the Bear Stearns collapse, and the novel in verse, good as it might be, appealed to no one but Pushkin scholars, those hardcore Seth enthusiasts who were riled or enthused by the comparisons, and the usual subcategory of suburban super-literates looking to out-wow their fellow book-clubbers. He asked for a tour but was politely informed that no one in the company had ever heard of an author tour that paid for itself, or, for that matter, deserved the writer's investment of time. He told Bethany that he didn't care about that. He just wanted to put his book into people's hands. It was a book that needed to be read. To that end he'd sent a copy up to the Princess Patricia's Regiment in Winnipeg, where the four men he'd ridden with had been based. He wasn't exactly sure why he'd done this. *A tribute to the fallen*, he'd inscribed on the frontis-piece, but that, he knew, had been a bit of a stretch. It was, at least, a tip of the hat to those men. Maybe he'd been hoping for some sense of closure on the whole sad business. But after he posted it he let the thought slide from his mind.

Zack and Audrey were friends by this time. It hurt but it was better than nothing. He was still living in the same crappy hotel in East Harlem. In exchange for a reduced rate, he tended the front desk three nights a week. He met Audrey for coffee on Fridays. By then she'd split with Javier and met up with a married professor of hers named Bob most Wednesday afternoons. The book still hadn't earned out its modest advance. She had troubles of her own. So they'd get together and share their woes, bitch some, and help each other feel a little better. She complained about Bob's wife, Gail, how she'd been jealous of her husband's career since the day they'd married. She was smothering him. Zack found it hard to sympathize. Bob had got tenure at Columbia based on three lousy days of desk-reporting out of St. George's after the Grenada invasion back in 1983. Not with any undue cynicism, Zack drew Audrey's attention to this fact, to which she countered that Bob was the most generous lover she'd ever had. These were not always pleasant meetings. But it was the only thing he could do to be close to her. He steeled himself with a backup plan. When things got tough, such as with that generous lover comment, he called to mind one of his favorable reviews, inhaled deeply, and tried to remember that Bob, like Javier, was little more than a temporary fix in a big lonely city. He'd get her back up to Canada one way or another, one day, and she'd realize that Zack, and only Zack, was the right man for her.

He knew things had to change, and soon. He was still living off the last nickels of what might be the only money he would get for the book and the occasional check his brother sent down from Vancouver. But he swore he'd never go back to journalism. "Anyway," he said that last afternoon they met, "I've already got a job. If you hadn't noticed."

Trying to push that book of his was practically a full-time occupation, anyway. *Colby* had been out barely a year now and still had some life left in it yet, in his opinion. He was determined to move heaven and earth to put it into people's hands, to do whatever he could. And to that end he spent at least two full days a week going around to the bookstores offering his services—readings, poetry workshops, informal lectures on how to get published. He went to the high schools and community colleges, the libraries and the YMCAs. Sometimes he got as far as the store manager or head librarian. He always carried copies of the book in his red Adidas gym bag. He'd had his foot near blown off, spent two years slaving over those 667 sonnets, and he was damned if he was going to roll over and die just because his publishing house was run by a collection of spineless boobs who didn't have the first clue about marketing the most important novel of its type since *Eugene Onegin*.

"In fact, I'm going guerrilla. I've got a new approach."

"Onward, good soldier. Take the poetry to the people," she said.

"A book doesn't exist unless it's being read. Plus, I'm broke." He leaned forward, gave her a peck on the cheek. He produced a heavy hockey bag from under their table. "Say yo to Bob."

"I will," she said.

He limped out the door, the canvas bag hiked up on his back.

He walked along 7th Avenue, pleased with himself, watching the cavernous city streets open left and right as he labored south. Pleased because he thought he'd detected something in Audrey, a conditional surrender. Maybe things were looking up. Maybe she was getting tired of Bob, who hadn't done anything of note—other than sleep with Audrey—in the past twenty years.

Zack wasn't sure if Audrey had ever read his book, had been afraid to ask, in fact; but he knew—or was beginning to suspect, at least—that he was a fascinating mystery to her. How many people in the world had written a book like his? He could count them on one hand while holding a glass of water. Even if you hadn't read it, you had to shake your head in wonder. Why else would she agree to meet every Friday the way they did? How to explain that? He imagined her walking home now, in the opposite direction, and later taking down the copy of *Colby* from her bookshelf and falling in love with him, or at least his beautiful verse—that would do for now—and becoming mesmerized by how perfectly he'd captured the heart of the little girl who'd lost her father to the bomb that had reshaped his leg. Only a man who deserved love could write what he'd written. She would see that now.

It was just before seven o'clock when he began to set up on West 47th across from the Roxy Delicatessen in Times Square. He figured he'd get the tail end of the matinee crowd, which he thought might at least be semiliterate, or pretend to be, and the early-evening supper crowd, which might be feeling generous after a drink or two. He unfolded the portable table and Bristol-board placards from the big duffel bag, and stacked thirty-eight hardcover copies of *Colby* into four neat piles. The big duffel bag he folded and stored under the table. He slipped the two placards, which he'd built with his own two hands, over his head. The two sheets of Bristol board, inscribed with large black lettering, hung suspended from his shoulders, joined by sections of birthday ribbon he'd found in the hotel's basement. On the back board he'd stencilled *Poetry Is the Bomb* with a happy face drawn into an old-fashioned-looking circular cartoon bomb, wick sparkling with a red-marker flame. On the front he'd simply written, *Explode with Me.* He saw the superior grins of those who failed to understand the privileged sacrifice of a man who chooses to totally commit to his art. He saw the blank stares of the men and women who spent their lives lost or hiding from their own thoughts. He saw kids pointing and grandmothers frowning and the beautiful young hipsters too cool to notice anything but their own yesteryear hairdos. He saw Japanese tourists marveling at his American freedom. He saw a table of veterans eyeing him suspiciously from the window at Roxy's. He saw a pretty girl holding her boyfriend's hand. She stopped, picked up a copy, and told him good luck, the world needs more poets. She smiled at him warmly. He thanked her and let her take the book for free.

The humanity of the city was in full flush this evening. Throngs of people coursed by. He sold three copies in quick succession. Sixty dollars in his pocket. "Thank you," he said. "You bet. Hope you like it."

Things were looking good.

One man sidled up to the table, examined a copy, and said, "A novel? Written like a poem? Man, why not just shoot off the other foot?"

But Zack was buoyed. Zack was pumped. Four more copies went

in under ten minutes. He wondered why he hadn't thought of doing this earlier. It was possible he might even run out of copies.

He hauled out his cell and dialed Audrey's number. He didn't even care if she was with Bob. Hope was on his side this evening, and his hope, the hope of an artist in full flight, was indestructible. He felt better than he'd felt in a long time. Even the pain in his left leg was gone now.

Her voice flooded his ear. He waited for the beep to sound. He'd do his best to be cool, to cover the giddy optimism that welled within him. Not too strong, he cautioned himself. Don't come on too strong. But a voice, a female voice behind him, screamed suddenly. And then a chorus of voices rose and half of Times Square was running, and the other half was falling to the sidewalk and covering their heads. The police officer whom he'd seen walking across the square was running now and pulling something out from his side and waving those few people away who were still standing, and Zack, who'd dreamed the sound of weapons fire almost every night since driving the Kandahar Road, now heard the report of a single shot whistle through the air just as Audrey picked up. And he fell clutching the phone to his ear, one eye turned to the delicatessen, the other watching a pigeon cut the sky, and listened as if for the first time to the deep and luminous sound of his own breathing.

The
Last
Pages

Gretchen with her first husband, Bob Robbins, 1928.

When I was a boy I was in the habit of making up stories. I recall my father, in his heavily accented and grammatically incorrect English, talking to my mother at the kitchen table. "What is wrong with this boy?" he would say. "Everything is exaggeration and embellishing everything." Years later as a medical student, I was on rounds when my attending physician said, "Shushtari, go ahead and present the case. And stick to the facts, because if you start with one of your stories about the patient's life, I'm going to fail you." Somewhere along the way, I learned to concentrate on medical data and science, but I never lost the desire to tell good stories. Nor did I tire of hearing them, and

my father had plenty. The character of Bijan in "Vast Garden" was inspired by a person I never met, named Baba Hassan, pictured here with my father (in the foreground) and two of his brothers in Esfahan, Iran in 1926. Stories about Baba Hassan were fascinating to me, and I couldn't get enough of them. I'm fairly certain my father also engaged in hyperbole, but I loved it.

—*J. Kevin Shushtari*

" Improvised Explosive Device" started with a focus on voice. I wanted to find a narrator who could tell a bloody sad story with a bit of a smile on his face. Zack, the young lovelorn journalist with something to prove, turned out to be the perfect character to bring in. The ironic tone helped me edge the story believably closer to the world of the unlikely or the improbable; it opened up levels of plot and character that simply don't fly when you're working with a straight-up narrative voice. Now, Zack was suddenly a poet. Here I was in the company of a modern-day Wilfred Owen or Siegfried Sassoon and looking at the war in Afghanistan as Zack's great artistic challenge. He's determined to make something good of it and, like all great romantics, use this new talent to get the girl. Where the story carries Zack was a great surprise to me. Writing is a process of discovery. The question, "What happens next?" is always front and center for me. Without it to invite me into a character's life, I don't think I'd write at all. I had no idea where Zack's story would end, and only when I saw him entering Times Square with a load of books did I see the full picture. This voice opened up his world for me.

—*Dennis Bock*

My husband and I take a lot of road trips. He instigates these trips. He's a filmmaker and is generally restless and in search of inspiration. I drive, and he takes pictures. The one above is of me, jumping on a trampoline next to a plowed field in Bainbridge, Georgia, my father-in-law's hometown. On another trip, across the Panhandle and into the Louisiana Gulf Coast, I saw a teenage girl walking along the highway with a backpack and silver sneakers. She became the Sadie of my story.

—*Lydia Fitzpatrick*

Sometimes a story is born out of a moment and a place: the time it takes to drive a stretch of road outside Washtucna, Washington; pose for a picture in the Great Kiva at Pueblo Bonito; or walk the half-mile back to the house from the edge of a field where the combine's missed a few stray stalks of corn.

—*Paul Rawlins*

In 2003 I was in midtown Manhattan when the blackout occurred. Because the subways were down, I had to walk to downtown Manhattan and then cross over the Brooklyn Bridge to get back home. I wanted to write about this experience in some way, but every time I tried I couldn't find much of a story to go along with it. I set the idea aside, and for years pretty much forgot about it.

In 2009, during one of my numerous email exchanges with a good friend, Melanie Bishop (also a *Glimmer Train* contributor), Melanie mentioned a writing exercise she sometimes gives to her fiction students: choose three random things (objects, events, setting, people, you name it) and then write a story containing those three elements. I'd never written in this way before, so I asked Melanie to pick three things for me. Her choices: New Testament. SIDS. A jar. Immediately I went to work, and rather quickly characters and a situation began to take form: a man returning from work to a depressed wife who is paralyzed by the recent death of their baby. What a joy it was when the blackout story suddenly returned to me, and I realized that it belonged with the

current SIDS story, that *this* was what the man walking home during a blackout was returning to—a life that had been shut down for months. Once I made that connection, the story pretty much fell into place except for the last paragraph, the writing of which was a process of slow and laborious labor.

—*Robert Schirmer*

I have always been overly fascinated with speech, and the melody of dialogue. In another life I would have dedicated myself to voice acting. One of my biggest heroes when I was a kid was Mel Blanc, The Man of a Thousand Voices, the talent behind Bugs Bunny, Daffy Duck, and dozens of other Golden Age cartoon characters. And what began as an appreciation for the elasticity and dynamic ability of the human voice later developed into a fascination (obsession?) with the more subtle dance between two or more people simply talking with one another.

In "The Getaway Driver," the character Eli is a king-hell talker. He talks to get out of trouble, he talks to charm, he talks just for the sake of talking. Eli is supremely comfortable with his banter, with leading a conversation or holding one entirely on his own. I tried to do Eli justice in writing his dialogue, and did my best to convey his mastery of bullshit via the spoken word. When I got stuck I would think of Mr. Blanc, the man himself, and perhaps a combination of Foghorn Leghorn, Porky Pig, and Pepe LePew. Take those three, add a healthy dash of marijuana and a nasal whine, and you have something approaching Eli.

—*Nick Yribar*

Growing up in a big Irish Catholic family on the south shore of Massachusetts, the Church was always there, as were various forms of temptation, some fairly harmless and others not so much. Mason Finneran is probably more interested in recruiting soldiers than he is in defiling the Church, but in order for a new faith to be instilled, the old must be erased. I think for many people today faith in general creates an interesting paradox—a source of pride when alone or with fellow practitioners, and at times a source of shame when amongst others—and in mid-adolescence, Jack is just becoming aware of this. The first story I published in *Glimmer Train* was actually from Danny's point of view after he is grown, and I have several stories narrated from Jack's POV, so I do like to come back to them. In the Last Pages of my first *Glimmer Train* story, I put a picture of my daughter Molly, and in the second, her twin Katie, and as that created an outcry amongst some of my other little ones, here I figured the safest thing to do would be to include a picture of everybody. From left to right: Molly, my wife Suzanne, Kerrin, me, Katie, Matthew, Maggie, and Christina.

—*Sean Padraic McCarthy*

A few summers ago, I came home to find this frog stuck to my bedroom window. It stayed there until I went to sleep. When I woke up the next morning, it was gone.

For me, writing is like being that frog. It's being willing to press unexpected angles of yourself, your belly and the underside of your chin, against the glass. It's holding on when you don't know where you are or how you got there, far from the place you call home, with only tiny suction cups tethering you to the world. In charmed moments, you realize what little it takes to hold yourself up.

—*Joy Wood*

When someone dies, the mind plays tricks. You can no longer hold memories up to the measuring stick of lived experience. I started "Roadrunner" about a decade after my great-grandmother's death. I was missing her more than usual, and for some reason I started thinking about her fondness for the desert and wondering why she had loved it so much. Trying to learn or remember something is one way to start a story. I suppose trying to unlearn or forget something is another way.

It took a lot of drafts for me to realize that Lori wasn't *me* and her grandmother wasn't *my* great-grandmother. The story needed to find its own truths. In the first drafts there was no suicide, no bloody knuckles on the steering wheel. The characters lacked the naked ferocity of flesh-and-blood people. I was creating puppets, not protagonists; I had not pushed them hard enough to make them real. In the final version, only the most superficial details remain true: the organ, the respirator, the yucca trees.

"Roadrunner" was difficult to write, and I am grateful to Marc, Tracy, Marjorie, Keith, Malena, and Liz for asking the questions that pushed me to find the real story.

—*Kathryne Young*

PAST CONTRIBUTING AUTHORS AND ARTISTS

Robert A. Abel • David Abrams • Linsey Abrams • Steve Adams • Hubert Ahn • Lynn Ahrens • Diane King Akers • Daniel Alarcón • Susan Alenick • Xhenet Aliu • Ed Allen • Will Allison • Rosemary Altea • Julia Alvarez • Kyoko Amano • Brian Ames • Scott Alan Anderson • Selena Anderson • A. Manette Ansay • Margaret Atwood • Dalia Azim • Kevin Bacon • Michael Bahler • Doreen Baingana • Aida Baker • Kerry Neville Bakken • Carmiel Banasky • Olufunke Grace Bankole • Russell Banks • Brad Barkley • Andrea Barrett • Victoria Barrett • Ken Barris • Marc Basch • Kyle Ann Bates • Richard Bausch • Robert Bausch • Charles Baxter • Ann Beattie • Sean Beaudoin • Barbara Bechtold • Cathie Beck • Jeff Becker • Janet Belding • Janet Benton • Sallie Bingham • Kristen Birchett • Melanie Bishop • James Carlos Blake • Victoria Blake • Corinne Demas Bliss • Valerie Block • Carol Bly • Will Boast • Belle Boggs • Joan Bohorfoush • Matt Bondurant • David Borofka • Robin Bradford • Harold Brodkey • Barbara Brooks • Kim Brooks • Oliver Broudy • Carrie Brown • Danit Brown • Kurt McGinnis Brown • Nic Brown • Paul Brownfield • Gabriel Brownstein • Ayşe Papatya Bucak • Judy Budnitz • Susanna Bullock • Christopher Bundy • Jenny A. Burkholder • Evan Christopher Burton • Robert Olen Butler • Michael Byers • Christine Byl • Gerard Byrne • Jack Cady • Annie Callan • Joshua Canipe • Kevin Canty • Peter Carey • Ioanna Carlsen • Ron Carlson • Aaron Carmichael • H.G. Carroll • Paul Carroll • Nona Caspers • David Allan Cates • Marjorie Celona • Jeremiah Chamberlin • Brian Champeau • Vikram Chandra • Diane Chang • Mike Chasar • Xiaofei Chen • Yunny Chen • Terrence Cheng • Robert Chibka • Chieh Chieng • Jon Chopan • Carolyn Chute • Christi Clancy • George Makana Clark • Rikki Clark • Dennis Clemmens • Christopher Coake • Aaron Cohen • Andrea Cohen • Robert Cohen • Evan S. Connell • Joan Connor • K.L. Cook • Ellen Cooney • Rand Richards Cooper • Lydia E. Copeland • Michelle Coppedge • Rita D. Costello • Wendy Counsil • Frances Ya-Chu Cowhig • Doug Crandell • Lindsey Crittenden • M. Allen Cunningham • Colleen Curran • Ronald F. Currie Jr. • William J. Cyr • Quinn Dalton • Edwidge Danticat • Bilal Dardai • Tristan Davies • Bill Davis • C.V. Davis • Annie Dawid • Erica Johnson Debeljak • Laurence de Looze • Anne de Marcken • Toi Derricotte • Janet Desaulniers • Tiziana di Marina • Junot Díaz • Stephanie Dickinson • Stephen Dixon • Matthew Doherty • Leslie Dormen • Michael Dorris • Siobhan Dowd • Greg Downs • Eugenie Doyle • Tiffany Drever • Alan Arthur Drew • Andre Dubus • Andre Dubus III • E.A. Durden • Stuart Dybek • Wayne Dyer • Melodie S. Edwards • Ron Egatz • Barbara Eiswerth • Mary Relindes Ellis • Sherry Ellis • Susan Engberg • Lin Enger • James English • Tony Eprile • Louise Erdrich • Zoë Evamy • Eli S. Evans • Nomi Eve • George Fahey • Edward Falco • Anthony Farrington • Merrill Feitell • J. M. Ferguson Jr. • Lisa Fetchko • Joseph Flanagan • Charlotte Forbes • Alyson Foster • Patricia Foster • Susan Fox • Michael Frank • Stefanie Freele • Pete Fromm • Abby Frucht • Daniel Gabriel • Avital Gad-Cykman • Ernest Gaines • Mary Gaitskill • Riva Galchen • Tess Gallagher • Louis Gallo • Elizabeth Gallu • Kent Gardien • Abby Geni • Aaron Gilbreath • Ellen Gilchrist • Myla Goldberg • Allyson Goldin • D M Gordon • Mary Gordon • Peter Gordon • Trevor Gore • Amy S. Gottfried • Jean Colgan Gould • Elizabeth Graver • Lisa Graley • Jo-Ann Graziano • Andrew Sean Greer • Cynthia Gregory • Gail Greiner • John Griesemer • Zoë Griffith-Jones • Paul Griner • Lauren Groff • Cary Groner • Michael L. Guerra • Lucrecia Guerrero • Aaron Gwyn • L.B. Haas • Rawi Hage • Garth Risk Hallberg • Patricia Hampl • Christian Hansen • Ann Harleman • Elizabeth Logan Harris • Marina Harris • Erin Hart • Kent Haruf • Ethan Hauser • Jake Hawkes • Daniel Hayes • David Haynes • Daniel Hecht • Ursula Hegi • Amy Hempel • Joshua Henkin • Patricia Henley • Cristina Henríquez • Nellie Hermann • David Hicks • Patrick Hicks • Julie Hirsch • Andee Hochman • Rolaine Hochstein • Alice Hoffman • Cary Holladay • Jack Holland • Noy Holland • Travis Holland • Lucy Honig • Ann Hood • Linda Hornbuckle • Kuangyan Huang • David Huddle • Sandra Hunter • Tim Hurd • Siri Hustvedt • Quang Huynh • Frances Hwang • Leo Hwang • Catherine Ryan Hyde • Stewart David Ikeda • Lawson Fusao Inada • Elizabeth Inness-Brown • Debra Innocenti • Bruce Jacobson • Andrea Jeyaveeran • Ha Jin • Charles Johnson • Cheri Johnson • E.B. Johnson • Leslie Johnson • Sarah Anne Johnson • Wayne Johnson • Bret Anthony Johnston • Allen Morris Jones • Nalini Jones • Thom Jones • Cyril Jones-Kellet • Elizabeth Judd • Tom Miller Juvik • Jiri Kajanë • Anita Shah Kapadia • Hester Kaplan • Wayne Karlin • Amy Karr • Ariana-Sophia Kartsonis • Andrew Kass • Kate Kasten • Ken Kaye • Tom Kealey • David Kear • John M. Keller • Andrea King Kelly • Jenny Kennedy • Thomas E. Kennedy • Tim Keppel • Jamaica Kincaid • Lily King • Dana Kinstler • Maina wa Kinyatti • Carolyn Kizer • Perri Klass • Rachel Klein • Carrie Knowles • Clark E. Knowles • Elizabeth Koch • N.S. Köenings • Jonathan

Kooker • David Koon • Karen Kovacik • Justin Kramon • Jake Kreilkamp • Nita Krevans • Anasuya Krishnaswamy • Erika Krouse • Marilyn Krysl • Frances Kuffel • Evan Kuhlman • Mandy Dawn Kuntz • Anatoly Kurchatkin • W. Tsung-yan Kwong • J.P. Lacrampe • Victoria Lancelotta • Christiana Langenberg • Rattawut Lapcharoensap • Jenni Lapidus • Danielle Lavaque-Manty • Doug Lawson • David Leavitt • Don Lee • Frances Lefkowitz • Peter Lefcourt • Jon Leon • Doris Lessing • Jennifer Levasseur • Debra Levy • Janice Levy • Yiyun Li • Christine Liotta • Rosina Lippi-Green • David Long • Nathan Long • Salvatore Diego Lopez • Melissa Lowver • William Luvaas • Barry Lyga • David H. Lynn • Richard Lyons • Bruce Machart • Jeff MacNelly • R. Kevin Maler • Kelly Malone • Paul Mandelbaum • George Manner • Jana Martin • Lee Martin • Valerie Martin • Juan Martinez • Daniel Mason • Brendan Mathews • Alice Mattison • Bruce McAllister • Jane McCafferty • Colum McCann • Sean Padraic McCarthy • Judith McClain • Cammie McGovern • Cate McGowan • Eileen McGuire • Jay McInerney • Susan McInnis • Gregory McNamee • Jenny Drake McPhee • Amalia Melis • Askold Melnyczuk • Matthew Mercier • Susan Messer • Frank Michel • Paul Michel • Nancy Middleton • Alyce Miller • Greg Miller • Katherine Min • Mary McGarry Morris • Ted Morrissey • Mary Morrissy • Jennifer Moses • Bernard Mulligan • Abdelrahman Munif • Manuel Muñoz • Karen Munro • Scott Nadelson • Paula Nangle • Jim Nashold • Antonya Nelson • Kent Nelson • Randy F. Nelson • Lucia Nevai • Thisbe Nissen • Katherin Nolte • Miriam Novogrodsky • Sigrid Nunez • N. Nye • Ron Nyren • Joyce Carol Oates • Tim O'Brien • Vana O'Brien • Gina Ochsner • Mary O'Dell • Chris Offutt • Jennifer Oh • Laura Oliver • Felicia Olivera • Jimmy Olsen • Thomas O'Malley • Stewart O'Nan • Elizabeth Oness • Karen Outen • Mary Overton • Ruth Ozeki • Patricia Page • Ashley Paige • Ann Pancake • Michael Parker • Alexander Parsons • Peter Parsons • Roy Parvin • Karenmary Penn • Susan Perabo • Benjamin Percy • Marissa Perry • Susan Petrone • Dawn Karima Pettigrew • Jessi Phillips • Constance Pierce • William Pierce • D.B.C. Pierre • Angela Pneuman • Steven Polansky • Michael Poore • John Prendergast • Jessica Printz • Melissa Pritchard • Annie Proulx • Eric Puchner • Lindsay Purves • Kevin Rabalais • Jonathan Raban • George Rabasa • Margo Rabb • Mark Rader • Paul Rawlins • Yosefa Raz • Karen Regen-Tuero • Frederick Reiken • Nancy Reisman • Yelizaveta P. Renfro • Adam Theron-Lee Rensch • Linda Reynolds • Kurt Rheinheimer • Anne Rice • Michelle Richmond • Alberto Ríos • Roxana Robinson • Anya Robyak • Susan Jackson Rodgers • Andrew Roe • Paulette Roeske • Stan Rogal • Carol Roh-Spaulding • Frank Ronan • Emma Roper-Evans • Julie Rose • Sari Rose • Elizabeth Rosen • Janice Rosenberg • Jane Rosenzweig • David Rothman • Sam Ruddick • Elissa Minor Rust • Karen Sagstetter • Kiran Kaur Saini • Mark Salzman • Mark Sanders • Ron Savage • Carl Schaffer • R. K. Scher • Michael Schiavone • Robert Schirmer • Libby Schmais • Samantha Schoech • Natalie Schoen • Scott Schrader • Adam Schuitema • Jim Schumock • Lynn Sharon Schwartz • Barbara Scot • Andrew Scott • Andrew Thomas Scott • Peter Selgin • Amy Selwyn • James Sepsey • Catherine Seto • Bob Shacochis • Evelyn Sharenov • Karen Shepard • Maggie Shipstead • Sally Shivnan • Evan Shopper • Daryl Siegel • Ami Silber • Al Sim • Mark Sindecuse • George Singleton • Hasanthika Sirisena • Johanna Skibsrud • Floyd Skloot • Brian Slattery • Aria Beth Sloss • Louise Farmer Smith • Janice D. Soderling • Roland Sodowsky • Stephanie Soileau • Scott Southwick • R. Clifton Spargo • Gregory Spatz • Diana Spechler • Brent Spencer • L.M. Spencer • Lara Stapleton • John Stazinski • Lori Ann Stephens • Barbara Stevens • John Stinson • George Stolz • William Styron • Virgil Suárez • Karen Swenson • Liz Szabla • Shimon Tanaka • Mika Tanner • Deborah Tarnoff • Lois Taylor • Paul Theroux • Abigail Thomas • Randolph Thomas • Jackie Thomas-Kennedy • Joyce Thompson • Patrick Tierney • Aaron Tillman • Tamara B. Titus • Andrew Toos • Daniel Torday • Justin Torres • Pauls Toutonghi • Johnny Townsend • Vu Tran • Patricia Traxler • Jessica Treadway • Eric Trethewey • Doug Trevor • William Trevor • Rob Trucks • Kathryn Trueblood • Eric Scot Tryon • Jennifer Tseng • Carol Turner • Christine Turner • Kathleen Tyau • Michael Upchurch • Lee Upton • Laura Valeri • Vauhini Vara • Gerard Varni • Katherine Vaz • A.J. Verdelle • Daniel Villasenor • Robert Vivian • Sergio Gabriel Waisman • John S. Walker • Daniel Wallace • Ren Wanding • Eric Wasserman • Mary Yukari Waters • Jonathan Wei • Josh Weil • Eric Weinberger • Jamie Weisman • Lance Weller • Ed Weyhing • J. Patrice Whetsell • Sara Whyatt • Joan Wickersham • Vinnie Wilhelm • Margo Williams • Lex Williford • Gary Wilson • Robin Winick • Mark Wisniewski • Terry Wolverton • Monica Wood • Christopher Woods • Leslie A. Wootten • wormser • Celia Wren • Callie Wright • Calvin Wright • Brennen Wysong • Geoff Wyss • June Unjoo Yang • Rolf Yngve • Paul Yoon • Nancy Zafris • Yuvi Zalkow • Jenny Zhang • Silas Zobal • Jane Zwinger

Starting anew after the 1946 heart attack. McAndrews Road, Medford.

COMING SOON

That Davis had lost one eye in an auto crash, married interracially, hugged Richard Nixon, and suffered from recurrent bouts of "lifestyle related" liver and kidney problems endeared him to the Maurants.

from "When the Wind Blows the Water Gray" by Clayton Luz

Every household in the river knows how the height of the river affects them—what footage means a wet yard, a saturated garage, a soaked living room, a drenched attic. In about another foot, she'll be stuffing every crack with towels, not that it will do any good.

from "While Surrounded by Water" by Stefanie Freele

In a few years, the remaining mills would finally sputter out, though the city, unlike most of the rust belt, would survive with some measure of grace: a neutered economy of hospitals and service, free of the sweat, the carcinogenic burning and puffing required in the manufacture of solid goods.

from "Insurance" by James F. Sidel

There was a chance the baby was normal. There was a chance the baby was not.

from "Chance" by Peter Ho Davies